Berkley Prime Crime titles by Christy Fifield

MURDER BUYS A T-SHIRT
MURDER HOOKS A MERMAID
MURDER SENDS A POSTCARD

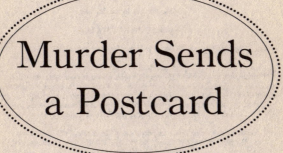

Murder Sends a Postcard

Christy Fifield

BERKLEY PRIME CRIME, NEW YORK

THE BERKLEY PUBLISHING GROUP
Published by the Penguin Group
Penguin Group (USA) LLC
375 Hudson Street, New York, New York 10014

USA • Canada • UK • Ireland • Australia • New Zealand • India • South Africa • China

penguin.com

A Penguin Random House Company

MURDER SENDS A POSTCARD

A Berkley Prime Crime Book / published by arrangement with the author

Berkley Prime Crime Books are published by The Berkley Publishing Group.
BERKLEY® PRIME CRIME and the PRIME CRIME logo are trademarks of
Penguin Group (USA) LLC.

For information, address: The Berkley Publishing Group,
a division of Penguin Group (USA) LLC,
375 Hudson Street, New York, New York 10014.

ISBN: 978-0-425-25229-1

PUBLISHING HISTORY
Berkley Prime Crime mass-market edition / January 2014

PRINTED IN THE UNITED STATES OF AMERICA

10 9 8 7 6 5 4 3 2 1

Cover illustration by Ben Perini.
Cover design by Sarah Oberrender.
Interior text design by Kristin del Rosario.

This one's for you, Mom.
Lois Jeanne Nouguier Fifield, 1931–2012.
You will live forever in my heart.

Acknowledgments

In a perfect world, a writer sits down in an immaculate garden full of unicorns and rainbows and creates a perfect book. Unfortunately, this writer lives in the real, far-from-perfect world. Fortunately, I have incredible people helping me navigate that world.

When I should have been in my perfect garden, I was instead learning firsthand the meaning of "Code 3." It really does mean the ambulance driver gets to use the lights and siren all the way to the hospital—even if it's ninety miles away. I also learned many new medical terms, and got up close and personal with amazing advances in medical technology.

I am indebted to the physicians, surgeons, nurses, and technicians at Oregon Health & Science University, especially Dr. Patrick Worth (my personal guardian angel), my amazing home health nurse, Erik, and all the wound care staff. I cannot imagine the last months without your help.

My thanks, also, to everyone who helped at home: Sue

and Sue (both of them!), Dan, Kris, Dean, and Debbie. And to the many people who provided much-needed support for my husband, especially Sean and Rose, Stephanie, Greg, Scott, Lynette, and Colleen.

And as always, I am grateful for the usual cast and crew: Michelle, incredibly savvy—and patient—editor; Susannah, dedicated agent; Colleen (again), first reader, cheerleader, chauffeur; the Oregon Writers Network crowd, especially Dean and Kris; my sisters, Jan, Jeri, and Jeri (yep, there are two of them), who did more than I could have ever asked.

And most of all to Steve, who saved my life.

Literally this time.

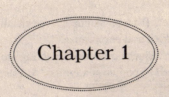

Chapter 1

I KNEW WHO BRIDGET MCKENNA WAS THE INSTANT she stepped through the door of Southern Treasures. Not because she'd been in the gift shop I owned here in Keyhole Bay, Florida, but because she hadn't.

I'd only heard about her.

Our tourists usually fit in one of several categories: the young and single, the families, and the empty nesters, with the occasional girls'-weekend-without-the-husbands group.

Bridget was none of those. With her designer suits and stiletto heels, she appeared overdressed for the Florida panhandle. Careful makeup masked her age, though I suspected she was a few years north of my mid-thirties.

She looked good. Good enough to earn a wolf-whistle from Bluebeard, the parrot I'd inherited along with my 55 percent of Southern Treasures. My cousin Peter owned the other 45 percent, but he lived in Montgomery and didn't work in the store. He just meddled from a hundred miles away.

"Bluebeard!"

Harassing customers wasn't good for business, and he knew better.

To my relief, Bridget laughed, a clear, almost musical sound. "I'll take it as a compliment."

"Pretty girl," Bluebeard cooed, shooting me a triumphant look. He seemed so human sometimes. At least now I understood why.

"What's your name?" she asked, approaching his perch.

For one crazy moment I actually expected him to say "Louis," the name of my great-uncle, the previous owner of Southern Treasures—and the ghost who lived in the shop.

Uncle Louis used Bluebeard as a spokesbird, and I was never quite sure when he might decide he had something to say.

Fortunately, today Uncle Louis decided to stay quiet.

"Bluebeard," the parrot and I answered in unison.

"Well, I'm very glad to meet you, Bluebeard," she said, a smile in her voice. She turned around to face me. "And you, too."

She walked back across the shop to where I stood behind the counter, and stuck out her hand. "Bridget McKenna."

I shook her outstretched hand, answering her smile with one of my own. "Gloryanna," I said. "Gloryanna Martine, owner of this place and the rude parrot."

Up close, I could see my estimate of her age was at least five years low, maybe more. Her hair, expertly streaked dark honey-blond, hung low over her forehead, concealing the beginnings of frown lines between her perfectly arched eyebrows.

Her handshake was firm, and her friendly smile reached her eyes, instead of stopping at the empty gesture of her lips.

"Welcome to Keyhole Bay," I said.

She glanced down at her suit and shoes, so out of place in our little tourist town. "That obvious, huh?"

"Well," I admitted with a grin, "I already heard about you." I shrugged. "It's a small town."

It wasn't such a small town in the middle of summer, actually. Tourists swelled our population and a steady stream of people came through the door. Quiet, even just long enough to say hello, was rare.

Her expression sobered. "I'm not surprised. Big-city woman coming down from Minnesota to take over the local bank."

Candid *and* perceptive. I instantly liked Bridget McKenna.

I started to ask another question, but the bell over the door interrupted as a gaggle of youngsters poured in, followed by a harried-looking woman.

The gaggle surrounded the toy rack, the mass of suntanned arms and legs sorting themselves out into three kids: a boy about twelve, a girl of seven or eight, and a boy whose gap-toothed grin pegged him as five or six.

Their mother quickly took the two younger ones by the hand, pulling them back a step from the display. "Look with your eyes," she said. "Not with your hands."

It was a phrase Memaw used to use when she took me shopping, and I smiled at the memory.

I turned back to say something to Bridget, but she had

walked over to the postcard spinner and was gazing at the offerings. She glanced up and smiled briefly, then went back to her perusal.

"Getting busy again?" a voice asked behind me.

I turned to see Julie Nelson, my part-time clerk, coming from the storage area behind the shop. "Rose Ann's settled down, I can take over," she said.

Rose Ann was Julie's daughter, born just a few months earlier. In an effort to keep Julie working at the store, we had set up a small nursery—really little more than an alcove with partitions—for Rose Ann. The baby spent several days a week with her grandmother, but there was a place for her on the days Anita Nelson wasn't available.

"You sure?" I checked the time. Julie still had a couple hours on her shift.

She nodded.

I trudged up the stairs to my apartment over Southern Treasures. Summer had hit full force, and this morning's rain shower combined with the midday ninety-degree heat to drain all my energy.

Unfortunately, it was my turn to host our regular Thursday dinner. My three best friends would arrive at six thirty, expecting a traditional Southern meal, and it was too blasted hot even to think about cooking.

Fortunately, I had remembered something my mother used to make when I was a kid. *Cold supper*, she called it. A meal that involved very little actual cooking, all of it done in advance.

So while Julie watched the store, I was headed upstairs to put the finishing touches on tonight's meal.

I'd left the apartment closed and dark when I opened the store at nine, but by midafternoon the heat had seeped in around the tightly drawn drapes.

In an attempt to capture the afternoon breezes, I opened the windows overlooking the main drag in front of the store and the sliding door to my miniature balcony in back. From the balcony I could watch the boats in the tiny bay that gave Keyhole Bay its name.

The cross-ventilation helped, though the open windows also let in the traffic noise. A week before Fourth of July there was a lot of traffic.

I should be grateful, I told myself. It was exactly that traffic that kept me in business. Tourist season provided the revenue to keep our small town going through the quiet months.

We all complained about the traffic, and the noise, and the stupid tourist tricks, but we also knew they were the source of our income.

It was a love-hate relationship common to tourist towns everywhere, but most of the people who came through Southern Treasures were actually pretty nice. Like the woman downstairs with the three kids she kept from tearing up my display.

And at least the ones who weren't so nice made for funny stories later.

I checked the fresh peach ice cream in the freezer. It was set, ready to serve with the no-bake cookies I'd made the night before.

I turned up the volume on the intercom system I'd recently installed, in case Julie needed me. In three months,

Rose Ann had settled into a routine, and she should sleep the rest of the afternoon. But as I was learning, babies didn't always do what they should.

The refrigerator was packed with an array of cold dishes: deviled eggs for an appetizer, chicken salad as the main course, potato salad, coleslaw, three-bean salad, and macaroni salad. I just needed to put together a fruit salad, and make a fresh batch of sweet tea.

I put a big jug of water on the balcony, and dropped in a half-dozen tea bags. Memaw would have pitched a fit about me not properly boiling water for the sweet tea. But Memaw passed many years ago, so I figured I was safe.

Then again, I knew there was at least one ghost in Southern Treasures. I hoped he was the only one.

I cut the chilled melons and popped fat green and red grapes off their stems. With the addition of sliced kiwi, an array of fresh berries, and slices of perfectly ripe peaches, the salad was ready to go back in the refrigerator to allow the flavors to mellow.

We could debate all evening whether it was traditional Southern cooking, but I had managed to avoid heating up the apartment, so I called it a win.

I was starting to set the table when I heard Rose Ann fussing. Her nursery was at the bottom of the stairs, just a few steps from the sales counter, where her mother worked.

I abandoned my preparations, grateful to have accomplished as much as I had, and hurried back downstairs to relieve Julie.

Glancing up at the black-and-white cartoon cat clock on the wall of the store, I realized Julie's shift had ended half an hour earlier. I felt a stab of guilt for keeping her past her quitting time.

"Sorry!" I said, sliding behind the counter. "You should have hollered."

Julie laughed. "And wake up the baby? Not a chance! I figure if she wants to sleep, I'll let her." She tucked a strand of long blond hair behind her ear and grinned at me.

From across the shop, a sharp whistle caught my attention. "Baby crying," Bluebeard said.

Julie shot him an amused glance. He turned into a real nag where Rose Ann's care was concerned. Like an indulgent old uncle.

"By the way," she said as she packed up her various bags, "your cousin called. He wanted to talk to you about something, but I didn't want to bother you while you were cooking. I told him I'd have you call back later."

"Thanks," I said. I was looking forward to a fun evening with my friends; there was no way I was going to call Peter tonight. Whatever he had to say, I wouldn't like it. It could wait until tomorrow. Or next week. Or next month. Heck, maybe I would just wait until he phoned me again.

A few minutes later Julie called out to tell me she was leaving. She went in and out the back door a couple times, carrying baby gear to her car before she liberated Rose Ann from her crib. With a final shouted "Bye!" they were gone. I listened to make sure the door locked behind them.

A late rush of customers kept me busy through the last couple hours and left a satisfying stack of bills in the cash drawer at the end of the day.

I locked the front door, flipped the sign from "Open" to

"Closed," and emptied the cash drawer into the big safe under the stairs. I was still taking care of Bluebeard when I heard a knock at the front door.

I looked over to see my best friend, Karen Freed—otherwise known as "The Voice of the Shores" newscaster on local radio station WBBY.

With her shoulder-length auburn curls and a body that still fit into her high school jeans—though she wouldn't be caught dead in anything that out of style—she could have been a TV reporter. If she'd been willing to put up with the restrictions that went with the job. Instead she stayed at the local radio station, where she had a larger say in what stories she reported.

Bluebeard wolf-whistled when I let Karen in. She immediately went over and gave him a scratch on top of his head. He rubbed against her hand, enjoying the attention.

"You're only encouraging him," I complained as she talked softly to the bird. "I can't get him to stop whistling, and you just reinforce his bad behavior."

I relocked the door. Ernie and Felipe weren't due for another half hour. I signaled Karen to follow me and headed for the stairs. She gave Bluebeard a last pat and came up the stairs behind me.

While we waited, Karen finished setting the table while I added sugar to the tea and put it in a big spigot jar with lots and lots of ice.

"No Jake tonight?" she asked, counting the four places at the table.

"He's keeping the store open late," I answered. Jake Robinson owned Beach Books, across the street from Southern

Treasures. We were edging closer to being a couple, although there were still a lot of unanswered questions. He'd been a frequent visitor at our Thursday dinners, but he wasn't a permanent member of the group. Yet.

"How about Riley?" I countered. Karen's ex-husband wasn't so *ex* lately, and he'd been to several of our dinners in recent weeks. "You said he couldn't make it tonight?"

"Family obligation," she said. "Bobby's birthday is Monday, so they're celebrating tonight, before the holiday weekend craziness."

I had to admit the Freeds had a lot to celebrate. Bobby, Riley's younger brother, had been accused of murdering a federal agent a few months earlier, and the Freeds were only now getting back to a semblance of normal family life.

"Too late," I said, thinking of the crowds I'd seen earlier in the day. "And you didn't go with him?"

She shook her head. "I didn't want to miss dinner. It's the only time I see Felipe and Ernie once summer starts."

Felipe Vargas and Ernie Jourdain owned Carousel Antiques. Once the summer crowds arrived, the two of them worked nearly every waking hour. The four of us rotated hosting duties every Thursday—had for several years—and it was the only night they closed early during the lucrative summer season.

The phone rang and I picked it up.

"Hello, darlin'," Ernie drawled. "We're running a few minutes late getting out of here, but we are on our way. Felipe is driving like a crazy man, so in two minutes we will either be at your door or we will be dead."

I laughed. "I'll open the door."

Karen started down the stairs before I could hang up the phone. "Got it," she called over her shoulder.

Minutes later I heard the three of them coming back up. Ernie looked elegant as always, the pale green of his crisp Oxford cloth shirt contrasting with his dark skin, his long legs covered with fashionably faded denim.

The man made blue jeans look like a tuxedo. I sighed. Some people just knew how to exude style, and I wasn't one of them. I kept my wardrobe simple—jeans and T-shirts mostly. I tried to look approachable when someone came in the store. That meant dressing just a step above the beach-wear customers, with a casual hairstyle, light makeup, and minimal jewelry. Felipe was right behind his partner, carrying a six-pack of frosty longnecks, and Karen brought up the rear. Felipe immediately open four beers and passed them around as we all exchanged greetings.

Ernie instantly took in the lack of activity in the kitchen. "Where's the food?" he asked. "Did you give up and order out?"

I put the plate of deviled eggs on the table and planted my fists on my hips in mock outrage. "How dare you? I've been cooking for two days."

Behind me, Felipe swung open the refrigerator door to stash the last two beers. His startled "Wow" was all the corroboration I needed.

"How many people do you think you're feeding, girl?"

Chapter 2

ERNIE LOOKED OVER MY SHOULDER AND LET OUT A long, low whistle. "I take it all back. You *have* been cooking."

"Of course," I answered sweetly. "Would you care for an appetizer?" I gestured toward the eggs.

We nibbled on the eggs as we took the rest of the food from the refrigerator, arranged the unmatched bowls on the table, and sat down on an assortment of kitchen chairs.

Most of my apartment had been furnished with bits and pieces from my inventory downstairs. Searching the piney woods of north Florida and south Alabama for vintage furniture, kitchenware, and magazines was one of the best parts of running Southern Treasures. Occasionally I found a piece I couldn't bear to part with. At least until I found the next piece and had to move something out to make room.

As I expected, we spent the first hour debating the authenticity of a "cold supper."

"I really don't know," I finally admitted. "I have no idea how far back the idea goes. But my mother used to make cold meals when it got too hot to cook."

Karen admitted she remembered my mom's cold suppers when we were in high school. "She wasn't the only one either. Mrs. Freed used to do cold suppers sometimes."

The mention of Riley's mother snagged Felipe's attention. "Which reminds me, where is your *Mr.* Freed tonight?"

"He's not *my* Mr. Freed," Karen protested. Her red face contradicted her words as she repeated her earlier explanation, but we didn't bother to point it out.

"How is the shop doing?" she asked Ernie in an attempt to change the subject. "Are the tourists being good to you?"

"Pretty good," Ernie answered. "Good thing, too, since we've lost several of our best local customers."

"You mean the Andersons?" I asked, helping myself to another scoop of potato salad.

"Them," Ernie agreed, "and Lacey Simon. And Jennifer Marshall." He shook his head. "This bank mess is spilling over the whole town."

"That reminds me," I said, remembering my afternoon visitor. "I met the bank auditor, the McKenna woman. She came in the shop this afternoon."

My three dinner companions all stared at me for a silent moment, then everyone spoke at once.

"What's she like?"

"How old is she really?"

"How much did she spend?"

The last question made me laugh. Trust Felipe to cut to the heart of the matter.

"I don't know. I was upstairs fixing dinner when she left, and Julie would have taken care of her." I answered Felipe's query first, then I turned to Karen. "At least forty, I'd guess, maybe a little older." I told them about the careful makeup, the designer suit, and the stiletto heels. "Her haircut probably cost as much as any of us spends on haircuts in a year."

It was a pretty safe bet. Karen and I both visited the local beauty school a couple times a year, and the guys mostly cut each other's hair. In fact, Felipe had become a wizard with a pair of scissors.

"But what's she like?" Ernie repeated his question.

"Smart." I had only exchanged a few words with Bridget McKenna, but it was the one word that instantly came to mind. "Seems genuinely friendly, but she speaks her mind."

"That isn't exactly a news flash," Ernie said. "Last Merchants' Association meeting we got an earful from Andrew Marshall. Rumor has it his wife kicked him out, so maybe his views on women are a little skewed, but he was blaming the McKenna woman, and her bank, for everything that's happened."

"Marshall was a mess," Felipe said. "And I think he'd started happy hour a wee bit early, if you know what I mean."

Ernie nodded, and continued. "He acted like a guy who's lost everything. Which you would know if you'd been there."

He delivered the verbal jab with a resigned air. It was a ritual every Thursday, nagging me because I refused to join. But I wasn't one of the good ol' boys, and I didn't want to be.

"Marshall's already had a couple run-ins with her," Felipe added. "Said she has a bad temper, real short fuse, and a tongue sharp enough to slice bread."

"Well, he may have an attitude, too," Karen said. "After all, Bayvue Estates is the real reason she's here to begin with. If Marshall hadn't borrowed so much money from Back Bay for that development, the bank wouldn't be in trouble."

I shook my head. "You know it's more than that, Karen. Back Bay didn't have to lend that much to him. Or to anybody else. From what I hear, there were a lot of loans that were too big. Besides that, the Andersons treated the place like it was their own private piggy bank."

Felipe nodded, leaning back in his chair and clasping his hands over his stomach. "True that. Felicia Anderson never met an antique she didn't think she should have. Usually with some story about how it once belonged to old General Anderson, so we should give her a discount because it was really hers to begin with." He made a rude noise. "She only married into the family a couple years ago, but she acts like she's been here since plantation days."

It was a slight exaggeration. Billy Anderson had been a year ahead of Karen and me in school, and he'd married Felicia right out of college. So closer to fifteen years than just a couple.

The Andersons claimed they were descended from Civil War General Richard Anderson, based on evidence no one could confirm, and acted accordingly. To hear them tell it, we were all little more than sharecroppers and squatters on their ancestral estate.

Felipe's description wasn't far off. Felicia Anderson might have started out as a Yankee schoolgirl, but she quickly acquired a synthetic Southern drawl and the Andersons' superior attitude.

It was Karen's turn to sigh. "Billy's grandpa would just die to see what Billy's done to that bank. I remember the old man coming to school and starting us all on savings accounts when we were first-graders. Real proud of all the things he did for the community."

Karen stood up and waved away the topic of Billy and Felicia Anderson. "Anything else about the bank woman?" she asked as she started gathering the dirty dishes.

I shook my head. "I only talked to her for a couple minutes. She did like Bluebeard, though."

"Everybody likes Bluebeard." Felipe laughed. "What's more important is whether he liked her. He thought for a second, then continued, "Or whether Louis did."

"Indeed," Ernie agreed. "What did Louis think?"

"Glory said she was attractive," Karen called over her shoulder from the counter, where she was stacking dishes. "Of course Louis liked her."

I laughed. "He is a sucker for a pretty face," I conceded, "but he still has his standards." *Was I actually defending the judgment of a ghost?* I guess I was. "She did get a whistle, so he at least approved that much."

We cleared the table quickly, stashing leftovers in the fridge. Ernie filled the sink with soapy water and washed the plates and silver—someday I'd get a dishwasher!—while I started a pot of coffee. It didn't matter if it was a hundred degrees out, Felipe would want coffee with his dessert.

I scooped ice cream into bowls and put a plate of cookies in the middle of the table. They looked like messy chocolate blobs, but I knew from my taste testing the night before that they would be good.

Karen eyed the plate, then looked up at me. "Are those what I think they are?"

I nodded.

She grabbed a cookie and took a bite. "I haven't had one of these in a million years!" she exclaimed around a mouthful of chocolate and oatmeal.

"What are they?" Felipe asked. He gave the brown blob a suspicious look.

"Lunchroom cookies," Karen and I answered in unison.

"What?"

As hostess, it was my job to explain. "I don't know what other people call them, although I'm sure they have a real name. We just call them lunchroom cookies because they used to have them in the school lunchroom when we were little kids."

Felipe didn't look like he was sold on the idea, but he took a tentative bite, chewing carefully. "Tastes kind of like fudge-coated oatmeal."

"You're pretty close," I agreed. "It's cocoa, sugar, butter, oatmeal, and peanut butter."

Felipe snapped his fingers. "Peanut butter! I knew there was something else. Just couldn't place it."

"The best part is they don't take much cooking. Cook the sugar, butter, and cocoa into a syrup, boil it for a minute, mix it with the oatmeal and peanut butter, and drop spoonfuls on waxed paper to cool."

Karen quizzed me about the recipe, and I fetched the copies I'd made for my guests. We always gave one another our recipes at the end of dinner. Over the years my Thursday notebook had grown fat with things I would cook someday.

"I haven't been able to come up with a definitive origin for the cookies," I admitted. "But I do have my own theory of why they were so common in the lunchroom."

My friends looked at me expectantly, and I explained. "When we were in grade school, there was a commodities program that provided food to the school lunch program. I don't know a lot about it, but I seem to remember a lot of peanut butter and butter in the cafeteria, and oatmeal. I'm guessing that most of the ingredients came from that program."

Karen nodded. "Keyhole Bay was definitely a rural school district back then," she told Felipe and Ernie. "We bused kids in from way out in the country."

As always, we talked far too late, catching up on the week's news and eventually circling back to the impending takeover of Back Bay Bank.

"Is it really that bad?" Ernie asked.

Karen nodded. As the lead reporter for WBBY, she took her news-gathering duties seriously, and usually had the inside track on whatever was happening in town. "I think it is," she said. "They sent down one of their big guns to run the audit, in the middle of the high season. Even at top rates they couldn't find her a hotel room."

"Then where is she staying?" I asked. "Pensacola's got to be worse."

"In one of the model homes," Karen answered. She yawned and stretched her arms over her head before standing up. "The bank owns the houses"—she shrugged—"so I guess it makes sense. Got some rental furniture out of one of those discount places over by Eglin, and moved in." She gathered up the oversized bag she carried with her everywhere. "Early morning tomorrow. I need to be getting home."

Felipe and Ernie were on their feet, too. Ernie carried the ice cream bowls to the sink, but I waved him away. "You've done enough already," I said. "I can take care of the rest of this."

I walked them downstairs and said good night, carefully locking the door behind them and arming the alarm system. I'd become a fanatic about the alarm in the last year.

I checked on Bluebeard, giving him a shredded-wheat biscuit for a treat. He nibbled the biscuit, then dropped the rest of it in his dish and hopped onto my arm. Bumping against my chin, he asked "Coffee?"

I shook my head. "You know the answer," I said, stroking his head. He leaned into me, as though the show of affection would change my mind.

I petted him for another minute or two, but I was already yawning, and it was time to go to bed.

I urged Bluebeard back into his cage, gave him a few seeds to assuage my guilt over the coffee, and made sure he was settled down for the night.

Through the wide front window I could see the lights still on across the street in Beach Books.

I made a quick mental calculation of the leftovers in the refrigerator. There were a *lot* of leftovers, I realized. I'd wanted to be sure I had enough of everything, but because I'd made so many dishes, I had ended up with a refrigerator full of food.

I picked up the phone and dialed Jake's cell number.

"Hi," I said when he answered. "You hungry?"

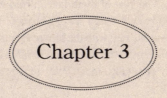

Chapter 3

FIVE MINUTES AFTER I HUNG UP, THE LIGHTS WENT out in Beach Books, and two minutes after that, Jake was at the front door.

I let him in, and Bluebeard squawked a greeting. Jake, understanding his duties as guest, went directly to the parrot to say hello.

"He's already had his biscuit," I warned Jake as he reached in his pocket. Jake often carried treats for the cantankerous bird.

"Not a @#%^$%#% biscuit," Bluebeard shot back, fixing me with a beady stare.

"Language!" I cautioned. Bluebeard could swear like, well, like a pirate, and I hadn't had much luck breaking him of his lifelong habit.

He muttered for a minute, the words indistinguishable but the tone crystal clear, then turned back to Jake. "Pretty boy," he cooed and quickly exited his cage.

Jake looked at me, his glance quizzical. I shook my head in resignation. The two of them had started ganging up on me lately, and I knew I didn't stand a chance.

Privately I was pleased with the turn of events. Bluebeard—and Uncle Louis—were the only blood family I had left, if you didn't count my annoying cousin Peter and his parents, which I usually didn't.

Whether Jake and I were actually a couple was still up for debate, but neither of us was seeing anyone else. So the apparent approval of my great-uncle, even when it came via his spokesbird, was treasured.

I watched Jake pull out a small plastic bag of plump green grapes and put them in Bluebeard's dish. He was rewarded with a quick head butt and another cooed "Pretty boy" before Bluebeard hopped over to the dish and greedily consumed the grapes.

When he had devoured his second treat, Bluebeard went back into his large cage and settled on his perch for the night. I left the door open, which we both preferred, but I draped the cage with a blanket to block the streetlights coming through the big front windows.

"'Night," I whispered.

Bluebeard murmured something soft and indistinct, already on his way to parrot dreamland. I wondered if parrots dreamed. And if Bluebeard didn't dream, did Uncle Louis? I still had no idea what the rules were for ghosts, and Uncle

Louis had done very little to enlighten me. Mostly he flirted with customers and swore a lot.

Having given Bluebeard his due, Jake turned his attention back to me, giving me a hug and a quick kiss. As we climbed the stairs to my apartment, I told him about dinner and asked him what he'd like to eat.

"How am I supposed to choose? It all sounds good!"

I gestured to the table. "Sit down, I'll fix you a plate."

Jake protested, but I shook my head. "I had plenty of help with cleanup, and you were stuck working. I'll get it."

"It's not like I was that stuck," he said. But he settled for getting himself some silverware before he sat and watched me put samples of several salads on a plate. I put the plate on the table, along with a tall glass of sweet tea for each of us.

While Jake ate, making appreciative noises with each bite, I filled him in on everything I'd learned over dinner.

He shook his head at my description of Felicia Anderson. "Fifteen years, and she's still a Yankee?" He lifted his hands in a gesture of surrender that was marred by the potato salad that fell off his fork and plopped back onto his plate. "There's no hope for me then, is there?"

"Probably not," I agreed. "But you're at least a Westerner, not a true Yankee." Though Jake's background was still a bit sketchy, I knew he'd grown up on the West Coast. "Felicia's from somewhere in Connecticut, and even Mark Twain said people from there were Yankees."

"Two points," Jake said, "for a literary reference. Very good."

"But it's all about family," I continued. "Who your family is, who you're related to, how long you've lived here."

Families in Keyhole Bay measured their residence in generations, not years. I knew people whose families had lived in the area for more than two centuries. Family history was a popular topic of conversation, always had been. Which meant I knew hours' worth of stories about families like the Andersons.

"Felicia will always be a Yankee in the eyes of the old families around here." I shrugged. "You will, too—not that it matters to me."

I grinned at him. "Think you can live with that?"

Jake returned my grin. "I guess I can manage," he said. He scraped up the last bite of coleslaw. "Do I get dessert, since I ate all my dinner?" he asked with mock innocence. He already knew there were cookies and homemade peach ice cream, and I knew he had a sweet tooth.

I snagged another cookie for myself when I brought Jake his dessert. He looked askance at the cookies, and I had to explain their history.

"I don't think they're exactly traditional," I admitted. "But I loved them when I was a kid."

While Jake finished dessert, I tried unsuccessfully to stifle a yawn.

"You're tired," he said. "I need to get out of here and let you get some sleep."

I didn't argue. We weren't at the staying-over stage, still far from it, and I wasn't in any hurry to get there.

I let Jake out the front door, and watched as he loped across the deserted street to the front door of his shop before I trudged back upstairs and fell into bed.

* * *

IT WAS NEARLY CLOSING TIME ON FRIDAY WHEN Bridget McKenna came back in the shop. She went straight to Bluebeard's perch and said hello, even remembering to use his name.

A few minutes later, after making a circuit of the shop, inspecting the handmade quilts and thumbing through the vintage magazines, she came to the counter with a couple postcards and a garish T-shirt in a size small. "I should have packed some weekend clothes," she said, handing me the T-shirt. "Usually I plan better than this."

"You travel a lot?" I asked, ringing up her purchases.

She nodded. "It used to be long-term assignments, but over the last few months it's been every other week, with a week at home in between. This time"—she paused to dig in her wallet for a credit card—"it's going to take a little longer than expected, so I'm stuck here over the weekend."

I took the postcards and turned them over to scan the price codes. "I'd swear I bought postcards when I was in here yesterday," she said. "But when I got home, they were nowhere to be found."

I vaguely remembered seeing her standing at the spinner rack the afternoon before when I had gone upstairs to fix dinner. I thought she'd had postcards in her hand, though I couldn't be sure.

It might not be our mistake, but I bought the cards by the hundreds, and they didn't cost a lot. Call it a gesture of goodwill, I could afford to give away a few postcards.

"These are on me," I said as I slipped the postcards into a small bag. "You want to put these in your purse?"

She took the small bag and slid it into a side pocket of her purse.

"Thank you," she said. "If I find the others, I will be sure to return them to you."

"Not necessary. Consider it a gift," I said as I handed her the large bag with the T-shirt.

She glanced around, as though making sure there weren't any other customers in the store. "So what's to do on the weekends around here?"

"Depends on what you like," I replied. "Boat tours, museums, beaches if you can stand the crowds." I ignored the shudder that passed through me at the thought and added, "Lots of scuba diving in the Gulf.

"You have a car, right?"

She nodded.

"Biloxi's just a couple hours west, if you want a casino. Another hour or so to New Orleans, a couple more and you're in Cajun country, if you want to do some driving. There are some lovely places in southern Louisiana: bayous, plantations, there's even a couple places that have sternwheeler cruises. And there's always a festival or something."

She thought for a moment, then asked, "Where would you go?"

"Biloxi, I guess, because I haven't been there in a while," I answered. "I usually go over a couple times a year with friends. Catch a show, gamble a little, maybe stay over one night. But mostly I can't be gone longer than a day," I said, glancing around the shop.

I also couldn't afford to gamble if I wanted to continue saving for my secret goal: to buy out my annoying cousin Peter. Which reminded me he had called the day before. My mother would be scandalized that I was ignoring the social obligation of returning his call, but my mother hadn't had to deal with Peter the way I did.

"One more question. Where around here is good for dinner? I've been living on takeout all week."

I shook my head. "Wish I had a good answer to that one. There are a couple great places, but everything's packed on a Friday night in the summer."

She sighed. "Guess it's another evening of fish and chips, or burgers. I am so not ready to fight crowds." She glanced around again. "Besides, I know I'm not exactly welcome around here."

The ghost of a grin played around her mouth. "Not like that's anything new."

I don't know what possessed me, but before I could stop myself, I blurted out, "If you don't mind leftovers, I've got plenty to share."

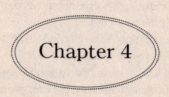

Chapter 4

BRIDGET—AFTER MY HASTY INVITATION, I HAD TO start thinking of her on a first-name basis—considered my offer for several seconds, but she answered before I could rescind it.

"That's very generous, but I wouldn't want to put you out. Are you sure you want to do this?"

My brain was screaming "No!" but the manners drilled into me by generations of Martine and Beaumont women wouldn't let me take back an offer of hospitality.

"Of course," I lied, smiling in what I hoped was a sincere way. "I'll just need to tidy up a little." I frantically tried to remember if I had made the bed that morning, or washed the rest of last night's dishes.

"Are those leftovers portable?" she asked.

"Uh, yeah, I guess so. Why?"

"Why don't you bring them out to Bayvue, and we can eat

there? I have a huge house all to myself. Besides"—she lowered her voice conspiratorially—"I know everybody around here wants to see what those houses look like. Unless you've been out there already?"

I shook my head. The houses had been completed just as Marshall Development cratered. Nobody from Keyhole Bay got a chance to see the models before they were locked up tight. Since then, only the bank examiners had been allowed on the property.

"I have to admit I'm curious," I said. I knew that my curiosity sometimes got me into trouble, but I couldn't see any harm in getting a tour of the notorious model home. "Why don't I give you a call when I'm ready to drive out?"

There wasn't any way I could get in trouble just going out to see those houses, was there? And how could I resist the opportunity to get a close-up look at the development that was causing so much dissention?

As soon as Bridget was out the door, I grabbed the phone and called Karen. The call went to voice mail, and I instinctively checked the time; it was five minutes past the hour, time for Karen's local news segment on WBBY.

While I turned on the radio to catch her broadcast, I left a message. "Call me ASAP."

For the next ten minutes, I listened to Karen. She interviewed a local author who just happened to have a signing scheduled at Beach Books on Saturday, reported on the fresh catch at the fishing piers, and presented a recorded segment of her ongoing coverage of Keyhole Bay history.

Karen kept her boss happy by doing the stories he wanted, the ones that cast his advertisers and listeners in a good light.

But she also liked to do what she called *real reporting.* Digging into stories with an edge energized her more than a triple espresso, and she managed to get them on the air even when the portrayal was less than flattering.

It took her another fifteen minutes to return my call. "Only have a few minutes," she said without preamble. "Meeting with the station manager in five."

"Well, whatever plans you had for tonight, cancel them."

She didn't argue. We'd been best friends for decades, and she knew I would have a good reason. But that didn't stop her from asking, "Why?"

"You want to see the inside of one of the Bayvue Estates model homes." It wasn't a question; I knew she'd want to go. The fact that I needed some moral support had nothing to do with anything. Much.

"When?"

"Soon as you're off. We're taking the leftovers from last night. Oh, and we'll need a main dish to fill out the menu. There isn't much chicken salad left. 'Bye!" I broke the connection, knowing she wouldn't delay her meeting to call me back.

I could deal with the fallout while we got ready to go out to Bayvue Estates. Besides, I was the one with the invitation. She wouldn't get to see the house without me.

My hands shook as I put the phone back in place. I didn't spontaneously invite strangers to dinner, or boss Karen around. If anything, Karen bossed *me* around. And everyone else. It was one of the main reasons she and Riley couldn't seem to live together. Riley owned his own fishing boat, and he was used to being the boss. Having two bosses in one house had led to some interesting times. And a divorce.

So where did all this gumption come from?

That was the exact question Karen asked when she showed up at my door an hour later.

I was just closing up for the night when her SUV slid in next to the curb. How *did* she manage to find the exact perfect parking spot, no matter where she went? It was as if the universe acknowledged that she was in a hurry and it catered to her needs. It was part of her charm that she simply accepted her good fortune as her due.

She came through the front door with a grocery bag in her hand, her giant shoulder bag slung over her shoulder, and a bemused look on her face.

"Who was that strange woman who called me an hour ago and started giving orders?" she asked with a laugh in her voice as she locked the door behind her. "I don't believe I know her."

"I don't either," I admitted. "But I need your help, and I knew you'd want to go with me."

"With you where?" She shook her head. "You can explain while we take care of this." She waved the grocery bag in my direction. "An extra pound of chicken salad from the deli at Frank's. We'll mix it with whatever's left of yours and no one's the wiser."

She was halfway up the stairs before I caught up with her.

I pulled the leftovers out of the refrigerator, gauging whether there was enough food for three people. I decided it was probably fine. Bridget wasn't tiny, but she was slender, and I would bet she wasn't a big eater.

I don't know what I was concerned about. Last night I had a refrigerator so full I didn't know what to do. And now I was worrying over how much Bridget would eat, in case I didn't have enough. But a good Southern hostess always served way more food than her guests would eat.

Karen took my bowl of chicken salad and added in her contribution from Frank's Foods. She mixed the two together and tasted, then transferred it to a clean bowl. I debated doing the same with the other salads, but they were all in refrigerator containers with secure lids, and they would travel better that way.

I tried not to imagine what Memaw would have said about serving food from a plastic box. It simply wouldn't have happened in her house.

As we worked, I explained to Karen how the invitation had come about. "She sounded kind of lonely," I said, "and the idea of take-out burgers, even good ones, every night?" It didn't appeal to me, and I was certain it hadn't appealed to Bridget. Why else would she have said yes to an invitation from a complete stranger?

"Did you tell her I was coming with you?" Karen asked. The challenge in her voice told me she already knew the answer.

"I will," I said, trying not to sound defensive.

Karen was packing the boxes and bowls into a couple canvas shopping bags. "Well, you better get on that, since we're about ready to leave."

We were ready, but I suddenly felt hesitant about the whole enterprise. What were we doing, really?

I shoved aside my trepidation and picked up the phone. It rang twice, then I heard Bridget say, "Hello."

"Hi, Ms. McKenna. This is Glory Martine from Southern Treasures. I'm just closing up the shop. We still on for dinner?"

"Of course. And please call me Bridget. I'm only Ms. McKenna to clients and my boss."

"Okay," I said. "Just one thing. I forgot I was going to see a friend tonight. Do you mind if I bring her along? I think you'll like her."

"I'm sure I will." I could hear Bridget's smile, and an undertone of something—relief?—in her voice. "Do you need directions?"

I told her no, and said we'd see her in a few minutes.

Bayvue Estates was a couple miles beyond the city limits, but nowhere in Keyhole Bay was much more than five minutes from anywhere else.

Except in summer traffic.

Karen offered to drive her SUV, but I wanted to take my truck and she agreed to ride with me. The truck was my pride and joy, purchased a few months earlier from my friend Sly.

It was really more of a gift, though Sly would insist I had paid a fair price. The 1949 Ford pickup had belonged to Uncle Louis before Sly bought it, and he'd sold it to me for what he'd spent on it. It had just come back from the lettering shop with the name and number of my store emblazoned in old-fashioned gold script on the dark forest green paint. According to Sly, it was just the way it had been when Uncle Louis owned it.

I thought it was the most beautiful truck in the South.

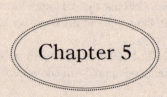

Chapter 5

WE CREPT THROUGH THE EARLY EVENING TRAFFIC with the windows rolled down. Auto air-conditioning was unheard of in 1949, and in spite of the Florida heat, I couldn't bear the idea of adding it. The truck was completely original and I wanted to keep it that way. So we drove with the windows open.

"Thanks for coming with me," I said to Karen. "This could be really awkward, just the two of us. But you can talk to anyone anytime."

"I can ask nosy questions, you mean."

"That, too," I answered. "But I think you'll like Bridget. Besides, you might get something that will make a good news story down the road."

Traffic thinned as we moved away from the crush of motels, restaurants, and souvenir shops. Most people never got off the main drag, never saw the homes and schools that made Keyhole Bay a real town.

We passed the city limit, turned north on a county road, and spotted the brick gateposts that marked the entrance to Bayvue Estates. They guarded the entrance to an unfenced swath of bare land with a single paved road leading away from the highway.

There weren't many estates, just two model homes surrounded by empty lots. And there wasn't a view of the bay either.

A tall magnolia tree, its base hidden beneath fallen leaves and waxy white blossoms, stood in front of one house. The rest of the front yard, overgrown with tall grass, gave the new construction an air of defeat and abandonment. The only sign of human occupation was a midsize sedan parked in the driveway.

The paving petered out a few yards beyond the model homes, the remainder of the streets in the development nothing more than graded dirt paths wandering between the vacant lots.

I pulled the truck up next to the sedan, and we clambered out with the bags of food. As we approached the front door, it swung open and Bridget called out a greeting, as though she had been listening for our arrival. She had changed from her suit and stilettos into a pair of fashionable jeans and a casual tank top that probably cost more than my entire wardrobe.

"Hi," I answered. "We brought a cold supper, since it's too hot to cook." I nodded to Karen. "Bridget, this is my best friend, Karen Freed. If you've listened to WBBY since you've been here, you've probably heard her newscasts.

"Karen, this is Bridget McKenna."

Karen managed to shift the grocery bag to her left hand and extended her right hand to Bridget.

"I'm that evil woman from up North," Bridget said with the same warm smile I'd seen the day before. "Glad to meet you." She glanced over at me. "And yes, I have heard her on the radio." She held the door for us. "Come on in."

I waved away Bridget's offer to take my bag and followed her toward the kitchen with Karen right behind me. As we crossed the two-story-tall entry, I took in the marble floor and the view across the broad living room to the backyard.

Without landscaping, the backyard looked even more desolate than the front. I could imagine what it might look like if a professional landscape architect had been able to finish the job with native grasses, flowering bushes, and tropical plants.

Bridget led us through the empty dining room and into the kitchen. Speckled black granite counters topped honey-colored wood cabinets. Glass doors, meant to display china and crystal, exposed empty shelves. A six-burner gas range under a top-of-the-line microwave–range hood combination dominated one wall, and a three-door refrigerator stood within easy reach of the butcher-block-topped central island. I could see where a big chunk of Back Bay's money had gone.

Next to the deep farmhouse sink, a roll of paper towels stood on end by a cheap toaster and coffeemaker, which seemed out of place in the high-end kitchen. They were the only things that looked as though they had been used.

"Cold supper sounds like an excellent idea," Bridget said

as we unpacked the bags and laid out plastic boxes and bowls on the island next to a collection of plates and silverware. "Food first?" she asked. "Or would you rather have the grand tour?"

I didn't wait for Karen's answer. "Tour first."

We stuffed the food into the nearly empty refrigerator, battling the door that closed on us the minute we let go of it.

"It needs to be leveled," Bridget said. "It's on my to-do list."

Karen shot her a quizzical glance.

"The bank wants to liquidate as soon as possible, to get our money back out. They asked me to evaluate the property—get an appraisal if I need to—and see what it will take to unload the houses and the empty lots."

Bridget led us through the house. Upstairs, a huge master suite opened to an expansive balcony running along the entire back of the house, and overlooking the barren backyard. Windows in the master bathroom surrounded the jetted tub set on a ceramic-tiled pedestal, and shared the same view.

Karen let out a low whistle. "Could have been gorgeous," she said, "if the yard was finished."

We saw two smaller bedrooms on the second floor with a Jack-and-Jill bathroom between them. In the shared bathroom there were no faucets or towel bars, and the vessel sinks still had manufacturer's stickers on the outside.

In the closet of the back bedroom, one wall had been lined in cedar, and a stack of planks on the floor looked as though the carpenter had left at the end of the workday and never come back. Which, I suppose, was pretty close to the truth.

Back in the central hallway, the door to the hall cabinet sagged open. Karen had pushed it closed as we walked past, but it had swung open again. Either the house had a ghost, or the cabinet door had been hung improperly. I suspected the latter. On the other hand, I had some firsthand experience with ghosts. I was convinced Uncle Louis sometimes did things like that just to mess with me.

Back downstairs Bridget showed us the home office with its own entrance around the corner of the house from the front door. It was a room full of built-in dark oak cabinets and bookcases, tucked behind the soaring entry.

Karen eyed the office appraisingly. "Nice setup for someone who works from home," she said. "A lawyer, or an architect. Something like that."

In contrast to the open plan, huge windows, and light colors of the rest of the house, this room had a cozy, private feel to it. It was my favorite room in the house, one where I could have happily settled down and filled the shelves with books. But as we left the room, I noticed how uneven the textured finish of the walls looked.

The house was a study in contradictions. The kitchen was completely finished, filled with custom cabinets and high-end appliances befitting a sales display for expensive homes, the beautiful office storage units were clearly custom-fitted to the room, and the smell of new carpet still permeated the entire structure. But the upstairs hadn't been completed, and in several places work had been done in such a hurry that it wasn't properly finished, like the sagging closet door and faulty texturing.

As we trooped back down the stairs, the doorbell rang.

Bridget shot us a questioning glance. We both shook our heads and followed her to the door.

It couldn't be anyone from Keyhole Bay; no one was that ill-mannered, not even Felicia Anderson. Showing up at someone's home—if you weren't family, or as good as—without an invitation was considered rude, but without even calling first was ever so much worse.

Before we reached the bottom of the stairs, the bell rang again. A fist pounded against the door, and from outside a deep voice yelled, "Marshall, are you in there? I want to talk to you!"

The three of us exchanged a quick look. "You know who he's looking for, right?" I asked Bridget.

She nodded. "The developer, Andrew Marshall. But he's never lived here. Nobody has."

"Yeah," Karen said as we crossed the entry hall, "I thought they just used it as the sales model."

"That's right," Bridget answered. "They had a construction trailer out here when they started. Moved it when they had these places close to finished. That was about a week before the hammer fell."

She stopped at the door and took a moment to draw a deep breath. In an instant she transformed from the relaxed and friendly woman we'd been talking to into an executive with a commanding air of authority.

All the while the pounding and screaming continued, with the addition of some rather inventive cursing that would have impressed even Bluebeard.

Bridget took one last deep breath and opened the door.

"Can I help you?" she asked in a tone that implied she probably couldn't. Or wouldn't.

The man paused for a second, then yelled, "Where is that thieving SOB?"

I had been right. He definitely wasn't from Keyhole Bay. Sixtysomething, with the ruddy face and veined nose of a longtime drinker, his pale skin branded him as a Northerner as surely as his bad manners did. He wore custom-tailored white slacks and a pastel golf shirt that strained across his beer belly, with an expensive and ostentatious watch clasped around his wrist.

He stood on the porch, his head thrust forward in the challenging posture of a lifelong bully. A man with a lot of money, very little class, and no tact at all.

I stood back and watched as Bridget carefully dismantled his air of superiority.

"I'm afraid I have no idea where Mr. Marshall is," she said calmly, as though she hadn't heard his outburst. "He has no interest in this property. There is no reason for him to be here."

Somehow, despite the fact that the man was at least six inches taller, she appeared to look down her nose at him. "Will there be anything else?"

"There damn well will be!" he shouted. Like most bullies, volume was one of his favorite weapons.

"And that is?" Bridget made a show of suppressing a sigh, as though her boredom threshold had long been passed. She turned and looked at us, the gesture broad and theatrical. Taking the cue, we both shrugged elaborately.

"I want my damned house! If he's not here, then maybe you better be turning it over to me, honey."

I saw Bridget's spine stiffen at the casual condescension in his tone, and the familiarity of his words. But she didn't let him see it.

"Well," she said, her voice still controlled, her posture deliberately relaxed, and her tone deceptively cheery, "since I don't know who you are, or why I should give you anything, particularly the house where I am currently residing, I don't see how that is going to happen."

"I gave that SOB a hefty deposit on this house." He had stopped screaming, though he was still loud. "He said it'd be ready for us to move in by the first of July. Now I get here and I find you living in my house, Marshall's nowhere to be found, and my wife is raising hell." He gestured toward the expensive sedan parked in the road in front of the house.

I assumed his wife was in the car, though the tinted windows obscured any view of his passenger.

Bridget shook her head. "You did not put a deposit on this house. This house was never for sale. You put a deposit on a house in this development. *This* house"—she waved her arm as though displaying a prize on a TV game show—"belongs to the bank that financed Mr. Marshall's venture. And so does the rest of the development."

She stared him down. "If you have any other questions, I suggest you make an appointment to see me in my office at Back Bay Bank. You can call my secretary on Monday morning. Bring your receipts and contracts. And maybe your lawyer.

"In the meantime, I suggest you get off my porch and out of my yard. You're trespassing."

She didn't wait for his answer.

She shut the door in his face. She didn't slam it, just closed it swiftly and firmly, and shot the dead bolt as soon as the latch clicked into place.

From the porch we could hear the man continuing to yell. He pounded on the door and leaned on the doorbell for several minutes at a time.

Bridget waited until he was getting hoarse from the shouting, and the pounding grew weaker. Whoever her visitor was, he wasn't a young man, and he didn't have the stamina for a sustained attack.

As he started another round of pounding, she whipped the door open. His arm was in midstrike, and without the solid surface of the door, the momentum of his swing threw him off balance.

For long seconds he flailed around, nearly falling in a heap on the doorstep. She just stared at him as he struggled to stay on his feet.

Once he was stable, she looked him up and down, then spoke. "By the way, can I get your name? For my report?"

His answer would have made Bluebeard blush, and contained several suggestions that I didn't think were physically possible. He finally turned to leave, but stopped long enough to stare back at her.

"You'll pay for that."

For the first time since he'd appeared, I was frightened.

Bridget didn't appear the least bit afraid, but fury bubbled in her every word and gesture. "The worst part is, I have no idea if he's the only one, or how many there might be. Three? Five? A dozen? Back Bay doesn't have a record of how many deposits Marshall took, or how much they were." She slammed her fist against the door, an echo of the man's tantrum on the porch.

"Dammit! I do not want to have to hire security guards again."

Karen looked startled. "Again?"

Bridget sighed, and I could see her anger ebbing. "Yeah. It's one of the hazards of the job. You're messing with people's money and their lives.

"Desperate people sometimes do desperate things. Once in a while I've needed a little extra help getting through some of the worst situations.

"Come on," she said, waving toward the kitchen. "Let's see what you brought. Confrontations make me hungry."

She laughed, her tone and attitude dismissing the angry bully who never did give her his name, and she led the way through the house.

Back in the kitchen, we retrieved the food and spread it across the butcher block. As we filled our plates, I explained the various dishes to Bridget, which led to a discussion of our Thursday night dinner.

"It started out as a way to keep in touch during the summer, when we were all really busy," Karen said after we were settled at the small dining table tucked into a corner of the kitchen. "And then we just kept going. After a while it kind of became a tradition, and now we can't stop."

Bridget looked wistful. "Sounds great to me. I travel so much I could never keep up with a schedule like that."

"Well, we do sometimes miss a week, if someone's on vacation or something," I said.

"Like you ever take a vacation," Karen said.

"I do. But when you work for yourself, the boss won't give you much time off."

"A real slave driver, eh?" Bridget asked.

"Sure is," Karen answered before I could. "She never really takes a day for herself."

"Not true," I said. "We went to De Funiak—"

"A year ago," Karen interrupted. "And even then it wasn't a day off. It was a treasure-hunting expedition and you bought a bunch of inventory for the store."

"But that's fun for me," I protested.

"So, Bridget," I said, trying to steer the conversation away from my supposed obsession with work, "did you decide what you're going to do with your days off?"

Bridget hesitated, as though reconsidering her options. "I think," she said finally, "I may go over to Biloxi for the day, maybe even stay over one night." She glanced around the sparsely furnished house. "It might be good to get away from here, especially after my visitor. At least for a few hours."

She had a point. The house might someday be a lovely home, but right now it was downright depressing. The rental furniture was low-end commercial: a basic bedroom set, a bare-bones living room set, and the dining table and chairs. I didn't like a lot of clutter—my apartment was far too small for tons of knickknacks or mementos—but I had books in my bookcases, pictures on the walls, and canisters on my kitchen counter.

Even a hotel room would feel homier than Bayvue Estates.

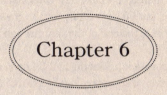

Chapter 6

"BILOXI SOUNDS LIKE FUN," KAREN SAID WHEN WE pulled out of Bridget's driveway. "We ought to go again soon."

"Yeah, right," I answered dryly. "In my copious free time."

"You have Julie," she countered. "I know you can't go in the summer, but September's only a couple months away."

I pulled out of the deserted development past the brick gateposts, turning south onto the county road. Far behind me I saw a pair of headlights, the only other vehicle on what most tourists would consider a back road. Once you got off the highway, you could travel for miles without seeing another car.

We turned onto the highway, heading back into the center of town. The midsummer sun was just setting, and waiting crowds spilled out of restaurants onto the sidewalk, a reminder of what Bridget would have encountered in her search for dinner.

As we drove through, I mentally tallied the number of hotels and motels with red neon signs blazing "No Vacancy." It was a good indication of what to expect for the weekend. Near as I could tell, the town was 100 percent full.

Tomorrow should be a busy day. Biloxi was sounding better all the time, but I'd be wishing for the crowds when business dropped off at the end of the summer and I still had bills to pay.

It was my constant balancing act. I'd been orphaned by a hit-and-run driver at seventeen, and I felt like I'd been pretty much on my own since then. Paying the bills and taking care of myself topped my list of priorities, and had for over fifteen years. It often didn't leave a lot of time for other things.

I had accepted the responsibility long ago. I'd chosen to run Southern Treasures myself, and I usually preferred it that way. But it didn't stop me from occasionally chafing under my self-imposed restrictions.

I pulled into the parking area behind the shop and shut off the engine. "Wine?" I asked Karen as we climbed out of the truck.

She shook her head. "After I ditched Riley to go with you, I better not," she said. "I promised him I'd be home before it got too late."

I stopped at the back door, key in hand. "Home? He's checking up on you?"

She hesitated, and I prodded some more. "What's really going on with you two? *Really?*"

"It's complicated," she answered.

I shook my head. "That's not an answer, Freed." As I said it, I realized something that had somehow eluded me for years. Karen had divorced Riley, but she had kept his name. At the time she had claimed it was for professional reasons: she was known on air as Karen Freed and she didn't want to lose that identity. Now I wasn't sure I completely believed her.

"And don't tell me you're 'taking it slow' again. That isn't an answer either."

Karen's unhappy frown didn't deflect my question. I stood my ground, not yet unlocking the door while I waited for an answer.

Finally she sighed and looked away. "We're not together, if that's what you're asking," she said without looking at me. "But we are seeing a lot of each other, and we aren't seeing anyone else."

She hesitated and took another deep breath. "And he's stayed at the house a few times. *That* was never a problem."

"Are you crazy?" I asked. I kept my voice low, concerned, not challenging. "You divorced him once, and now you're going right back into"—I struggled for the right word—"into whatever this is. You two keep splitting up and getting back together, and now he's staying over? Do you not remember how upset he got when you went to Jacksonville alone?"

I reached out, put my hand on her arm. "You got hurt bad the first time, hon. Can you handle that again when you break up for good?"

"*If*," she insisted. "*If* we break up, not when. We're adults this time. Sure, Riley got upset when I went to Jacksonville, but we talked it out instead of fighting. That's progress, isn't it?

"We know where the pitfalls are, Glory, and we're trying to find ways around them. So we *are* taking it slow, even if you don't think that's an answer."

I squeezed her arm. There wasn't anything I could say that was going to change her mind, and she knew full well the risk she was taking. And maybe they could make it work. I hoped so, for both their sakes.

"Okay," I said. "I'll be here if you need me." As if there was any question. We'd always been there for each other, ever since grade school.

I unlocked the door.

I followed Karen inside, stopping to double-check the locks on the back door, then moving through the storage room to let her out the front, where her SUV waited at the curb.

"Thanks again for going with me," I said.

"Glad to," she answered with a grin. "You were right, you know. I did like her. Too bad she'll be gone again in a couple weeks."

"Who knows?" I answered. "Maybe she'll come back and work here when the sale goes through. We could start a girls' network, have our own answer to the good ol' boys."

"Yeah, sure." Sarcasm dripped from her words. "I won't hold my breath."

I laughed. "Someday."

I locked the door behind her, and went to check on Bluebeard.

I changed his water and fed him a shredded-wheat biscuit from the can underneath his cage.

"Coffee?" he asked hopefully.

"No, Bluebeard, parrots do not get coffee. *I* don't even get coffee at this hour." I gave him a couple scritches, checked the locks again, and headed upstairs.

* * *

I WAS DOWNSTAIRS WORKING ON A T-SHIRT ORDER when Julie arrived the next morning. She let herself in and turned over the "Closed" sign.

"Morning, boss," she said, sliding behind the counter next to me. She pointed to an image on the computer screen. "That one's been really popular this summer," she said. "You might want to order a few extra in kid sizes. For some reason, that's one they want to buy as matching mother-daughter sets."

"Thanks," I said, clicking back on the design and adding two dozen in mixed sizes before checking the totals and clicking on the "Order" button.

"There was one other thing," Julie said. "I've been getting a lot of people asking about stuff with Bluebeard on it. T-shirts, shot glasses, postcards, stuff like that. Some of them say they saw him on the website and they are disappointed we don't have anything."

I'd spent months learning about websites, working for hours experimenting with ways to display my merchandise and promote the store. Adding Bluebeard's picture to the pages had been Jake's suggestion, a good one.

Now Julie offered a way to take it a step further.

"I'll give Mandy a call, if you'd like," Julie said.

"Mandy?"

"A friend of mine. She works over at Coast Custom Printers. They do the shirts for Mermaid Grotto. Started out as a uniform for the staff, but customers kept asking if they could buy them. They put a stack at the register and she says their order gets bigger every month."

She started to say more, but the bell over the door rang as a tourist couple came in. She gave them her dazzling, cheerleader smile and called out, "Hi, y'all! Can I help you find something special?"

They shook their heads. "Just looking," the wife said.

"Sure thing," Julie said, still smiling. "Let me know if there's anything you need."

She made a show of going back to straightening the shelves behind the counter. She'd learned quickly that the fastest way to drive a customer out the door was to hover, to make them feel like they were being watched, even when they were.

Across the street, Jake's "Closed" sign still hung in the front window. He'd changed his hours, opening later in the morning and staying open later at night every Saturday, and he said the new hours had boosted sales.

Jake emerged from his front door and crossed the street to my front door. He glanced around, spotting the one couple flipping through the vintage magazine rack against the back wall. "Got time for coffee?" he asked.

I looked at Julie, who nodded. "I'll call if it gets busy," she said.

I made sure I had my cell phone, and followed Jake next door to Lighthouse Coffee.

Chloe put out two vanilla lattes and two lemon scones as soon as we reached the counter. "The usual," she said. "Saw you coming." She grinned.

Jake tossed a twenty on the counter. "Keep it," he said,

waving away the change she offered him. "I had a good day yesterday. Besides"—he grinned back at her—"come winter, there may be no tips at all."

Chloe shook her head. "I don't think that's even possible for you," she said. "You're far too nice to stiff the barista."

"You'd be surprised," he teased her, but I knew she was right. Jake was one of the most considerate people I'd ever known.

Out of habit, we sat by the front window, where Jake could watch the front door of Beach Books, even though the "Closed" sign was still up.

I took a sip of the sweet coffee. "Thanks. A good day yesterday, huh?"

Jake nodded. "I don't know why, but the store was busy from open to close. You?"

I shrugged. "Good. Not a blockbuster, but a good day. The evening got a little strange, though."

"Oh?" Jake cocked an eyebrow. "What happened?"

I told him about Bridget coming back into the shop, and my impulsive invitation.

"You had her over for dinner?" he asked, surprised.

I shook my head. "Not exactly."

Jake listened while I gave him a quick summary of the previous night's adventure. He looked alarmed when I told him about the guy pounding on the door.

"You didn't call the cops?" he asked.

I shook my head. "Bridget chased him off, and he left. There wasn't much they could have done anyway. Warned him, maybe, or cited him for trespassing. But the property isn't marked, so I don't know if they could even charge him with trespassing unless he came back after she told him to go away."

Jake looked thoughtful. "I don't know. I guess it depends on what the law is. I don't even know if that's a local ordinance or a state law."

"I don't know either." I ate the last bite of my scone, and took a sip of lukewarm latte. "I've never had to worry about it, but I bet Karen knows. I'll have to ask her. Not that it matters, but now I am curious."

Jake drained his coffee cup and glanced at his watch. "Time to go open up," he said, gathering his trash.

I looked up, intending to answer, and saw Bridget coming through the door. Dressed in the gaudy T-shirt she'd bought the day before, she had on a pair of jeans that looked like they'd been custom-made for her. Judging by what I'd seen of her wardrobe, maybe they had been.

She spotted me and waved, heading for our table.

"Hi, Glory," she said. She turned to Jake, who had started to stand. "Don't get up on my account," she said with a smile. "I'm on my way out of town, just stopped to return Glory's dishes."

She turned back to me. "I took them to the shop, and that sweet girl said you were over here having coffee. I just wanted to say thanks again for the meal, and the company."

"You're welcome," I said. I gestured to Jake. "Bridget, this is Jake Robinson. He owns the bookstore across the street. Jake, this is Bridget McKenna."

I didn't bother to explain Bridget's position. Jake, like everyone else in town, knew *exactly* who she was.

Jake was already on his feet, and shook her outstretched

hand. "Glad to meet you, Ms. McKenna. Don't mean to be rude, but I really was on my way out. Time to open up."

"Not at all," she answered. "I'm actually heading out myself. Taking Glory's suggestion and going over to Biloxi for a little R and R."

Jake nodded. "Have fun," he said. "Glory"—he looked at me—"talk to you later." He turned and waved over his shoulder as he walked out the door.

I gestured to the empty chair across from me. "I need to get back, but I have a minute if you want."

Bridget shook her head. "I should get on the road, I think. How about a rain check? One morning next week?"

She glanced out the window, watching Jake stride across the street, and smiled back at me. "That one looks like a keeper."

I felt a blush creep up my face. "Yeah. Maybe."

Bridget laughed. "See you next week."

I followed her out the door and went back to Southern Treasures.

More customers came in as the morning wore on. Julie and I handled questions, sales, and special requests. Bluebeard whistled and squawked and was rewarded with giggles, finger-pointing, and occasional shrieks from teenaged girls.

He had his picture taken with a steady stream of visitors, flirted with every woman, and only had to be reprimanded for his vocabulary a couple times.

The foot traffic thinned in the early afternoon as the temperature climbed and the tourists retreated to swimming pools and air-conditioned hotel rooms, or prostrated themselves on the blistering sand. Julie came back from her break, and I was free for a few minutes.

I stuck my cell phone in my pocket and headed for the front door. "Call if you need me," I said as I went out. "Otherwise I'll be back in twenty minutes or so."

My first stop was back to Lighthouse, for a trio of frozen mochas. Then I walked past Southern Treasures on my way to the Grog Shop.

I tried to check in with Linda, the owner, every couple days. Linda had been a friend of my mother's and was like the older sister I never had. She and her husband, Guy, had taken me in when my parents were killed, and she was the person I turned to when I needed advice.

Linda was at the register, ringing up a sale. I put two drinks on the counter, and wandered into the back looking for Guy. I found him checking off delivery sheets and hoisting cases of beer onto racks in their small warehouse space.

I put my drink down and started stacking cases as he marked them off. "Yours is up front, if Linda doesn't drink both of them before you claim it."

"She wouldn't dare," he growled.

I didn't believe his act for a minute. He and Linda were as devoted a couple as I had ever seen, a relationship I both envied and aspired to. If and when I found the right man. The image of Jake, grinning as he handed me my latte, flashed through my memory. I shoved the idea into the back closet of my mind and slammed the door. Too soon. Way too soon.

"How's it going?" I asked.

"Doing good," he replied. "Definitely beer weather."

I looked around, taking in the nearly empty shelves. "Looks like it."

Guy kept working as he talked. "Would you believe I already had two deliveries this week, and I had to call for another one this morning?" He ticked off the last case and I put it on the shelf. "Not that I'm complaining, mind you. Always good when people are buying."

Guy maneuvered a hand truck loaded with more cases toward the door. "Get that for me, would you?" he asked.

I grabbed my coffee and held the door while he steered the load through it and toward the giant walk-in cooler at the back of the store. I opened the cooler door, and he pushed the hand truck through, letting the door close behind him.

Linda was alone at the counter, and I walked behind it to give her a hug.

"Thanks for the mocha," she said.

We talked for a couple minutes, catching up on what we'd been doing the last few days. I told her about our Thursday dinner, and about taking the leftovers out to Bayvue Estates the night before.

"You went out there with that woman?" She sounded shocked. "What made you go all the way out there, all alone with a total stranger?"

"She seems really nice." Okay, that sounded lame, even to me. "I took Karen with me. And we got to see one of the model homes."

"Was it as deluxe as everybody said it was?"

I hated to disappoint her, but I had to say no. "Oh, they tried," I told her. "But the work wasn't done right. A lot of stuff looked like it was done in a hurry, or just not finished at all. It was sad, and kind of creepy.

"Like something had died out there."

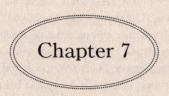

Chapter 7

I WANTED TO TALK TO LINDA ABOUT KAREN AND Riley, to have her reassure me that my best friend wasn't heading for a fall. It was the kind of conversation I imagined most women had with their mothers or sisters, and Linda was the closest thing I had to either one. But a steady stream of customers cut our visit short. That conversation would have to wait until we both closed for the night, or for another day.

I waved good-bye and went back to work. At least I got a cold drink, a jolt of caffeine, and a change of scenery for a few minutes.

By the time we closed up for the day, I was too tired to talk to anybody. It took me another couple hours to close out the register, balance the books, and get the store ready for the next day. When I was through, all I wanted to do was crawl upstairs and collapse in a heap. Even fixing dinner sounded like too much work.

And I wasn't the only one. As I was checking the locks

and setting the alarm, the store phone rang. I ignored it, letting it go to voice mail. I'd check the message before I went upstairs and decide if it could wait until morning.

A few seconds later my cell phone rang.

"Hello?"

"Pizza's on the way," Jake said. "Want some?"

"Thank you, yes. I was just thinking I was too tired to cook, so it was going to be corn flakes for dinner."

"Neil's said they'd have it here in half an hour, if that works for you." There was a pause, then he continued. "I gave them your address for the delivery."

"That's some nerve, Mr. Robinson. What if I'd had other plans? It's Saturday night. I might have had a date," I teased.

"Saturday night in July," he answered. "You never go out on the weekends in the summer. That was one of the first rules you taught me about being a local."

"Got me," I said. "I'll unlock the door, if you're coming over soon."

"On my way," he replied.

True to his word, I saw him emerge from his door onto the sidewalk, heading for the crosswalk in front of his store.

I dropped the phone in my pocket and went to take care of Bluebeard. He'd had a long day of customers, and he was as tuckered out as I was.

Bluebeard spotted Jake through the big front windows, approaching my door. "Pretty boy," he said, in a voice eerily like that of my great-uncle Louis Georges. I hadn't heard Uncle Louis since he passed away when I was ten, but I recognized his voice coming from Bluebeard, and I knew he wasn't talking about himself.

"Hush!" I said. "You keep your nose out of my business. Or your beak. Whatever. Just butt out, okay?"

Bluebeard cast a beady eye around the shop before glaring at me and uttering a clear profanity.

"Language, Bluebeard!"

He quieted to a low mutter, but I'd known this parrot a long time. Other people might not hear it, but I could make out several words he knew he wasn't supposed to use. I guess I should be glad he chose to wait until there were no customers in the store.

Jake locked the door behind himself and made his way between the display racks to where I stood.

"Arguing with Bluebeard again?" he asked, slipping an arm around my shoulders for a quick hug. He seemed to hesitate about any display of affection in front of Bluebeard.

I wanted to deny it, but he was right. I was arguing. *With a bird.* Okay, it was a bird who occasionally channeled the ghost of Uncle Louis, but it was still ridiculous.

"Bluebeard's misbehaving again, if that's what you mean," I said, sidestepping any admission of guilt. "He needs to learn to mind his own business."

Jake cocked an eyebrow at Bluebeard. "Trying to keep her out of trouble?"

Jake knew about Uncle Louis, and it amused him to think my great-uncle chose to meddle in my life. I wondered if he would think it was so funny if he knew Bluebeard was talking about him.

"Mostly he's tired and cranky," I said. "He's had a long hard day of being a celebrity." I remembered Julie's suggestion from that morning. "Speaking of which, what would you think about shirts and postcards with Bluebeard on them? We could use the same pictures we used for the website. It was Julie's idea," I added, not wanting to take credit that wasn't mine.

"Brilliant! Those oughta sell like crazy, if you can make the numbers work out."

"I don't know about the costs yet," I said. "Julie said she had a friend at a print shop where they do the shirts for Mermaid Grotto."

Jake's eyes widened for a moment. "Of course. I saw those at the hostess stand the night we were there. Don't know why I didn't think of doing them for Southern Treasures."

"You were busy taking in the atmosphere." Mermaid Grotto was all about the atmosphere. A giant fish tank separated the restaurant from the bar. The tank was home to a live mermaid show when I was a kid; now it held tropical fish and aquatic plants.

It had also had one very unwilling swimmer. I'd become far too familiar with that tank a few months earlier when I'd been shoved into it, and a shudder passed over me at the memory.

Jake put a comforting arm around me and drew me close to his side. Clearly he was remembering my visit to the mermaid tank, too.

I shook off the memory, refusing to dwell on an unhappy might-have-been.

"What kind of pizza did you order?"

"Pepperoni and tomato with extra onion and bell pepper. Right?"

I was impressed. Jake had clearly been paying attention.

In a few minutes Neil's delivery van pulled up in front and a kid jumped out holding an insulated carrier. Jake met him at the door with his wallet in hand.

Soon we were upstairs with hot pizza and cold beer. A far better end to the day than I had imagined possible.

We talked about watching a movie, but neither of us could work up enough enthusiasm to actually pick out something and put it in the player.

Instead we hung out eating pizza and talking about putting Bluebeard's image on T-shirts and postcards.

"You could also do mugs," Jake said. "See what other things the printer has, and what they cost."

"I wonder what Mermaid Grotto sells their shirts for," I said.

The question began to eat at me, and I had to get up and find my laptop. "Maybe they have them on their website."

"If they have a website," Jake said.

"Everybody has a website, according to you," I said. "You said I had to have one, because everyone else did. So they better have something."

It took me a couple minutes of searching, but I finally connected to the Mermaid Grotto site. "Look," I said, briefly turning the screen so he could see it, "here's their page. Lunch menus, dinner menus, entertainment . . ."

I ran the cursor along the tabs at the top of the page, stopping over the one that said *Merchandise*. I clicked and a new page loaded showing shirts, mugs, decals, and calendars.

Jake moved to share the display, coming close enough that I could feel the warmth of his shoulder pressed against mine. I liked the feeling.

We checked out the prices on the shirts. They were comparable to the graphic shirts I already sold at Southern Treasures. Definitely something I should look into.

But it would have to wait for Monday when Julie came back to work. I shut the laptop and leaned against Jake's shoulder, stifling a yawn.

"I saw that," he said, kissing me gently. "You need to get some sleep, and I need to get home."

I kissed him back, tempted to ask him to stay, but the reality of our respective responsibilities quickly drove the idea from my mind.

"I'll walk you down."

"You don't have to come downstairs," Jake replied, closing the pizza box and taking it to the refrigerator. "I can lock up."

I shook my head. Even though I'd given him the alarm codes, I couldn't relax without my daily ritual. "You know I have to check the locks and alarms for myself."

I followed him down. We checked the back door and the alarms, and kissed good night at the bottom of the stairs. We walked silently to the front door so as not to wake Bluebeard. I locked the door and watched Jake lope across the street and around the building to where he parked his car.

Bluebeard, however, wasn't nearly as cooperative. He stuck his head out of his cage and glared through the dim light.

"Trying to $&#$&$% sleep here."

I took the hint and went back upstairs.

Chapter 8

A FREAK SUNDAY MORNING THUNDERSTORM CHASED the tourists off the beach and into coffee shops and stores like mine. As soon as the sun broke through, though, the shop emptied as the crowds headed for the water.

In the lull that followed, I straightened and restocked the shelves, filling in the bare spots with merchandise from the warehouse. The shirts were stacked, the mugs and glassware lined up, and I was refilling the postcard rack when I heard Bluebeard mutter, "Uh-oh."

I glanced at him, realized he was staring at the door, and turned to see what caused his distress.

Peter.

Peter was coming through the front door, with his family close behind. Peggy waved at me, a harried look on her face as she headed directly for the back of the shop, seven-year-old Matthew clinging to her hand. Judging from Matthew's awkward gait, I suspected they were headed for the small bathroom tucked into a corner of the warehouse. Eleven-year-old Melissa followed at a more leisurely pace, her expression making it quite clear that she considered her brother's distress an affront to proper etiquette.

"Peter?" My voice came out with a quaver. I swallowed hard and tried again. "Peter, what a surprise! What brings you here?"

Peter shrugged, not meeting my eye. "We were visiting the folks for the weekend, and the kids wanted to come to the beach, so we figured we'd come down for the day."

There was more to it than that, I was sure, but I knew Peter—and he would take his time getting around to the real reason for his visit. Meanwhile, I was stuck with him, Peggy, Matthew, and Melissa in the store.

I asked Peter how he'd been, and let him rattle on about his job while I worked on the postcard rack. I wasn't listening carefully, but I gathered his success was just beginning and he would undoubtedly be running the company soon.

After a few minutes of Peter's chatter, Peggy returned from the bathroom with Matthew still in tow.

Melissa trailed behind, as though trying to keep as much distance between herself and the rest of the family as possible without risking a public scolding. Clearly, adolescence had hit full force. Going to the beach was good. Going with your parents was barely tolerable. Going with your little brother was clearly unacceptable.

I'd always gotten on well with Melissa when she was younger and I was the cool independent auntie with an apartment, a store, and a parrot. But I hadn't seen her in nearly a year, and it looked like I had joined the ranks of the other adults in her life.

The verdict was crystal clear when she greeted me with "Hello, Aunt Gloryanna. It's good to see you." Gone were the excited hugs, the "Auntie Glory," the begging to feed Bluebeard. I bit back a sigh. Most kids went through this stage; I had just hoped it would be different for Melissa and me.

"Good to see you, too"—I hesitated—"Melissa." Somehow, calling her Mel, which I had always done, felt wrong. She gave me a perfunctory hug, immediately pulling away as though anxious that someone might see her. With a shock I realized she was nearly as tall as me. When did that happen?

When you were busy avoiding her father, Martine.

Fortunately for my bruised ego, Matthew still thought I was cool. He waited impatiently until I released Melissa, then charged up and grabbed me around the waist. "Hi, Glory!"

Peter cleared his throat and looked hard at Matthew. His smile slipped and he released me. "Hello, Aunt Gloryanna," he said.

Ignoring Peter, I crouched down to Matthew's eye level and gave him a quick hug. "Hi, Matthew. I'm very glad to see you."

I stood back up and patted his mop of unruly sun-bleached hair. "How are you?"

"Good. Can I feed your bird?"

Bluebeard muttered again. I think Melissa had hurt his feelings, and I was grateful for Matthew's little-boy enthusiasm.

I led Matthew to the biscuit tin and let him extract a couple of the shredded-wheat squares that were Bluebeard's usual treat. Looking at the parrot, I said, "If he behaves himself, I'll let you give him some banana a little later."

His grin told me I had scored some important auntie points.

Peggy hadn't spoken a word since she'd emerged from the back of the shop. In fact, she didn't seem able to even look me in the eye. Her gaze seemed rooted somewhere around my navel, her brow furrowed as though she was trying to unravel a particularly puzzling problem.

"Peggy?" I said.

Her eyes flickered to my face and then back down.

"Honey?" Even Peter, oblivious as ever, had noticed her concern. "Is something wrong?"

Peggy pulled her lips in, biting them as if to prevent her thoughts from spilling out. She shook her head slightly and unclenched her lips. "No," she said, but she didn't sound convinced.

Matthew was feeding Bluebeard, ignoring the grown-up drama taking place a few feet behind his back, and Melissa had moved several paces away as though once again putting as much distance as possible between herself and the adults.

Silence stretched as we waited for Peggy to continue. Something was clearly bothering her, but I didn't know what, and Peter, as always, didn't have a clue.

Finally Melissa broke the uncomfortable silence with a dramatic sigh. "Mom, just *ask*, for God's sake!"

"Melissa! Do not take the Lord's name in vain!" Peter seized on his daughter's expression as a way to extract himself from whatever was upsetting his wife. But Melissa wasn't having any of it.

"Oh, Dad," she said in her most disgusted almost-a-teenager tone. "Really? Mom is about to lose it, and you're worried about my language?" She shook her head, clearly incredulous that her parents could be so clueless.

Peggy, meanwhile, still hadn't spoken, and didn't look as though she was going to.

Melissa tossed her long dark hair over her shoulder with a flip of her head, dismissing her father. "Mom, if you won't ask, I will."

Peggy didn't respond. Melissa turned and looked at me. Something in her expression told me I was being tested. I hoped I wouldn't fail.

"Aunt Gloryanna, why is there a baby crib in your back room?"

It took a few seconds for her question, and the meaning of Peggy's stare, to sink in. I started to laugh, but before I could explain, Peter broke in angrily.

"Is that why you wouldn't come visit Mother and Dad? Why you've been avoiding us? Glory, what were you *thinking?*"

I stopped laughing, anger bubbling in my stomach like a cup of bad coffee. I felt my face flush and my hands clenched into fists.

"Oh, no," Bluebeard said softly.

I had to control my temper.

One.

Two.

Three.

I couldn't punch Peter in front of his wife and kids, much as I wanted to.

64

Four.

Five.

I would not swear at him with Melissa and Matthew listening.

Six.

Seven.

Eight.

Even if he was being a judgmental asshat.

Nine.

Ten.

Like hell I wouldn't.

"What the hell?" My voice was loud, but I didn't scream, and my language was milder than it might have been. I'd had Bluebeard as an example, after all. But I got my point across.

"A—a crib?" Peter stammered.

"So what if there is?" I shot back. "Would you just hold off on your judgmental BS for a minute?"

I turned my back on Peter and addressed Melissa. "Yes, there's a baby crib back there. And a changing table, a rocking chair, and a chest full of diapers. They are for my friend Julie who works here part-time, so she can bring her baby with her when she doesn't have a babysitter."

I felt a hand on my arm. I turned and found Peggy standing at my side. "Sorry," she said, a blush in her cheeks. "I just saw the crib, and I thought . . ." She hesitated, then shook her head. "I didn't know quite what I thought, or how to ask about it. I'm sorry."

Melissa's attitude relented. "That is so cool, Aunt Glory! You really let your employee bring her baby to work?"

I nodded. "Rose Ann usually stays with her grandma, but some days her grandma can't keep her and she comes here. She's a very good baby."

I turned to Peter. "Do you have any other questions?"

Peter didn't answer. Not that I expected him to.

In a too-bright voice, Peggy tried to change the subject. "Have you been busy, Glory? There was a lot of traffic on the way down."

"It was a pretty good morning," I answered. She was trying desperately to ignore the tension that remained after her husband's outburst, and I went along. But in the back of my mind another strike was added to Peter's list of offenses. It was growing into a long list. "You're getting your reports and checks all right every month, aren't you?"

"Of course we are." Peter spoke up again, now that his wife had smoothed things over. "In fact, that was one of the things I wanted to talk to you about." He looked at Peggy, a clear reminder that she had a specific role to play in his little performance.

She looked relieved, and called to the children. "Let's go!" She turned back to me, her cool, impassive mask back in place. "I promised the children ice cream when we got here. We'll be back in a jiffy," she said with an insincere smile.

Obviously, her moment of embarrassment had passed. She took Matthew by the hand and led the way back to the sidewalk, Melissa trailing along in her wake.

Melissa looked at her father and me over her shoulder, her expression telling me quite clearly that she would rather listen in on our conversation than hang out at the ice cream shop with her mother and little brother.

A rush of warm air flowed through the door, then the three of them were outside and the door closed behind them.

The old air conditioner droned on, battling against the heat, its constant whirring the only sound in the shop. Even Bluebeard remained silent, waiting to see what fool thing would come out of Peter's mouth next.

But I didn't get a chance to find out why Peter had dropped in. He got as far as "I wanted to talk to you," when the bell sounded over the door and a trio of thirtysomething women came in.

I smiled at the new arrivals. "Can I help you find something?" I asked in a friendly voice. Even if Peter had angered me beyond endurance, I couldn't let it change the way I treated my customers.

"Thanks," said a leggy blonde, clearly the alpha of their little group. "Just looking for some souvenirs for the family before we have to head back."

The other two giggled in a way that said "girls' weekend" more clearly than their sunburns and the slight air of one-too-many umbrella drinks last night that clung to them.

"Anything in particular?" I asked, stepping closer. "Kid stuff, or something for the men in your life?" I had stopped using *husband* and *boyfriend* a few years back, in a moment of extreme caution, and the habit had stuck.

"Kids," the blonde's companions said in unison, and burst into giggles again, which the blonde didn't share. I revised the umbrella drink hypothesis to mimosas with brunch, with the blonde as designated driver.

I moved to the spinner rack full of T-shirts and hoodies with garish slogans emblazoned across them. I was already wishing I had Bluebeard T-shirts. These women would have snatched them up. "Boys or girls?"

Before the giggling women had a chance to answer, Peter clamped his hand on my arm. "We need to talk," he said. "But this isn't the time. Let's have dinner together. I'll call and tell you where to meet us."

Without waiting for an answer, he hurried out onto the sidewalk just as Peggy and the kids approached from down the block.

I turned back to my customers, wondering just what it was we had to talk about.

Chapter 9

TRUE TO HIS WORD, PETER CALLED JUST BEFORE I closed up for the night.

"We have reservations at Mermaid Grotto in an hour," he said. "Can you meet us there, or do we need to pick you up?"

How did he do that? Somehow, in his own bumbling way, Peter had managed to choose the one place in Keyhole Bay where I never wanted to go again. Even without knowing about my adventure, he'd zeroed in on the worst possible choice. And unless I wanted to tell him why, there wasn't any easy way around it.

"We loved going there when we were kids, remember, Glory?" he went on. "I thought it would be great to go again, and to introduce Matthew and Melissa to one of our favorite places. They don't have mermaids anymore, of course."

If you only knew!

"I'll meet you there," I told Peter. If I had to go to Mermaid Grotto, I at least wanted to have my own car with me.

And I didn't really want to go alone. Not when I would be facing Peter and Peggy and both kids.

I could call Karen, but I'd already intruded on her Friday night, and there were limits to what I could ask, even from my best friend. My gaze went to the shop across the street, as it did more and more lately. Jake knew about Peter, and about my secret plan to buy him out. But Beach Books still had an "Open" sign in the front window, and there were people in the store.

I thought about asking Felipe, or Ernie, but Sunday night was their time to relax and regroup after the weekend. Same for Linda and Guy. Although I knew Linda would drop whatever she was doing to go with me if I needed her, it wasn't fair of me to ask.

I locked the store, and went to take care of Bluebeard. "Looks like I'm going to have to face him alone," I said as I filled his water and checked his food dish. "Not that I can't do it, but I hate being outnumbered."

I put a few grapes and a piece of banana in Bluebeard's dish. He'd had a long weekend, too, and he deserved a treat.

"Won't be the first time," I continued.

Bluebeard cocked his head and looked at me with his beady black eyes. He looked so human when he did that, as though he was thinking hard about his response. But it wasn't the parrot who answered.

"Sylvester." The name came from the bird, but the voice was Uncle Louis's. "Sylvester," he repeated.

I felt a slow smile spread across my face as I considered

his suggestion. Sly was the one person I knew who had known my great-uncle well. Though I had only met him recently, he felt like a long-lost uncle. He wasn't blood, but I trusted and respected Sly a lot more than Peter, who was.

"Perfect!" I said. I gave Bluebeard another piece of banana. "Good boy!"

I called Sly and asked him if he'd like to have dinner with me. His enthusiasm dimmed somewhat when I explained about Peter and his family, but he agreed to be my date. I said I'd pick him up in half an hour.

Then I called Peter back. "Hope you don't mind," I said in a rushed tone. "I'm bringing a friend along to dinner. I had plans with him," I lied, "so I'll just bring him with. I'm sure there isn't anything you need to tell me that he can't hear."

I didn't wait for Peter to break his stunned silence. "Gotta run. See you in a little bit." I broke the connection and charged upstairs to change. My phone rang as I reached the top of the stairs and the caller ID said it was Peter.

I didn't answer.

Twenty minutes later, showered and wearing a cool cotton dress and a pair of flat sandals, my hair pulled into a loose ponytail that kept it off my neck, I ran back downstairs. I said good-bye to Bluebeard, checked the locks and alarms, and hurried out the back door to where my truck was parked behind the shop.

Five minutes later I pulled into the junkyard behind Fowler's Auto Sales. I congratualted myself on knowing all the back roads, and avoiding the parking lot that Main Street became on a summer weekend. One of the benefits of living in Keyhole Bay all my life.

A grin split Sly's face when he saw the truck gleaming in the late afternoon sun. He may have sold her to me, but I knew she held a special place in his heart.

I tossed him the keys. "Want to drive?"

He snatched the keys out of the air with the dexterity of a man forty years younger, and the grin grew wider.

"Guess I could do that for you, girl," he said. But the joy in his voice belied the casual words, and made me smile.

"By the way, if Peter asks, we had plans."

He nodded.

Sly slid behind the big steering wheel and started the engine. He cocked his head, listening carefully to the muted rumble. After a minute of concentration he nodded, as though satisfied the truck was performing properly, and expertly released the clutch.

I watched his face as he drove the few blocks to Mermaid Grotto. His delight in driving the old truck was evident, and I felt a lump in my throat as I realized how much the old man had come to mean to me.

He pulled into the far corner of the lot, as far from other vehicles as possible, and parked protectively next to a curb. It was exactly what I would have done.

We climbed out of the cab, and I caught Sly patting the hood when he thought I wasn't looking. "Just making sure she isn't running too hot," he said. I didn't believe it for a second.

I walked across the parking lot, through the shimmering waves of heat rising from the blacktop. As we neared the front door, my steps slowed.

Facing Peter was bad enough, but I hadn't been through the front door of Mermaid Grotto since the afternoon Sly had sold me the truck. Since that afternoon in the old mermaid tank that had nearly been my last.

"You have to face it sometime," Sly said, offering me his arm. "But it don't have to be today. Up to you, girl."

I took his arm with my left hand and straightened my slumping shoulders. "No, you're right. And today's as good a day as any." I patted his arm with my right hand. "Thanks for being here," I said softly.

"Any time you need me," he answered. "Now let's go meet that cousin of yours and see what damn fool scheme he's got in his head this time."

I grinned. Trust Sly to cut to the heart of the matter.

But even with Sly at my side, walking into Mermaid Grotto turned my stomach and weakened my knees. I stopped just inside the door, unable to take another step for fear my legs would give out and send me tumbling to the floor.

"It don't have to be today," Sly repeated in a whisper.

I closed my eyes for a second and took a deep breath, steeling myself against the sight of the mermaid tank. "Yes, it does," I whispered back, opening my eyes and looking around. "Or I have to explain to Peter why not. And I do not want to discuss my swim in that tank with him. Ever."

"Up to you," Sly replied.

I stood my ground, and Sly stayed at my side.

After a few seconds I felt stronger, and we moved toward the hostess stand. I distracted myself by examining the T-shirts on display. The graphics were excellent, and the shirts appeared to be high quality.

"Did I tell you we might be doing T-shirts with Bluebeard on them?" I asked Sly.

He shook his head. "You didn't, but it sounds like a great idea. Heck, you might even get me to wear one."

The idea made me smile. Sly may have worn coveralls in the junkyard, but they always looked as though they had started the day clean and freshly pressed. When he wasn't working, he wore sharply creased khakis and long-sleeved sport shirts with the sleeves rolled up to expose his sinewy forearms.

I had never seen him in anything as casual as a T-shirt. Especially one with a parrot on the front.

"I'll give you one, if you promise to wear it," I teased.

"You got a deal," he answered.

The hostess gave me an inquiring glance, and I told her we had a reservation.

"Name?" she asked, looking at her list.

I realized belatedly that Peter hadn't told me what name he'd given them. I gave her Peter's name, but there wasn't anything. I tried Peggy. It would be just like my cousin to delegate the actual work to his wife. No joy.

I was about to abandon my quest and just wait for Peter and his family to arrive when I had one more idea. "Southern Treasures?" I asked.

The girl glanced down at her list and back up with a polite smile. "That's it," she said, as though I was a small child that had finally given the correct answer to a question. A frown creased her perfect brow. "But it says three adults and two children?"

"Actually there are four adults," I said, returning her false smile. "The others should be along any minute. We're just a little early."

She eyed me for a moment longer, than motioned us to follow her. I gripped Sly's arm tighter, and kept my gaze on the hostess's back as she led us to a large round table near the enormous fish tank.

Sly immediately pulled out the chair that faced away from the tank and held it for me. "We should let the guests watch the tank, don't you think?" he said, taking the chair next to mine.

I nodded, but couldn't find my voice to answer. I could feel the mass of water at my back, and I shivered with a chill that had nothing to do with the temperature of the room.

Within seconds ice water appeared, and a young man took our order for sweet tea. After he left to fetch the drinks, Sly gave me a concerned look. "Sure you're okay? You look like you seen a ghost."

I laughed, or at least I tried. What came out of my throat was closer to a gargle. "No, I only talk to a ghost."

"You know what I mean."

"I do, Sly," I croaked. I took a long drink of water and tried again. "Really, I'll be fine."

To distract us both from our surroundings, I began to tell Sly about Peter and Peggy's visit to the shop. I got as far as Peggy's return from the restroom when Sly shook his head slightly and looked over my shoulder.

I turned to follow his glance, and saw the hostess approaching our table with Peter, Peggy, Melissa, and Matthew trailing along behind her.

The next few minutes were a chaos of introductions and musical chairs, as the kids jockeyed for the seats facing the fish tank, and Peter tried to control everyone's movements.

Sly acknowledged the children with the courtly manners of an earlier generation, and practically bowed over Peggy's hand when she offered it to him.

Peter maneuvered himself into the chair on my left. He leaned close as the kids and Peggy were exclaiming over the fish tank and took advantage of the hubbub to whisper, "Don't you think we should talk about our business in private, Gloryanna?"

I forced an innocent smile onto my face. "Whatever do you mean, Peter? You said you wanted to talk, but you never actually said it was about business."

He glared, but I wasn't finished. "You know, Sly is an old friend of Uncle Louis, and he's kind of taken to looking out for me, since I'm alone down here."

I stopped and bit my lip, trying to look sincere. It wasn't exactly a lie; Sly did kind of look out for me. Not because I was alone, or because I needed looking after, but because he was my friend.

"You know we wanted to have you move up closer to your family," he said. "You could have come and stayed with Mom and Dad when your folks . . ." He left the rest of the sentence dangling, as though he was too considerate to actually say something indelicate.

"No, I couldn't have, Peter. We've had that conversation a million times. But that's ancient history. Sly is here, and there isn't anything you can say that you can't say in front of him."

"You're sure you want our family business discussed in front of *him?*" Peter's voice rose slightly, and he clamped his mouth shut as though trying to stop the flow of words.

"It won't bother me," I said, maintaining my innocent tone. Truth be told, I kind of wanted a witness to whatever Peter had planned, and I trusted Sly to be objective. Even though he'd called Peter's ideas "damn fool schemes."

Some things were just self-evident.

Peter, as usual, had to stall for a while before he could actually get to his point. He made a show of examining the menu, and asked me a series of questions about the offerings. Had I tried a particular dish? Did I remember if that was on the menu when we were kids? Had I been here lately?

It was the one question I hoped he wouldn't ask but knew he would. Like his choice of restaurant, he'd managed to find the most inane question with the most painful associations.

"I was here for dinner a few months back," I answered. "Before spring break. But I avoid places like this during the tourist season, they're usually very crowded." I neglected to mention my subsequent visit, and tried to deflect further questions. "Which reminds me, how in heaven's name did you manage to wrangle an actual reservation? Usually they don't take them; it's first come, first served, and the lines are monstrous on the weekends."

It worked. Peter launched into a long-winded explanation about how he'd impressed the hostess and the manager and talked them into allowing him to put his name on the list and arrange to return at a particular time. "You can usually get what you want," he said smugly, "if you know how to play the game."

He smiled knowingly. "That's how it works in the city."

I turned my head and caught Sly's eye. His warning frown kept me from bursting into hysterical laughter. It was the standard procedure at the Grotto during the summer, when their clientele tended toward families with children, who couldn't wait in the bar. It wasn't a reservation exactly, but it let them manage the waiting crowd a little better.

While I tried to figure out how to answer Peter's arrogance, the waitress appeared to take our orders. I was grateful for the interruption.

Peter, naturally, had to modify everything he selected for his dinner, so it took several minutes to get the order exactly to his specifications. Eventually, though, he was satisfied and the waitress left.

She returned in a couple minutes with a glass of white wine for Peggy and sodas for the rest of the family. I envied Peggy; if I had to spend much longer around Peter, I'd need something a lot stronger than wine.

But that would have to wait until I got home.

For the next few minutes, Peter held court, explaining the fish tank and its history to his family. I could see the kids rapidly losing interest, until Peter started talking about the mermaids that used to swim in the tank.

"Real mermaids? Really?" Matthew asked, his eyes alight with the prospect.

"There's no such thing as a mermaid," Melissa said, with barely concealed contempt. "Everybody knows that."

"They were real enough," Peter said. "Ladies with tails and long hair. They swam around the tank in a kind of slow dance, and they did flips and loops and all sorts of things. They were all really beautiful, and really amazing swimmers, and they did a show every half hour, I think it was, all day and all night. It was really something to see." He turned and looked at me. "You remember that, don't you, Glory? Way back, when there were people swimming in the tank?"

For one insane second I considered telling him it had only been a few months since someone went swimming in the tank, but the impulse passed.

So I nodded in agreement, and motioned for him to go on.

Peter chattered on about the mermaids, and how their show was famous all along the Gulf. I sat with my back to the tank and let his voice wash over me, wondering when he would finally get to the point of his visit.

Dinner arrived, fish and chips for the kids, grilled shrimp for Sly, salads for Peggy and me, and a highly modified sampler platter for Peter. Everything looked and smelled good, and the conversation died away quickly as we tucked into the meal.

Peter ate quickly, nodding appreciatively. "It's as good as I remember," he said when he pushed the empty platter away with a contented sigh.

"When was the last time you were here?" I asked, searching for some way to restart the conversation.

"Not since I was a teenager," Peter said. He stared off into space, as though trying to remember. But the details didn't come, and he shrugged. "A long time anyway."

Peter drew a deep breath and turned in his chair to look at me. "I want to talk to you about the store."

"I presumed as much," I said dryly. "Especially when you made the reservation in the name of the store."

Peter shrugged. "It just seemed appropriate. Anyway," he

went on, "I thought I'd talk to you while we were down here, and after our visit to the shop, well . . ." His voice trailed off, as though I should know what he meant.

"Well, what?" I played dumb. I wasn't sure what he had in mind, but I suspected it had to do with Rose Ann's nursery. I wasn't wrong.

"I think we need more merchandise," Peter said. "Revenue is up a little, but it could be better. Have you thought about expanding?"

"There isn't any space. The places on either side of me have been there for years, they're doing well, and neither one is going anywhere. I can't expand." I dismissed his suggestion. "Maybe someday, but not right now."

Peter shook his head. "I thought about that, but after I looked the place over again today, I think there's room to bring in more merchandise.

"If you don't need the space in the back for warehouse space, if you can waste that area, and our money, on a nursery for a part-time employee, you can use it for more displays and more merchandise."

Even though I was expecting him to say something along these lines, his pronouncement stunned me into silence. Wrong in so many ways. I felt anger start to bubble, but I forced it back. I'd already yelled at Peter once today, with no apparent affect. It was time for a different approach. "I understand that you aren't around the store much," I said. Beneath the table I clenched my hands into fists, my fingernails digging into my palms in an effort to control my temper. "You have no way of knowing what works and what doesn't. And you have no way of knowing how that nursery came to be. But believe me, there is no waste of 'our' space, and I did not spend any of the store's money."

He started to speak, but I cut him off. "The nursery was a gift from many of Julie's friends, a way to allow her to keep her job. Which, I want to point out, she is very, *very* good at, though you have no way of knowing that either."

Ignoring most of what I said, Peter shot back, "Well, maybe I need to be more involved then. Maybe I should spend some time here, see what works. I'm sure you could profit from a fresh pair of eyes on the operation." He sniffed indignantly. "Of course, I have a very important job that keeps me busy."

He shook his head. "There isn't any way I can personally supervise your operation."

He cocked his head to the side and tried to pretend he'd just had an idea. I knew we were finally getting to his real mission. And I knew I wasn't going to like it.

Chapter 10

"SINCE I CAN'T BE HERE MYSELF," HE CONTINUED, "maybe I can get someone else to take a look at the operation. A consultant maybe?"

I controlled my mounting anger. Peter's interference had reached a new height. He had always worked for a large corporation, and he had trouble translating what was appropriate for a big company into what worked for a small store. I had to keep that in mind, or I would explode.

"We've talked about consultants before, Peter," I reminded him. "The expense far outweighs anything they could do for a company this small."

"But there must be something," Peter replied.

I should have come up with an alternative, but I couldn't think of anything that would pacify Peter. Which gave him time to come up with something on his own.

I could see the wheels turning as he searched for another

plan. Clearly he hadn't been prepared to discuss other ideas, and didn't have a Plan B. But that didn't stop him from saying the first thing that popped into his head.

"What if Peggy comes down for a few weeks? While the kids are out of school."

"What?" Peggy clearly hadn't heard this idea before, and judging from her tone, she wasn't on board with it. "I can't possibly be away from the children."

Peter glanced over at her. "You could bring them with you. It would be like an extended vacation for all of you."

I glanced at Peggy, assuring myself she would be my ally in shooting down this latest scheme.

"There are about a million reasons that is not a good idea," I said. "It's obvious Peggy has a few of her own, and I could give you a long list. Starting with, where will they stay? Summer rentals are completely booked, and even if you found a cancellation, the rates are massively expensive."

Before I could offer any other arguments, Peggy spoke up again. "Peter, there is no way I am going to spend the rest of the summer down here with the children, staying Lord-knows-where, and leaving them alone while I work in some tacky shop."

She tossed me an apologetic glance. "Not that *your* shop is really tacky, Glory, but it's the idea of the place."

She turned her attention back to Peter. "That is not a good idea, and you should have at least talked to me first."

She looked toward the children, then back at her husband. "We can talk about this. Later. But spending the summer down here simply isn't going to work."

Sly had held his tongue all through the conversation,

though his presence had helped calm me. Now he spoke up. "I knew your uncle, Mr. Peter," he said quietly. "He was a good man, but he knew his limits. That's why he never made that store no bigger. Kept it small enough to run by hisself; or with his little sister helping." He nodded in answer to the question he saw on my face. "That was your granny. But he never did hire anyone else."

Peter tried to interrupt, but Sly waved him to silence. "Mr. Louis was plenty smart. Knew what he was about, all the time. And he made a success of that little shop. Still in business all these years later, isn't it?

"So you might want to think real careful before you go messing with what Mr. Louis started. You know the old saying, 'If it ain't broke, don't fix it.'"

Sly sat back and fell silent. He'd spoken his piece, and he was done. He pulled a worn leather wallet from his pants pocket, counted out some bills, and left them on the table.

"I believe I'll wait in the car, Miss Glory. If that's okay with you?"

I nodded, ignoring Peter. "I'll be right along, Sylvester. Just let me say good night to my family."

Peter tried to draw me into another discussion after Sly walked away, but I had nothing more to say. "I understand that you want the shop to grow," I said. "But there isn't a good way to do it, and this isn't the time. Maybe in the future, if Pansy decides to close up Lighthouse, or Guy and Linda want to retire, then we can talk about it. But not right now."

I added some bills to the stack Sly had left by his plate. "It was good to see all of you, but I have to be up early tomorrow."

I turned to Peter with a sober expression. "You have a

demanding job. So do I. I have not had a day off since before summer started. And I won't have one until at least September or October. That's what keeps your earnings checks coming every month. I love it, and I'm darned good at it.

"Just trust me, Peter. I know what I'm doing."

With that I turned my back and walked toward the door. I had held my temper in check for as long as I possibly could. If I didn't get away from Peter—and out of the restaurant crowded with bad memories—I was going to explode.

When I got to the truck, Sly had the doors open, letting the evening breeze cool off the interior. I ducked my head into the cab and quickly popped back out. It would be a few more minutes before we'd be going anywhere.

"You did good, Miss Glory," Sly said. "Mr. Louis would be proud of you."

"Thanks. You didn't do so bad yourself."

"Just speakin' the truth. A man's got to know his limits, that's all."

We climbed in the truck, Sly behind the wheel, and he started the engine. Peter and his family hadn't come out of the restaurant when we pulled out into traffic and started back to Sly's cottage in the junkyard.

"There is one thing I still don't understand," I said as Sly expertly maneuvered through the crowded streets. "Uncle Louis left the store to Peter and me instead of our parents, his niece and nephew. And he didn't leave us equal shares. That's never made any sense to me."

Sly didn't answer right away. He finessed his way between two carloads of way-lost tourists, one trying to turn left across the steady stream of traffic and the other waiting to turn right while a gaggle of teenagers straggled across the street in front of them, oblivious to the traffic.

We turned into the lot at Fowler's Auto Sales and drove around back to the fenced-off junkyard before Sly finally answered me.

"It was because of the tuition," he said, as though that explained everything. It explained nothing.

"What tuition?" I asked.

"Your uncle Andrew's."

"Peter's dad?" I asked. "What does his tuition have to do with anything?" I paused and thought for a minute. "He didn't even go to college, did he?"

"Nope."

Sly parked the truck outside the gate and jumped down out of the cab. He walked up to the gate and dragged a key ring from his pocket. Selecting a key, he opened the padlock that held the gate closed.

At the sound of the key, Bobo came running from somewhere deep in the shadows of the junkyard. Even though I knew and loved Sly's dog, I had to admit he looked pretty intimidating coming at us out of the dark. If I didn't have any good reason to be in that yard, I would have been running. Fast.

Sly climbed back in the truck and pulled into the yard, leaving the gate open behind us. He knew I wouldn't be staying long.

"So," I said once the truck stopped inside the gate, "what about Uncle Andrew's tuition? What has that got to do with Southern Treasures?"

Sly stared into the darkness, as though looking at something only he could see. In a way that was true; he was looking at memories from before I was born.

"Mr. Andrew took a long time figuring out what he wanted to do with hisself. He tried a couple things around here, even thought about lettin' me teach him mechanicing." He grinned as though remembering an old joke. "Bet you can just imagine how popular *that* idea would have been."

He shook his head and went back to his story. "But nothing ever quite took. Not until he started messing with that old aeroplane. Pretty soon he was out at the airfield every spare minute. It was real clear that boy purely loved planes, and there weren't nothing else he wanted to do."

"I know he works on planes," I said. "But I always thought he was kind of an airplane mechanic. Isn't it all the same thing?"

"Yes and no," Sly answered. "The engines work the same way. Sort of. But they're more different than they are the same. At least according to Mr. Andrew.

"Anyway, when he put his mind to a thing, that was the end of it, and he decided he wanted to work on planes. But to do that, he had to go to school, and school cost money."

"Which Uncle Andrew didn't have?" I guessed aloud.

"Which Mr. Andrew didn't have," Sly agreed. "And his daddy didn't have it, neither. So he went looking for some way to come up with the money."

"And Uncle Louis had something to do with it?"

"You're right smart, girl." Sly chuckled. "Yep, Mr. Louis helped him out with the schooling. Lent him money and didn't pester him about paying it back.

"Your mama, though, didn't borrow anything from Mr.

Louis. Mr. Andrew did fine; he got married, then your mama got married, and Peter came along and then you."

"Uncle Andrew still owed Uncle Louis the money?" I asked.

"Yep, but he didn't forget about it. The two of them worked out a deal when Mr. Louis went to do his will: everything would be divided between you two, but you got a bigger share to make up for the tuition money."

He turned and looked at me. "So you can stop feeling guilty about getting more than Peter. The fact is, Peter got a lot more than you in the long run. And he keeps getting it without doing any work."

Sly's explanation made a lot of pieces fall into place. Things that had bothered me since I was a kid suddenly made sense. As I thought about it, I realized something else.

"Peter doesn't know, does he?"

"I doubt it," Sly answered. "Mr. Andrew kept things pretty close to his chest. Doubt he would have told the boy."

"Thanks, Sly," I said. "It helps a lot to know why things happened the way they did."

"Don't you let Mr. Louis know I told you," he said. "I don't know as he'd want me to be talkin' about all this."

I promised, and pulled out of the junkyard with my head spinning. I was more determined than ever to buy out Peter's share of Southern Treasures.

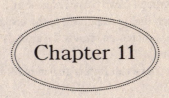

Chapter 11

IT WAS WEDNESDAY BEFORE I TALKED TO KAREN again. The store was busy, as it always was the week of the Fourth; busy enough I hadn't had time to worry about her.

I was working alone near closing time when she showed up. The sight of her SUV reminded me of the situation with her and Riley. I hoped everything was okay.

She sat in the car for a minute, and I realized she was listening to the police scanner. She kept one in the car, one at the station, and one in her house—all in case a story broke.

As I watched, she gestured impatiently at the machine, then jerked it free of the power connection and burst out of the car carrying the scanner, now running on battery power.

She slammed through the front door, tossed her bag on the counter, and hushed me when I tried to say hello. "Something's up," she said. "Don't know what, but something, and I want to hear it."

The scanner was quiet as we waited in silence. I had learned a long time ago to hold my tongue when Karen was listening to the scanner.

The tiny speaker buzzed and crackled with static, then a voice came through clearly. We listened as Boomer Hardy, the police chief, finally responded to the dispatcher.

"Keep your britches on, Travis. I was in the head. What's so dang important?"

"Just had a phone call from a guy up in Minnesota, works for that bank?"

Boomer—his name was Barclay, but no one ever called him that—didn't need to ask which bank. Everyone in town knew which bank had taken an interest in Keyhole Bay.

"What did he want that was so important you had to keep calling me?" Boomer's impatience came clearly through the transmission.

"He asked us to check up on that Yankee gal, the one's down here snooping around Back Bay. Says she hasn't checked in since Friday and she's not answering her phone."

Boomer snorted. "So he's got his panties in a bunch 'cause she hasn't called in a couple days? Tell him to call her at work; she's at the bank before they open and there 'til after they close."

"Well, that's just it, Boomer. He did try calling the bank. They said she hadn't been in all week. He sure didn't like the sound of that, acted like they should've let him know she hadn't shown up."

I wondered if something had happened on Bridget's trip to Biloxi. Car trouble maybe, or she could be sick in her hotel. There had to be a reasonable explanation.

There wasn't anything to worry about.

I caught Karen's eye; she was thinking the same thing I was, and we both had the same sick feeling.

Something had gone badly wrong.

"I'll go take a look, if it'll make him feel better," Boomer agreed, annoyance clear in his voice. "Can't have those Yankees worryin' about their little gal down here. Give me the location."

The dispatcher reeled off the address where Karen and I had been on Friday, and the image of the deserted subdivision full of empty and abandoned lots flashed in my mind. A chill passed through me, making me shiver.

I locked up while we waited, mentally ticking off the minutes until Boomer would reach Bayvue Estates.

"She's probably stuck in Biloxi," I said.

"Probably," Karen agreed. "But you'd think she'd at least call and let somebody know where she was."

"Who would she call?" I asked. "Nobody here would give a flip, probably just as glad she wasn't at the bank digging into their records."

"Still, you'd think there would be somebody."

I shrugged. "You'd think."

I wondered who would miss me if I didn't check in for a few days. Julie would notice on the days she was in the shop, but she only worked three days a week. I talked to Karen and Jake almost every day, but if they were busy, it might take a couple days before anyone realized I was gone.

It was a creepy thought.

The scanner crackled to life with Boomer's voice. "Travis, I'm out at the location you gave me. There's a car in the driveway, but no sign of anyone." He described Bridget's rental car and recited a license number. "Verify the renter on that, would you?"

"Roger that."

Another minute of silence, and then Travis confirmed what Karen and I already knew: The car had been rented by Bridget. She'd used a company credit card.

"Maybe she wasn't supposed to use the company car for a personal trip?" I said.

Karen shrugged. "That could be." She went into what I called her reporter mode, a distance that shielded against emotional distress. "After all the scrutiny banks have been under, a lot of them have adopted very stringent rules to avoid looking like anybody's getting away with anything."

"Call that guy up North," Boomer instructed over the radio. "Ask him what he wants us to do. It's his house, and his gal. In the meantime I'll take a look around."

Karen and I made small talk while we waited, not sure what we were waiting for. The scanner sputtered to life occasionally with routine business: patrol officers checking licenses and issuing warnings or citations, reports of shoplifting and noisy neighbors. All the usual summer calls.

Travis finally came back, calling for Boomer. "Chief Hardy? I talked to the guy in Minnesota. He said to go in and take a look around."

Boomer's reply was an unintelligible mutter, reminding me of Bluebeard. The words might not be clear, but the meaning was. He wasn't happy.

"Place is locked up," Boomer answered. "What does he want me to do about that?"

"He said if you couldn't get in, to do—I am quoting here—whatever is necessary."

"Got it," Boomer answered. He didn't sound any happier.

He sounded even less happy when he called back a few minutes later. "Travis, send a wagon and Dr. Frazier. I think I found her."

"Roger," Travis answered.

Karen and I stared wordlessly, hoping it wasn't Bridget. Not if Boomer was calling for Marlon Frazier. Dr. Frazier was the county coroner.

Whoever Boomer had found was dead.

Chapter 12

"I'M HEADING OUT THERE," KAREN SAID, GATHERING up her scanner and bag. "I'll call you when I know something more."

"I'll go with you," I offered.

"No. Stay here. This could be a long night, and I don't know where I'll end up. I promise I'll call."

I reluctantly agreed; there was a part of me that didn't want to see what was out at Bayvue Estates. Besides, Boomer might tolerate Karen doing her job, but he wouldn't be thrilled to see me with her.

"Please do," I said. "It's got to be some kind of mistake, or it's somebody else. Or something."

"I don't think it's a mistake; Boomer doesn't make very many. But I'll keep you posted."

I followed Karen out onto the sidewalk. She jumped into her SUV and pulled into traffic.

I didn't want to be alone quite yet, and I realized I was staring across the street again, looking for Jake. Since when did I think of him first when I needed company?

I didn't stop to consider the answer to that question. I made sure the door was locked, and seeing a break in traffic, I hurried across.

The door was locked, but I could see Jake inside, counting the register and checking it against his computer screen. I tapped on the window and he looked up with an annoyed frown, which disappeared as soon as he recognized me.

His welcoming smile faded, though, the minute he opened the door and saw my face. "Glory, what's wrong?"

I blurted out the news.

"Karen and I were out there on Friday night," I reminded him. "She seemed fine. Said she might go over to Biloxi for the day on Saturday. That's where she was headed when you and I saw her on Saturday morning. She didn't stay long after you left; she seemed to be ready to be on the road."

"Let me finish up here," he said. "We can talk while I work." He offered me a chair behind the counter and went back to closing out his register. "Do you know anything more?"

I shook my head. "Just what we heard on the scanner. Boomer was out there, said it was her, but that was all. Karen's gone to chase down the story and she promised to let me know what she finds out."

Jake tapped the computer keys, the printer whirred and spat out a few pages, and he shut down the machine. "Let's get out of here," he suggested. "We can pick up some burgers at Curly's and figure out what to do from there."

Jake drove. We considered and rejected a dozen places to eat as we drove toward Curly's. "We could just eat there," I said, unable to come up with a better idea.

But when we pulled in, the parking lot was packed and we knew the small dining room would be even worse. We pulled into the line of cars at the drive-through, still trying to come up with a place to take our burgers.

Jake handed me the bag after we reached the window, and pulled out of the lot. "How about we take them to my place?" he asked without looking at me.

He'd never invited me to his place before. We went out or he joined the Thursday dinner crew, and my place was convenient after work. But tonight was different.

"I think I'd like that," I said quietly. I didn't want to be out in a crowd, and I didn't want to go home.

Jake's small rental house was only a few blocks from Beach Books, on a dead end in a maze of narrow residential streets. The pale green single-story cottage with a covered carport sat only a few feet from the street, a white board fence defining the perimeter of the postage-stamp lot. Native grass filled the front yard, trimmed precisely around the cobblestone walkway and the fence line.

Jake pulled into the carport and unlocked a side door that led directly into an immaculate kitchen as tiny as Bridget's had been spacious. The counters were clear of clutter, the sink empty and scrubbed until it shone, and the tile countertops gleamed in the light from the overhead fixture.

On one side of the room sat a small wooden table painted a soft blue, and two dark blue kitchen chairs. I put the bag of burgers on the table as Jake pulled colorful pottery plates out of the cupboard and filled tall glasses with ice.

"Sweet tea?" he asked, taking a pitcher from the refrigerator. He filled the glasses without waiting for an answer.

We made small talk while we ate, and when we were done, Jake offered me a tour of his house. "There isn't much to it," he said, leading me through into the living room.

It was no surprise to find every inch of wall space covered with packed bookcases. "You know, Jake, you have an entire store full of books," I said, gesturing to the bulging shelves. "Isn't that enough?"

He grinned sheepishly. "These are just the keepers," he explained. "The books I want to have around forever."

I stepped close to the nearest shelf, reading titles. "I'll have to check this out, see what it is you can't live without." I stopped as I read a string of titles shelved together.

"You're really taking this volunteer fire department thing seriously!" I ran my finger along the spines neatly lined up together. Firefighting equipment. Fire investigation. Arson. At least a dozen titles.

Jake's laugh sounded forced. "Yeah, I guess." He nodded toward the hallway off the living room. "Want to see the rest of the house?" he said, moving in that direction.

Clearly this topic was closed for the moment, but I guessed we'd come back to it eventually. Why else would he have let me see that row of books?

Down the short hallway were a single bedroom and a

small bath, both as tidy as the kitchen. The real surprise, though, was at the end of the hall, where a pair of multipaned glass doors led to a screened patio.

We sat down on the patio chairs, watching the light slowly fade from the sky. A soft breeze blew through, carrying the scent of roses from an unseen bush in a nearby yard.

The neighborhood was quiet. "Your neighbors must not be home," I said.

Jake shook his head. "May not be home from work yet," he said, "but even when they are, it's pretty quiet around here. No vacation rentals, just a few weekenders, but mostly they're all permanent residents."

"No wonder you like it here," I replied, "if it's this peaceful all the time."

"Pretty much," he said. "Makes it a good place to live. I'm kind of hoping the landlord will consider selling the house. I think I could stay right here for a good long time."

I struggled to find an opening to bring up the firefighting books again. They appeared to be older editions, not what a newly minted volunteer would read, and they were important to Jake. I wanted to know why.

From inside the house I heard the faint ringing of my cell phone. I had left it in my purse, hanging from the back of a kitchen chair.

I got up quickly and hurried back down the hallway and through the living room, but by the time I reached my purse, the phone had stopped ringing.

Jake shot me a questioning glance as I checked the call log. "It was Karen," I said, quickly redialing her number.

She answered on the second ring. "I was just leaving you

a voice mail," she said. "Are you okay? It surprised me when you didn't answer."

"I left the phone in the other room," I explained, without giving her any details. "So what did you find out?"

Her voice shook a little as she answered me. "It's Bridget, for sure. Boomer recognized her, and he had her driver's license for confirmation."

She paused, and I could imagine her slipping into reporter mode, distancing herself from what she had seen. "They're trying to reach her next of kin, but no luck so far, so Boomer hasn't officially released her name."

"What happened?" I asked. "She seemed fine on Saturday when she stopped by on her way to Biloxi."

"She stopped by Saturday?"

"Just returning my food containers," I answered. "But what's going on out there? What happened to Bridget?"

"I don't know. Dr. Frazier's here, but he's not saying anything yet." Karen's façade slipped, and stress pushed her voice into a higher register. "I have to go, but I promised to call, so I did. I'll call you back as soon as I know anything more."

Chapter 13

"I HEARD," JAKE SAID, HIS HAND RESTING LIGHTLY ON my shoulder. "Are you okay?"

"Not really," I answered, leaning against him. "I didn't know her very well—really just met her a couple times—but she seemed nice, and a little lonely. I thought maybe we could be friends while she was here. Felt like she could use someone to talk to."

I stood for several minutes with my head resting against Jake's chest, feeling the warmth of his arms around me. He didn't speak, and I was grateful for his quiet strength, for the patience to let me deal with things in my own way.

Outside, the sunset had faded to full dark. The kitchen light turned the windows to shadowy mirrors, reflecting the image of Jake and me standing with our arms around each other.

I really didn't know why Bridget's death affected me so

strongly. I didn't know her for very long. We didn't have a lot in common, as far as I could tell. There was just something about her that had clicked, and now she was gone.

From a distance we heard the whine and boom of fireworks as night fell. The Fourth was still a day away, but legions of visiting children couldn't wait another minute. Tomorrow there would be a professional display at the football stadium, but tonight was strictly amateur hour. It reminded me why I didn't go out much this time of year.

I knew I should get home, but I wasn't ready to leave just yet. My internal debate was short-circuited by the squawk of Jake's radio. I hadn't noticed it before, silent on a shelf in the corner of the kitchen, but now it crackled to life and the voice of the dispatcher filled the room.

"Station Three, Engine One. Grass fire reported at Anderson Park. Engine One respond, Code Two."

Answers poured in almost before the dispatcher had finished the call. Volunteers at the station radioed they were on the way, and several others responded they would meet the unit on-site.

Jake released me and reached for the microphone. "Robinson, on call," he said. "Will report to station."

He turned back to me. "Time to go. I'm on call to cover the station in case of a call out."

I didn't need any more of an explanation. I threw my purse over my shoulder and followed him to the car.

He pulled out of the carport, and propped a portable flasher in the window. "With the holiday traffic, I may need this."

He was right. Getting onto the highway would have been

nearly impossible without the red and blue strobes clearing the way. As he turned onto the main drag, he glanced at me. "I can drop you at home, or you can come with me. But you have about twenty seconds to decide."

I didn't hesitate. "I'm going with you."

Jake threaded his way through the evening traffic to the low brick building that housed the volunteer fire department. Keyhole Bay could call for help and support from Pensacola, if needed, but mostly our own volunteers handled our emergencies, large and small.

The station was empty, the pumper truck and medical unit already calling in from Anderson Park. "Small grass fire," a voice reported. "Under control. No injuries. Medical unit returning to station."

"Roger," the dispatcher answered.

"I have to stay until they get back," Jake said. He led the way to the small kitchen behind the truck bays. "You want something while we wait?"

I accepted his offer of a bottle of water. I swallowed, and felt the cold slide down my throat, still tight with emotion.

I looked at Jake. He looked so at home in the station, as though he belonged there. I remembered the volumes on his living room shelf, and wondered again what they might reveal about him.

Whatever that was, though, I wasn't going to find out tonight. While we waited for the medical unit to return, the radio continued to broadcast one call after another.

The pumper rolled in, the crew sweating in their heavy turnouts. Jake handed me his keys with an apologetic shrug.

"Looks like a busy night," he said. "They're going to need me. Take my car. Drop the keys through the mail slot and I'll pick it up later, or in the morning." He gave me a quick kiss and sprinted for the truck.

I watched the activity in the station for a few minutes, flattening myself against the brick wall and trying to stay out of the way. It quickly became clear that Jake was right: the station was a buzz of activity, and he was needed.

I don't think he even noticed when I left.

I parked Jake's car behind the bookstore and crossed the street to the front door of Southern Treasures. In spite of all that had happened, it wasn't that late and I realized Linda and Guy were still open.

I walked past my front door and into the Grog Shop.

Guy waved a greeting from the back of the shop, where he was filling a shelf with giant bottles of daiquiri and margarita mix. Based on past history, those shelves would be bare before noon tomorrow.

Linda was behind the counter, ringing up a steady stream of customers preparing for their holiday celebrations. I walked back and gave Guy a hand with the stocking.

It was a job I'd done every weekend my last year of high school, when I had lived with Guy and Linda after my parents died, and in a strange way it comforted me.

A few minutes later the clock hit closing time. Linda checked out the last customers and locked the front door behind them before coming over to check on our progress.

"Haven't lost your touch," she said, admiring the neat rows of bottles.

Guy snagged three bottles of soda from the cooler, twisting off the caps and giving one to each of us, keeping one for himself. "Stocking is thirsty work," he proclaimed.

It was a little ritual we'd observed since I first started helping him when I was just a bored little kid who thought his store was a cool place to hang out. I didn't realize back then just how lucky I was to have Guy and Linda.

Linda gave me a questioning look. "Something wrong, Glory? You look upset."

I told her the same thing I'd told Jake. "Nobody knows what happened," I said before she could ask. "Boomer went out on a welfare check and he found her body."

"It's just sad, thinking of her out there all alone," I said, shrugging off any further discussion.

"I did have something I wanted to ask you about," I said to Linda, trying to change the subject.

Guy gave us a lopsided grin. "I know girl talk when I see it coming," he said. "I'm pretty sure I have some work to do in the back."

He moved quickly, as though we might be contagious. Linda watched him go, an affectionate grin lighting her face. I envied her.

"What's up, Glory?" Linda asked as soon as Guy was out of earshot. "You looked like you had something on your mind when you were here over the weekend, but we didn't get a chance to talk."

"It's Karen and Riley."

Linda rolled her eyes. "Those two! Glory, whatever is going on between them, there is nothing you can do to change it. You're just going to have to let them do whatever they do."

"I know," I said. "But I still worry about Karen."

Linda put an arm around me. "That's what friends are for. We worry about the people we care about, even if there isn't anything we can do." She gave my shoulders a squeeze. "Who knows? They just might surprise you."

I hoped she was right. They had been spectacularly unsuccessful at actually living together so far, but maybe Karen was right and things were different this time. I allowed myself a glimmer of hope that they would make it work.

We talked a few minutes longer, carefully avoiding the subject of Bridget. The whole time a part of me was waiting for the phone to ring, with an update from Karen.

I left Linda with a promise to keep her posted on whatever I heard, and went home to take care of Bluebeard.

And wait.

Chapter 14

I HAD GONE TO BED WITH THE PHONE CLOSE AT HAND,
but it was nearly midnight when Karen finally called. I
picked it up on the first ring.

"It's not too late, is it?"

"No, I couldn't sleep," I admitted, tucking a bookmark
into the paperback I'd been reading. "Where have you been?"

"I went out to Bayvue, which I told you. Stayed there until
Boomer chased everyone out and sealed the place. It'll stay
closed up until he has a preliminary cause of death."

"That sounds ominous."

"He swears it's just precautionary. Any unattended death
requires an autopsy. Anyway, nobody is in any hurry to get
into the house, so he's just covering his butt. No sense making the bankers think he isn't doing his job."

"Which bankers? The Andersons? Or the Yankees?"

"Either one," Karen shot back. "Dr. Frazier is supposed to do an autopsy tomorrow, so we should know more then."

"On the holiday? That ought to make him super happy."

"Like I said, Boomer wants to keep everybody off his back, much as he can. No sense picking a fight with anybody."

"What about Bridget's family?" It was the question that had lingered in the back of my mind ever since that first dispatch call. *Who would miss her?*

"According to what her boss told the dispatcher, there's a brother in Minneapolis. Boomer called the local police department, asked them to contact him."

I didn't have to imagine what that visit would be like. I knew. I'd experienced the knock on the door, the wall of uniforms on the porch asking if I was Gloryanna Martine, asking if they could come in, telling me to sit down. It was a memory that would never go away.

I shoved those thoughts into a deep corner of my mind, slamming a mental door on the pain. I hoped Bridget's brother had someone to help him through the coming weeks.

"I guess that's all we're going to get for tonight, huh?"

"Think so," Karen answered. "I'll see you tomorrow at dinner."

In all the stress of the evening, I had forgotten tomorrow was Thursday. Another late night.

JULIE HAD JUST RETURNED FROM A BREAK WHEN Jake came into Southern Treasures the next morning with two cups from Lighthouse. He nodded to me, and stopped to greet Bluebeard.

"Coffee?" Bluebeard asked, hopeful. He bobbed his head in excitement. I'd been told parrots didn't have much sense of smell, but he clearly knew what was in those cups.

"Sorry, buddy," Jake said. "We both know you're not supposed to have coffee. And you wouldn't want me to argue with the boss over there, would you?"

Bluebeard eyed me as though I might weaken. I shook my head. Coffee was dangerous for several reasons and I wouldn't take any risks where my parrot was concerned.

"Told you," Jake said. He reached under Bluebeard's cage and took a shredded-wheat biscuit from the can. "This is the best I can do right now."

Having paid his respects, Jake came back across the shop to where I stood behind the counter. "Vanilla latte," he said as he handed me one of the cups. "By way of apology and thanks."

"Apology? For what?"

Julie moved discreetly away and began dusting and straightening shelves.

"For dumping you last night," he said, looking away. "You wanted some company and I bailed on you."

"You were needed at the station. I understood."

He shook his head. "Don't let me off that easy," he said with an embarrassed laugh. "*You* needed me. I should have stayed with you."

I put my hand on his arm and squeezed gently. "I'm a big girl," I said. "I can take care of myself. I appreciate that you were there while you could be. That's enough for me."

Jake hesitated, as though there was more to say.

"Now, it's the middle of a holiday, and you have a business to run," I reminded him with a smile. "Thanks for the coffee, even if it wasn't necessary."

His look told me the subject wasn't closed, but he let it drop. "The other reason I came over was to let you know Felipe called and invited me to dinner tonight, if that's okay with you?"

"Of course it is. Felipe doesn't need my permission to include you."

"That wasn't him asking, it was me," Jake explained.

"Either way," I said. "It'll be fun to have you there."

"Good." He hesitated. "Will you ride with me? I promise not to abandon you this time."

"Don't promise," I warned him. "This could be another busy night for the department. Besides, if you have to leave, I can always ride home with Karen."

We agreed to meet at Beach Books at six, and Jake headed back to his store.

Julie came back behind the counter without a word, but her look said a lot.

"It wasn't anything, really," I said. "I just wanted somebody to talk to. We got burgers from Curly's and then he got called out."

Julie already knew what I had wanted to talk to Jake about. The news of Bridget's death was all over town; gossip was an industry second only to tourism in our small town, and we were good at it.

"They called the fire department out there?" Julie asked, puzzled. "Why would they do that if she was dead?"

"No, they got called to Anderson Park. A grass fire. But there were a bunch of calls just after dark, when the tourists started setting off their fireworks."

Julie's confused expression cleared. "Oh. That makes more sense."

A steady stream of customers kept us busy until closing time, and beyond. It was nearly six when the last ones straggled out the door with their T-shirts and postcards.

As the last group of customers milled around the entrance, holding the door open, an orange cat slipped in. Sydney, who lived a couple blocks over, the official greeter at Molly Young's B and B.

Sydney was supposed to be an indoor cat, but she sometimes managed to escape. And when she did, she went exploring.

The door closed. I quickly turned the lock, trapping Sydney inside the shop, and reached for the phone to call Molly.

"Molly's Magnolia Bed and Breakfast," Molly answered. "How can I help you?"

"Hey, Molly," I said. "How are you?" Even if I was rescuing her cat, good manners dictated that I at least ask after her.

"Doing fine, Glory," she said. "How about you?"

"Can't complain. The tourists are spending, and the weather's not too hot."

"I hear that," she chuckled. "What can I do for you, sugar?"

"Well, I thought I ought to let you know, Sydney's come calling. I locked the door behind her, but I know you'll be wanting to get her back home."

"I'll be there quick as I can," she said.

Before I could say good-bye properly, Bluebeard let out a shriek.

I turned around just in time to see him half jump, half fly toward one of the hanging light fixtures. The shop wasn't really big enough for him to fly, but he was clearly agitated and trying to get to as high a perch as he could.

The fluorescent lamp swung wildly, and Bluebeard slipped from his precarious spot, losing his footing.

"@&%&%%^* cat!" he screeched. "Cat here!"

He flapped his wings wildly, managing to slow his fall somewhat, and he landed clumsily on a stack of T-shirts, sending several of them cascading to the floor.

Sydney, curious about the commotion, jumped onto the lower shelf and batted at Bluebeard with one paw, as though playing with a particularly noisy toy.

Bluebeard leaped away, cursing nonstop, his outburst punctuated every few seconds with the phrase "$%^#%& cat."

Sydney followed her new prey across the shop, crouched low, tail twitching. She'd gone from curious to hunting, and while Bluebeard was bigger, stronger, and a lot more aggressive when he wanted to be, he wasn't a predator by nature.

Bluebeard lit on top of the postcard spinner, and Sydney leaped up against the rack, trying to claw her way up the slippery chrome rungs.

The spinner teetered, spilling cards out of the pockets, and unseating Bluebeard. He slipped off the rack and onto another display table, hopping quickly across the shop and into the relative safety of his cage.

I moved faster that I thought possible, beating Sydney to

the cage, and closing the door before she could follow Blue-beard inside.

She glared up at me, like I had interrupted an especially amusing game, then lay down and started grooming herself as though nothing had happened.

In the cage I could hear Bluebeard cursing and ranting. I reached over and rattled the cage door gently. "It's closed," I told him. "No one can bother you. Even the cat."

The cursing grew softer, more like his usual muttering, but it didn't stop and I didn't argue with him about it. This was the first time I'd seen him encounter a cat, and his obvious distress was far beyond anything I would have imagined. I wondered what had happened to make him react so badly, but that was a question for later.

Right now I had to deal with Miss Sydney.

I managed to pick the cat up and carry her back to the counter, where I'd left the phone. The line was dead, which didn't surprise me, though I had to wonder what Molly had heard before she hung up.

I put Sydney on the counter, holding her in place with one arm while I picked up the phone and called Molly again.

I identified myself, and Molly immediately asked, "What happened, sugar? You were talking, and then there was a terrible commotion and the call dropped. I was about to send Ronnie over to make sure you were okay!"

I thanked her for her concern, and reassured her that I was fine. "But Bluebeard apparently has a serious issue with cats. He pitched a huge fit when he saw Sydney. He's in his cage now, and she's just sitting here like nothing happened."

"I am leaving right this minute," she said. I heard her holler for Ronnie, and tell him she had to go out. She turned back to the phone and said she would be right over.

True to her word, she was at my door in about three minutes, her plump cheeks bright red, and huffing and puffing like she'd run the three blocks. In her hand was a cat carrier with "Sydney" written on it in marking pen.

Sydney wasn't happy about getting in the carrier, but Molly wrestled her in and slammed the door shut, scolding the cat in a singsong voice the entire time.

"She knows she's not supposed to go out," she said. "But since when does a cat care what she's supposed to do?"

I shook my head. I had no idea what a cat cared about. I'd never had a cat, and judging by Bluebeard's reaction, I never would.

I thanked Molly for coming so quickly, and she apologized for upsetting Bluebeard.

I shrugged. "I had no idea," I told her. "I don't know why he got so freaked out. But now I know to watch out for cats."

Molly left with Sydney in the carrier, her plaintive yowls clearly indicating her indignation at her treatment.

When they were gone, I opened Bluebeard's cage. I never closed it, giving him the freedom of the store, but this had been an emergency.

I reached my hand in. He came close enough for me to scratch his head, but he refused to leave the cage. The encounter had upset him badly, and he just needed to be left alone to recover. I retreated, and began repairing the damage to the displays. There were a few shirts to fold, but not much else.

Except for the postcards.

The postcard spinner rack was a disaster area, but I didn't

have time to straighten and stock it before dinner; it would have to wait for tomorrow morning.

I groaned at the thought of having to get up early to take care of it, but it was one of the delights of running my own business. In the end, it was all up to me.

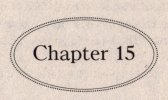

Chapter 15

JAKE WAS WAITING AT THE FRONT DOOR WHEN I crossed the street. On the drive to Felipe and Ernie's, Jake asked if I'd heard anything more from Karen.

"She didn't learn much. They were trying to reach Bridget's brother in Minneapolis, and Dr. Frazier was supposed to do the autopsy today."

We threaded our way slowly through the crush of tourist traffic, my usual back-road routes blocked. Normally the drive would take five minutes, but with the holiday swelling our population tenfold, we crawled along for closer to twenty.

I chuckled as we waited for yet another knot of visitors to dash across the street in the middle of the block, on their way to who-knows-where.

"What's so funny?" Jake asked, glaring impatiently as the last straggler passed in front of us.

"Those are the same people who were in the shop earlier today, asking how I could stand to live here with all this traffic." I chuckled again at the memory. "I didn't tell them it was only like this when they're here."

I shook my head at the scowl on his face. "Come on, you've been here long enough to know that. You've seen what it's like in the winter. These people go home, and we still live here.

"It's worth putting up with the traffic for a few weeks out of the year."

Jake crept forward with the slow-moving traffic. He glanced over and gave me a wry smile. "I suppose you're right," he said, turning back to watch the road. "But traffic has always been one of my hot buttons."

Hard to imagine that Jake, one of the calmest people I knew, even had hot buttons. Most people do, sure, but I hadn't seen anything upset him. Worried, yeah, like after my little adventure in the mermaid tank. But not upset or angry.

Then again, how much did I really know about Jake? He'd been in town a couple years, but I didn't know exactly where he came from, or what he did before he bought Beach Books. In many ways he was still a mystery.

We pulled up in front of Felipe and Ernie's tidy house, parking on the street behind Riley Freed's pickup. Looked like tonight was going to be a full house.

Ernie greeted us at the door in sharply creased khaki shorts and a garish Hawaiian shirt. No one should be able to make that outfit look elegant, but somehow he pulled it off.

On the patio out back, Felipe was hard at work over a top-of-the-line gas grill, his naturally olive complexion flushed with the heat and a bandanna tied jauntily around his brow to keep the sweat out of his eyes.

He waved a pair of grill tongs in our direction. "Hi! There's beer in the cooler. Help yourself!"

Before we could make a move, Riley grabbed a couple bottles from the bed of ice in the vintage metal cooler. He popped the tops and offered them to us.

"Thanks." Jake accepted the bottle, and clapped his other hand on Riley's shoulder. "Good to see you."

I thanked Riley for my beer with a hug. "How was Bobby's birthday party?"

"Great. Great," Riley answered, returning my hug. "You probably should have been there."

"No, it was a family time. You didn't need any outsiders."

His voice grew serious. "Glory, you'll always be family to us."

I gave him a last squeeze and pulled away. "Thanks for that. But there are times . . ."

I let my voice trail off. He knew what I meant.

"Speaking of family," I resumed, "wait 'til you hear what my cousin pulled this last weekend." I gave them a greatly abbreviated version of my Sunday encounter with Peter and his family.

"They thought the crib was for you?" Karen laughed.

I nodded.

"I'm trying to imagine the look on his face," Karen said between bursts of hilarity. "And you actually stood up to him? Good for you!"

Peter's scheme seemed forgotten in the midst of Karen's amusement. Just another of his crazy ideas.

Jake and I walked over to the grill to inspect Felipe's work. Chicken sizzled softly above the gas flame, glistening with a clear glaze.

Looking closer, I was able to identify the long needles of rosemary. I glanced back at Felipe. "Rosemary? Since when is that traditional Southern?"

"It's Independence Day, Glory. I am declaring myself independent of dinner rules for the day. We're having a grilled feast. Besides, you bent the rules last week. Or have you forgotten?"

"Bent, not broke," I argued. "It was something I remembered from my childhood. My *Southern* childhood," I added pointedly.

"Puerto Rico is south of here, *amiga*," he shot back. "And it is still too hot to cook inside."

"And New York is way north." I raised a hand in surrender. "But it *is* too hot," I agreed. "So what else is for dinner?"

Felipe pointed to a foil-covered baking dish tucked to one side of the grill. "Baked beans and"—he gestured at a tray of filled skewers waiting on the table beside the grill—"lots of vegetables. Grilled tomatoes. Tortillas." He held up a hand. "I *know* those aren't Southern, but they're good with the chicken."

Ernie appeared at my side with a plate of cocktail shrimp in tiny lettuce leaf bowls, topped with a spicy dressing. "Not traditional either," he said. "But tasty!"

I laughed and relaxed. The boys had invited Jake and Riley, and they had discarded our recent tradition for a far older one: the Fourth of July backyard barbeque. This was a night for a celebration with friends.

So be it.

We settled around a rustic picnic table on the screened porch, leaving the formal dining room and its mid-century modern furnishings for another night. And just like most Thursdays, we spent the first part of the meal talking about the food.

"The sauce is simple," Felipe said, passing the platter of juicy chicken pieces. "White wine, butter, rosemary, a little lemon juice. Careful grilling so it doesn't dry out, and you're done."

I helped myself to a skewer of vegetables from the pile on the tray in front of me. It held colorful peppers, onions, broccoli, mushrooms, several kinds of squash, and cherry tomatoes. Next to the tray of skewers were plates of grilled eggplant and grilled tomatoes.

"Delicious," Jake said, taking another piece of chicken and more tomatoes. He scooped part of the tomato into a tortilla, added chicken he'd pulled from the bone, and rolled it into a sort of taco.

I had to admit, traditional Southern or not, the food was sensational. Across from me, Karen and Riley sat close together on the wooden bench, their shoulders touching. They giggled as they occasionally stole bits of food from each other's plates.

When we had finished eating and I'd helped Ernie clear away the leftovers, we moved to the cushioned patio chairs clustered at one end of the porch. In an hour or so we would move outside, where we could watch the fireworks from the high school stadium as they exploded over the heads of the crowd. We were all content to watch from a distance, avoiding the crush of people and vehicles that filled the stadium.

Karen hadn't mentioned Bridget during dinner, but I had waited as long as I could. "Did you find out anything more about Bridget?" I asked her once we were seated.

"Not a lot. Boomer has finally released her name, now that he's talked to her brother."

Felipe and Ernie both sat forward. "So it was her? We'd heard rumors, but you can't always believe everything you hear," Ernie said.

"Even from the Merchants' Association?" I asked with false innocence. "I thought they had all the latest news."

He shot me a withering glance. "I trust what I hear officially at the meetings. Not so much what I hear fourth-hand from an individual with an agenda."

"Agenda?" Karen responded to the whiff of gossip. She always said that gossip meant a story, just like smoke meant fire.

"He means Felicia Anderson," Felipe cut in. "That woman was in the shop already today, nosing around some of the merchandise."

"But she can't really be planning any shopping," I blurted out. "Just because Bridget's"—I hesitated—"gone doesn't mean the bank won't send somebody else down here."

"Oh, she made all the right noises about 'that poor woman,'" Felipe said, his words dripping with contempt. "Not that I believed her for a minute. But she was right there, trying to talk me down on the price of an old chest that she was just *sure* used to belong to her husband's dear uncle, the General."

"You know, General Anderson never even lived in this area," I said. "I looked him up after we got to talking about

Felicia the other day. He commanded the troops when they attacked Fort Pickens, but he was only here for a short while. He never really lived here, and his wife and family were all in South Carolina."

Karen laughed out loud. "You know, I always just took their stories at face value," she said. "Never thought about checking them out. You know how it is down here"—she waved her arm, encompassing the entire region—"you measure your time by generations, and we all knew the Andersons had been here forever.

"I wonder who started that story," she said quietly. I could see the wheels already turning on the piece she'd write.

"But Felicia can't possibly think this ends here, can she?" I asked Ernie. "I mean, the bank is sure to send another auditor."

"I don't know what that"—Ernie paused, and I could see him struggle with the word he wanted to use—"that *witch* thinks. If she thinks at all. She just assumes she will get everything she wants because she always has."

"Oh, there will be another auditor," Karen said. The note of certainty in her voice told us there was more to the story. We all turned and looked at her expectantly.

She let the silence stretch out, taunting us with the hint of news to come. I let her have her moment, but impatience soon got the better of me. "Spill, Freed! I've been waiting all day to hear what you found out."

"Like I said, Boomer talked to her brother. He's on his way down. Apparently he works for the same bank, and he'll report to her manager about everything he finds down here."

She sat back with a sad little smile, and I knew she still hadn't told us everything.

"And?" I prompted.

"And," she said at last, "Dr. Frazier wouldn't give Boomer a definite cause of death until he gets the lab results. He hand-carried the samples to Pensacola for analysis.

"He said it looked like a drug overdose."

Chapter 16

I SHOOK MY HEAD, REFUSING TO BELIEVE WHAT SHE'D said. "Are you kidding? She wasn't taking drugs."

"Depends on what drugs," Jake said. "*Drug overdose* covers a lot of different possibilities."

"Glory's right, though," Karen said. "I was out there. I saw her and I saw that house. I've talked to a lot of people over the past few years, and I think I've seen about every kind of drug use around. She didn't have any of the signs."

"But it might have been something you *haven't* seen," Ernie said. "Maybe something that isn't common around here."

Karen shook her head, her expression stubborn. "I don't think that's likely, Ernie. Remember, we had a steroid problem here just last year." She shot me a sympathetic glance. I'd learned far more than I had ever wanted to know about 'roid rage, dealing with Julie's ex-husband.

"And this is a tourist town," she went on. "We get everything around here. Besides, she just wasn't the type."

"Type?" Felipe laughed, not an amused sound but a harsh bark. "There's no type. Not everybody who uses drugs is a meth head with their teeth falling out."

"He's right," Jake said. "And a drug overdose doesn't mean she was even doing anything illegal. People overdose on legal drugs. They take the wrong prescription, or they combine things they shouldn't. They forget they took their pills and take them again. Saying it looked like an overdose can mean a lot of things." He put his arm around me and patted my shoulder. "We won't really know until they get the lab results."

"Wouldn't Felicia Anderson just love that?" Ernie said. "Get rid of the auditor and discredit her all at once."

"You don't really think . . ." Riley's unfinished question, the same one that had occurred to me, hung in the air.

Ernie waved a dismissive hand. "Not really. Felicia wouldn't dirty her hands. But it sure wouldn't break her heart either."

"I still can't believe it was drugs," I muttered.

"Let's wait and see," Jake said softly, so close to my ear I could feel the warmth of his breath against my cheek. "The doctor could be wrong, too."

I nodded, just a slight brush of my face against his.

"Did you find out anything else about the brother?" I asked Karen, pushing the topic of drugs out of my mind. "Like when he'll get here, or what he does for the bank?"

Karen shook her head. "Boomer is being pretty close-mouthed about the whole thing."

"Then he's the only one," Ernie drawled. "Everyone else is certainly quacking their fool heads off about it."

Felipe nodded. "While Felicia was in the store today, she must have had a dozen calls. The rumor mill was working overtime, I can tell you that."

"Did you hear anything interesting?" Karen asked.

"Not much," Felipe said slowly as he stopped to think about it. "I tried not to eavesdrop, but it isn't easy when she's screeching away."

Ernie reached over to pat his partner's knee. "You could hear her all over the store," he said. "A lot of people noticed. You couldn't help hearing her entire conversation."

Felipe nodded at Ernie, grateful for his loyal defense. "She kept talking to people about how she'd heard that Bridget was on drugs. She was convinced that Bridget had gone to Biloxi because she certainly couldn't have bought anything like that here, in our fair city."

"Yeah, right." Ernie muttered.

Karen's derisive whoop of laughter interrupted Felipe's story. "Is she crazy?" She turned to me. "You remember a couple years ago, when Boomer had to shut down a party at the pool house? Right in the development where she made Billy build her that big new house? There were plenty of pills and powders and Lord knows what else out there that night, practically next door to her!"

I had to think for a minute, but I remembered the incident she was talking about. "I think it was more like four years," I said. "They built that house out there about the time I took over Southern Treasures completely. I remember because Shandra—my old manager—she went to work at the bank just in time to be invited to the housewarming."

"You sure?" Karen said.

"Yep. She bought the housewarming gift from me. Some old chamber pot I found up near Campground."

"Campground?" Jake asked. "What campground?"

"Not *a* campground," I explained. "Campground. It's a little town a ways north of here."

Felipe broke out laughing. "She gave them a *chamber pot* for a housewarming gift?"

I nodded. "She said she'd put flowers in it and Felicia wouldn't know the difference. And she was going to tell her she thought it had belonged to the General."

Jake whistled softly. "Wow! Apparently her employees don't like her very much."

Karen and I launched into an explanation of Felicia, and the Anderson family history, starting with the General. After a couple minutes, Jake held up his hand. "Much as I love your stories about everyone's family," he said, "if you don't skip a few generations, I will still be sitting here when the sun comes up."

"Okay. Fast-forward about a hundred years. Billy returns from college with a girlfriend. They announce their engagement at Christmas, and get married a year after Billy finishes grad school.

"Billy comes home and settles down to doing not much of anything, except collecting—and spending—dividend checks. His granddaddy had just passed—" The look on Jake's face stopped me in midsentence. "Sorry. Fast-forward another ten years. Felicia wants a new house, so Billy gets the bank board—basically his parents, him, and his younger sister—to raise the dividends. And he borrows a pot of money, too, if what I hear is right."

I explained about Felicia's fake drawl, her constant references to "the General," and how she put on airs around town. "Memaw always said, 'Pretty is as pretty does,'" I told him. "And by that standard, all the beauty salons in the world couldn't help that woman."

"So that's how the dreaded Felicia came to town," he said dryly. "I can see why she's so popular."

Karen picked up the story, telling Jake how Billy's ambition and greed had got him into some risky business ventures, culminating with the Bayvue Estates development.

"They got a couple model homes up, sold a bunch that weren't built yet, and then the bottom dropped out. They held on for a bit, but there was no way they could recover. So now we have this auditor for the new owners, and no one's happy."

Jake sighed. "What a mess."

"Oh, that's not all," Felipe said. "Not only are there people who bought houses that were never built—"

"We met one of them," I interjected. "Sort of. Friday night when we were out at Bayvue. Some man showed up looking for Andrew Marshall, and when he couldn't find him, he started yelling at us. He never did tell us his name, but he said he wanted his house and he made some pretty direct threats."

"I doubt seriously if he's the only one," Karen added.

"Exactly," Felipe said. "And there's a developer who's out of business, construction crews thrown out of work, a bank manager who lost his job—"

"And his house," Riley added.

"Really? How awful!" Karen's concern was genuine. We all knew Francis Simon had been fired over the Back Bay scandal, but we hadn't heard about the house.

Riley nodded. "My mom works with his wife at the drugstore. She heard the Simons have to move this month, that since Francis got fired, the bank is calling in their loans, and taking over their house."

Jake looked from one person to another around the room.

"This is more than just a mess," he said. "That development is jinxed for sure."

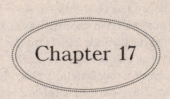

Chapter 17

WE LET THE SQUEAL AND BOOM OF FIREWORKS DRAW us out of the screened porch and into the backyard, leaving behind the discussion of Bridget, Back Bay, and the Andersons.

We stood there, three couples watching a visual display that we had each contributed to. Although the city collected a "donation" from those sitting in the stands, the majority of the cost was underwritten by the annual arm-twisting of the Merchants' Association. Members put donation jars on their counters for months beforehand, and we all tossed something in.

I had my differences with the Merchants' Association, but I still supported the fireworks. There was something about the scream and thunder, the shower of glittering lights, and the multicolor explosions that reminded me how much I loved this holiday.

In spite of the grown-up problems of traffic and crowds,

noisy neighbors with too much beer, and the inevitable mess the morning after, on the Fourth I was nine years old again, sitting in the stadium with Mom and Dad, watching the fireworks.

The final volley launched into the sky with clusters of brilliant light and color. We stood transfixed, listening to the growing quiet as the final sparkles faded from view.

After a moment, Felipe broke the silence. "Dessert?"

Everyone agreed it sounded like a great idea.

Felipe disappeared into the kitchen and emerged seconds later with a shallow bowl full of halved peaches. I had almost expected watermelon to top his grilled meal, but he had a bigger surprise in store.

With a flourish he raised the lid on the grill he'd heated while we were watching the fireworks, and laid the glistening peach halves on the rack.

He turned them once, the aroma of caramelizing sugar and pungent cinnamon teasing our noses as we watched. Within minutes he dished the halves onto elegant dessert plates, topping each with a dollop of sweet whipped cream.

For the next few minutes, conversation stopped except for an occasional question about his recipe. We were all too busy eating and murmuring approval to actually speak.

Finally, when the last plate had been scraped clean, Riley stood and stretched. "Wonderful meal, Felipe. A perfect Fourth of July." He reached for Karen's hand and pulled her up off the turquoise cushions of the sofa they had shared. "But some of us have to get up early."

Karen sighed and nodded. "Unfortunately." She made the

rounds, saying good night with hugs. When she got to me, she gave me an extra squeeze. "I'll let you know if I hear anything," she promised.

Jake and I soon followed their lead. It was getting late—the fireworks hadn't started until well after dark—and we both had to work in the morning. At least we had waited out most of the traffic from the stadium.

"Just be patient," Jake said when he parked in front of my store. "Boomer isn't a fool. He'll get to the truth."

"I hope so," I answered with a sigh.

"He will." Jake came around and opened my door, taking my hand to help me out of the car. I was perfectly capable of getting out of the car on my own, but I appreciated his gesture and liked letting him act the gentleman.

He waited while I unlocked my front door, and he followed me inside. It was a habit he'd developed after my break-in last year. I'd installed an alarm system, but Jake still wanted to check for himself, and I had to admit it was kind of nice to have someone looking out for me.

"Trying to #$$^$%$ sleep here!" Bluebeard hollered, sticking his head out of his cage.

"Just checking the alarm, Bluebeard," I said as I walked through to the storeroom, where the alarm lights glowed green. Set and secure.

I was about to head upstairs after saying good night to Jake when I remembered the postcard spinner. It had been a mess before I left, and I should go clean it up and restock it. But I was exhausted, and it was already way past my bedtime. I told myself the tourists would be getting a late start tomorrow after tonight's celebration. The postcards could wait until morning.

MORNING CAME FAR TOO EARLY. I WOKE BEFORE dawn from a fitful sleep filled with unpleasant dreams, and couldn't stop thinking about Bridget. How long had she been alone in that house, in the middle of an abandoned construction site? Did she suffer? Couldn't she have called for help?

Questions chased each other around my brain in the gray light until I gave up and crawled out of bed. I was still tired, but I knew I wouldn't get back to sleep.

If I had to be awake, I should do something constructive with the time. I promised myself a latte from Lighthouse, and maybe even one of Pansy's muffins, while I worked.

With that incentive, I was showered and dressed in just a few minutes. Lighthouse didn't open for another half hour, but Pansy, the eighty-one-year-old owner, came in every morning at three thirty to do the baking. Chloe, the barista, often came in early to help, in the hopes of someday prying Pansy's recipes out of her. So far she hadn't succeeded, but Chloe was ever optimistic.

Sure enough, when I went out my back door, I could smell the heady aroma of fresh cinnamon rolls wafting from Lighthouse.

I tapped on the open back door and stuck my head in. Chloe was just taking a tray of scones from the oven and sliding them into the cooling rack. She nodded at me to come in.

"You're up early," she said. "Need coffee?"

Pansy, all four-feet-nine of her, glanced over from the industrial mixer that was nearly as tall as she was. Dough hooks the size of cantaloupes slowly turned and stretched a batch of sweet dough that would become trays of sticky pecan buns. "Good morning, Gloryanna," she called cheerfully, waving a hand gnarled with arthritis as though being up before the sun was cause for celebration.

"Morning, Miss Pansy."

Chloe disappeared to the front and returned a minute later with a vanilla latte. She handed me the coffee, and a sample-sized scone. "We're trying out a new recipe," she explained. "Florida citrus is what Miss Pansy calls it, but she won't tell me exactly what's in it."

"Take two," Pansy said, hobbling over with another tiny pastry resting on her palm. "One for that handsome fella of yours. I'd like to know what he thinks, too."

I shook my head. "He's not my *fella*. He's just a friend," I lied. I had begun to secretly hope he was my fella, but I wasn't about to admit it. Especially to Pansy, who guarded her recipes like a dragon guards its treasure, but thrived on local gossip.

Pansy arched an eyebrow and made a disbelieving face. "Oh, he is. Don't you think for a minute you can tell me otherwise. I see the two of you in here, looking all googly-eyed at each other. I might have been born in the morning, but it wasn't *this* morning."

She went back to her mixer, throwing her last words over her bony shoulder. "You mark my words, girl! He's your fella."

Chloe just shrugged. "She's never wrong."

"Googly-eyed? Did she really say that?"

"Well . . ." Chloe drew the word out, as though hesitant to answer. "You *do* pay a lot of attention to each other."

"I may have to start getting my coffee somewhere else," I said darkly.

Chloe laughed. "We're the best, and you know it. Besides, it's the most convenient place for you and"—she drew a deep breath—"where else can you get a free latte before six A.M.?"

She had me and she knew it. "You win," I laughed. "But I'll have to be more careful about how I look at Jake from now on. And thanks for the coffee."

I went back to Southern Treasures and let myself in the back door. I still had to face the postcard mess, and get ready for what I hoped would be a busy Friday.

On my way through the storage area, I filled a box with postcards and note cards to restock the spinner and carried it out front.

"Coffee?" I don't know how Bluebeard knew I had coffee. No, I did know. I *always* had coffee first thing in the morning, although it was usually a mug from my French press upstairs, not a paper cup from Lighthouse. Generally, my latte intake began later in the day.

"No coffee," I answered. "But I will give you a treat."

I set my cup on the counter with the box of cards and broke off a small piece of my scone. Parrots shouldn't have much fat, and no sugar, but it wasn't toxic like coffee. I offered him the crumb of pastry, followed by his usual shredded-wheat biscuit.

The tiny treat earned me a head bump.

I pulled the spinning rack across the shop so I could

spread the cards out on the counter—another reason to do this before the customers arrived.

Several of the wire pockets were empty, and a couple more had no postcards, only note cards without envelopes, which was odd. I was used to a few of the cards going missing each time I filled the rack. People picked up the cards, admired the pictures on the front, and walked out with them, leaving the empty envelope on the rack. And sometimes I found note cards mixed in with postcards in other pockets.

But I didn't usually find cards without envelopes. Who would take an empty envelope?

Chapter 18

I EMPTIED ALL THE POCKETS, SORTING CARDS AND stacking them across the counter. Pictures of boats and beaches, silly sayings, tropical flowers, and vintage photos of Keyhole Bay.

I didn't find the missing envelopes, but by the time Julie arrived, the store was tidy, the postcard rack was fully stocked, and I was ready for a break. Not that I was going to get one. Not on the Friday of a holiday weekend, which was why Julie was working an extra day this week. I needed to take care of some errands, and I didn't dare close, even long enough to go to the bank.

I opened the safe to stock the till and was reminded that I had no reason to complain. It had been a good week so far, and the weekend looked promising. I made up a bank deposit, wrote a list of necessary errands, and stuck my wallet in my pocket with my driver's license.

I called Jake before I ducked out the back door. "You have a bank deposit?" I asked. "Or a change order? I'm heading over, be glad to take care of yours, too."

"Would you?" Jake sounded relieved. "I was already short of change, and the first customer through the door this morning spent ten bucks and gave me a hundred."

"Call in the order and I'll pick it up."

I hung up, told Julie what I was doing, and trotted across the street to pick up Jake's bank bag, and drop off Pansy's scone. *Not because he was my fella*, I told myself. *Just doing a favor for a friend.*

But as I came back across, I caught Chloe grinning at me through the big front window at Lighthouse and felt like I'd been caught. Doing what? I wasn't sure. I just knew I felt guilty.

I steered the Southern Treasures truck down back streets, avoiding the main drag as long as possible. I finally turned into traffic and crept the last few blocks to Back Bay Bank. As I parked the truck, I realized with a start that soon the signs would change and Back Bay would cease to exist.

I waited behind two other local merchants as Barbara counted their deposits and stamped their receipts. Everyone wanted to talk about the dead auditor and what it would mean for the transition.

"I really don't know yet," Barbara said to Cheryl Beauford. "There's supposed to be somebody from the bank coming down today, but who knows when he'll actually get here. You know what it's like trying to get a flight this time of year."

Cheryl nodded. "We don't travel during the summer, but we've had friends *try* to get here. It's ridiculous."

Cheryl stuffed her receipts in her bag and turned to leave.

"Hi, Glory," she said as she headed for the door. "How you doing?"

"Can't complain." I wiggled my zippered deposit bag. "Been a decent summer so far. How about you?"

"The Fourth's always good," she laughed. "Lots of cookouts and beer."

"Tell Frank I said hey," I told her, moving up as the person in front of me finished at the teller window. "I'll be by a little later, my cupboards are pretty bare."

"We'll be there," Cheryl said with an eye roll.

I laughed. Running the main grocery store in town meant they were there all day every day.

I stepped to the counter and handed over my deposits to Barbara. "Any word about Bridget?" I asked as she emptied the bag and started checking off the totals.

"Bridget?" Her head shot up and she gave me a puzzled look. "Did you know her?"

"A little," I said. "She came in the shop a couple times and we had dinner together the Friday before she died. Seemed like a nice gal."

Barbara shook her head. "I thought so, too."

She lowered her voice to a whisper. "Until I heard she was doing drugs out there. Is that true?"

She looked stricken as she realized what she'd just said. "Not that I thought you—I mean, you talked to her, maybe you got an impression or something."

"I did," I said, trying to contain the shock I felt. I knew the rumors were flying, but I hadn't heard them firsthand until now, and I certainly hadn't heard them associated with me. "To tell the truth, I don't believe it. She just didn't seem like that kind of person, and I didn't notice anything in the way she acted that made me think any different."

Barbara straightened up and went back to counting. I suspected my tone had been harsher than I'd intended, and she hadn't meant to accuse me of hanging out with a drug user. Still, her words stung.

I took my receipts and Jake's change order, and hurried back out to the truck. Traffic was already heavy, I absolutely had to go by Frank's Foods, and I needed to get the oil changed in the truck—though that would have to wait until next week.

On impulse, I pulled into Fowler's Auto Sales on my way to the grocery store. Not that I'd let any of those clowns touch my baby. Instead, I pulled around to the back of the lot and through the chain-link fence that marked the end of Fowler's property and the beginning of Sly's. I knew Fowler had his eye on the junkyard with the small cinderblock house in the middle, but Sly had said many times that he'd never get his hands on it. Sly didn't have much use for Matt Fowler, and neither did I.

Bobo, his teeth bared in a slobbery doggy grin, loped out from between the rows of trucks parked against the fence. I reached into the glove box of the pickup and retrieved a treat for him before I climbed out of the cab.

As I alighted, he sat expectantly, trying to control his excited wiggling. I remembered the first time I'd encountered Bobo, when I'd walked into the junkyard not knowing he, and Sly, lived there. All I saw that day was a head the size of a basketball, if basketballs had rows of large pointy teeth.

Since then I'd been accepted as part of his pack, and he treated me with affection and deference.

A few steps behind Bobo was Sly, his dark face split by a wide grin that exposed the gaps where several teeth used to be.

"Miz Glory! Didn't expect to see you again so soon."

"Hello, Sly." Anyone else I'd have greeted with a hug, but I wouldn't presume to violate his dignity. Sly was nearly seventy, after all, and had the courtly manners of a true Southern gentleman. Although he treated me with the affection of family, I still felt like I needed to maintain some reserve.

"What brings you here this morning?" he asked. "Seems like you ought to be pretty busy with your store."

"Julie's there, and Rose Ann is with her grandma. I had to go to the bank and stop at Frank's—Bluebeard is out of bananas and apples, and that's a crisis."

"He always was set in his ways," Sly said. I knew he wasn't talking about the parrot. Sly had been as close to a friend as Uncle Louis had in his later years.

"Anyway, I need an oil change, and since I was driving right by, I figured I'd stop and see when would be a good time for you."

"Any time. I could do it right now, if you like. Take me about twenty minutes."

I hesitated. I would love to stay and visit with Sly, but I'd promised Julie I'd be back quickly.

"Wish I could, Sly. I'd enjoy spending a little time with you and Bobo." I patted the patient hound and he rewarded my attention with a wag of his tail. "But I still need to get groceries, and I have to get back to the store."

"Well then, why don't you come back next time Julie's there to mind the store?"

I smiled. "She'll be in all day Monday. How about I bring lunch? Say, around noon?"

Sly nodded his agreement.

I headed back to the truck, but his voice stopped me. "Miz Glory? I don't mean to pry, but you look mighty down. Are you needin' something more than an oil change?"

The concern in his voice was what broke me. I couldn't bear to have Sly worrying about me.

I gave him a condensed version of the last few days, ending with my encounter at the bank. "I just can't believe she was doing drugs," I repeated for about the millionth time, "and I know I certainly wasn't! But now it looks like I could end up with the same things being said about me."

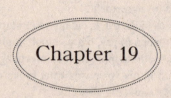

Chapter 19

SLY SCOWLED. "THEY BETTER NOT SAY ANYTHING like that where I can hear. Bobo neither."

Beside me Bobo rose to his feet and growled, as though he knew exactly what Sly had said.

The two of them coming to my defense reassured me. No one who knew me, even slightly, would have any doubt of my innocence. And everyone in town knew me.

"Thanks, Sly," I said. "And Bobo," I added with a pat on his broad head. "I know it will all get straightened out when they get the tests back from the lab."

I wished I felt as confident as I sounded.

"I'll bring the truck in on Monday," I said, climbing back in the cab. "Thanks!"

I waved at Sly through the windshield and put the truck into gear, backing out through the gate. I turned around and headed onto the road, in the direction of Frank's Foods.

The parking lot was busy, but not as jammed as it would be later in the day. I grabbed a couple cloth bags from behind the seat and hurried inside. I'd spent longer than I'd intended talking with Sly, and I needed to get back to the shop.

But in Keyhole Bay—like all small towns—nothing ever gets done fast. I ran into two different people in the bread aisle who wanted to talk about Back Bay and its troubles, and by the time I got to the produce section, I was beginning to regret my decision. Surely Bluebeard could have managed another day without a banana.

I quickly piled fruit and vegetables into my cart, anxious to get through with my shopping.

Frank appeared from the back, pushing a cart piled with melons, and called my name. "Just got a shipment of watermelon in," he said, "but one of 'em broke, and we can't eat it all. Would Bluebeard like some melon?"

"You know he would, Frank."

"Hang on." He ran into the storeroom and came running back a few seconds later with a plastic zip-seal bag from the fish counter. I could see chunks of bright red watermelon with juice puddling in the bag.

"Here you go."

"I owe you," I said as he scrawled his initials and the words *No Charge* across the heavy plastic.

He handed me the bag with a shrug. "No you don't."

Cheryl was ringing up another customer when I got in line, and a few minutes later I was handing her a check in exchange for my two bags of groceries.

"I know this is good," she joked as she slid the check in the bottom of the cash register. "Since I just saw you in the bank."

"Yeah. It's going to be strange, isn't it, when they take down the Back Bay signs."

"Sure is. Too bad about Francis and Lacey, too. He did what his bosses told him, and they just threw him to the wolves.

"Which reminds me," she went on, "have you heard anything about what they're going to do with Bayvue Estates? I know there are a bunch of the construction guys who are anxious to get in line if there's going to be work."

I slung the sacks over my shoulder and picked up the plastic bag of watermelon. "Wish I knew, Cheryl. It's terrible about all the people thrown out of work by this mess."

"You know, Frank and I actually thought about buying a lot out there. Maybe put up a place where we could retire one of these days," Cheryl said, shaking her head. "But then we went out and took a good look around. We knew we'd never be happy out there, not with what they had planned."

I hesitated. I should get home, but there was nobody in line, and I wanted to hear more. "What were they planning?"

"A bunch of patio homes. You know, big houses on lots so tiny that there's only room for a patio, with your neighbors living practically in your hip pocket. And a bunch of community stuff, like a pool and clubhouse, and eventually a golf course." She gave a little laugh. "Even if we could have afforded one of those overbuilt places—which we couldn't— we would have never fit in. It just felt cold and plastic and like it could be anywhere."

I couldn't imagine Frank and Cheryl in the kind of neighborhood she described. Nor could I picture the two of them, with their adored nephews and nieces who traipsed in and out of their home constantly, in the house I'd visited just a week ago.

"I can't even imagine y'all retiring," I told her. "Much less moving away from your family."

"Well, Glory, it's not like Bayvue Estates is that far away. It's just a few miles from where we are now."

"And your sister and her kids are right next door to where you are now."

She chuckled. "Got me."

I wanted to ask her who had showed her the development and talked to her about the plans, but just then a couple in shorts and loud shirts wheeled a cart up to the check stand. A quick glance at their cart loaded with wine, ice, and snack food pegged them as tourists.

I waved good-bye to Cheryl and went back to the truck. It was way past time I got back to the store.

I checked in with Julie, who assured me she had things under control, before I ran across the street to deliver Jake's change.

"Sorry it took so long," I said. "Long story, and neither of us has time for it right now."

"Tell me over dinner," he said, "once we're closed."

I accepted his invitation along with a promise to call a little later with dinner details.

Bluebeard gobbled down the watermelon when I put it in his dish, much to the delight of a couple little boys who were in the shop. Somehow the idea that the parrot was eating watermelon was one of the most entertaining things they had seen all day, and they begged to be able to feed him.

"I'm really sorry," I told them. "But he doesn't have very

good table manners sometimes, and he might hurt your fingers."

Bluebeard cursed softly behind my back, but fortunately he was quiet enough that I was the only one who heard him. Then he squawked loudly. "Good Bluebeard!"

The boys dissolved into fresh giggles and went running for their parents.

As they were leaving, the father asked in a tone that was only half joking if I would ever consider selling the bird.

I shook my head. "There isn't anyone I dislike that much," I said with a lighthearted laugh. "Parrots can be a handful, especially one like Bluebeard."

I didn't tell him about the ghost that came along with the bird, and made it impossible for me to part with him. I doubt he would have believed me.

A tall woman with cropped red hair came through the door, eliciting a wolf-whistle from Bluebeard.

Julie was around the counter, giving our visitor a warm hug, by the time I had admonished Bluebeard. It was a lost cause, I knew, but I still tried to curb his flirtatious behavior. Not everyone thought it was cute.

Our new arrival, though, didn't seem to notice. She was engaged in a rapid-fire conversation with Julie, and it was clear the two were old friends.

"Mandy," she said, pulling her friend over to where I stood behind the counter, "this is my boss, Gloryanna Martine. She owns this awesome place. Miss Glory, this is my friend Mandy Price. She works for Coast Custom Printers. You know, the place that does Mermaid Grotto's T-shirts."

"Glad to meet you, Miss Glory." Mandy handed me a

business card. "Julie told me you might be interested in some T-shirts?"

"We did talk a little about that," I said. I didn't tell her I'd forgotten we'd scheduled a meeting this afternoon. "Julie thought shirts with Bluebeard on them would sell well in the store."

"Pretty boy!" Bluebeard yelled.

Mandy noticed him this time. She turned and looked at the parrot across the shop. "May I?" she asked before she approached him.

"He's bad-mannered," I said. "But I couldn't have him in the store if he wasn't okay around the customers."

Julie led her friend across the shop and showed her where to find the shredded-wheat biscuits that he loved. One treat from an attractive lady and he practically melted.

Mandy gingerly touched his head and he rubbed against her hand. "Pretty girl."

"You're not too bad yourself, Bluebeard," she said.

"He likes pretty girls," Julie told her. "Especially the ones that give him treats," she added dryly.

Mandy laughed and came back to me. "So that's your star. I can see why Julie thinks he'd sell on a shirt. She's absolutely right. Mascots sell well, especially when it's one with a personality, and that he has in spades.

"So what did you have in mind?"

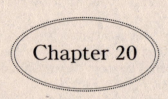

Chapter 20

I HAD TO HAND IT TO MANDY. SHE WAS ONE HECK OF a saleswoman. By the time she left, she had an order for five dozen shirts, a case of mugs, and several hundred postcards—all with full-color images of Bluebeard. And a deposit check for an amount that made me swallow hard.

She promised me that everything could be in the store in a week. Plenty of time, in her words, to "sell out and reorder before the end of the summer."

I truly hoped she was right. It was a gamble that would limit the money I could put in my Buy-Out-Peter Fund. On the other hand, if it was as successful as she expected, I would have a lot more in the Peter Fund at the end of the year.

That alone made it worth the risk.

While we were finalizing the order, a man walked through the door. He didn't fit in, just as Bridget hadn't a week earlier. Didn't seem interested in the merchandise exactly, just wandered around while I talked to Mandy and Julie waited on the customers who lined up at the register.

Julie walked Mandy out to her car, chattering about Rose Ann. I made a mental note that if the experiment was successful, she deserved a bonus for her idea, and a single mom could use all the help she could get.

The man who'd been wandering around finally approached me once we were alone. "Are you Miss Martine?" he asked.

His flat, Midwestern accent had a vaguely familiar tone. Lots of people come through Southern Treasures in the summer, and I'd probably talked to someone from his region recently. But he sounded exhausted, as though he hadn't slept in several days, and his manner was hesitant, almost deferential.

"Yes, I am."

"I, uh, I just wanted to thank you. My sister mentioned you and your parrot. She said he was quite flirty, but really sweet."

I must have looked puzzled, which I certainly was. What was this stranger thanking me for? And who was his sis—

"I'm so sorry—" I began as the pieces finally fell in place.

"I'm sorry," he said at the same time. "I should have introduced—"

We both stopped in one of those awkward conversational pauses, started to speak again, and stopped again. After a few seconds I rushed ahead.

"You're Bridget's brother." It was a statement, not a question. I could see a family resemblance. "I heard you were coming down. I'm so, so sorry. I really liked your sister."

He nodded and offered his hand. "Bradford McKenna—people call me Buddy."

I shook his hand. "Gloryanna Martine. Please call me Glory. And again, I am so sorry for your loss."

"Thank you," he said. He looked around the shop as if he didn't know quite what to say next. "She said it was a fun place," he continued, more to himself than to me. "Now I see what she meant."

From his perch, Bluebeard followed Buddy's movements with bright eyes. Did he see the same resemblance I did? Or was there more to his interest? I never knew when Uncle Louis would offer an opinion on something. Or someone.

Julie came back in, setting off the bell over the front door. At one time I had considered disabling that bell during the busy season, but I'd never got around to it. Right now, as the silence became uncomfortable, the interruption was welcome.

"Bridget told me about you." Buddy spoke suddenly, as though the words had escaped from his thoughts. "She said you and your friend were the first people that didn't treat her like she was trying to kill the town."

"She had a job to do," I answered, keeping my voice carefully neutral. Caution had returned when he mentioned Bridget's introduction to Keyhole Bay—his motives for coming in to Southern Treasures might not be as innocent as he claimed.

"It was more than that."

Silence stretched again. Julie fiddled casually with a display, her back to us, but I saw her fingering her cell phone in her pocket and I understood the gesture. She had my back in case of a confrontation.

"She got that a lot," Buddy continued. "And she understood it. When the big guns from out of town arrived, people got nervous and scared. They didn't know what the outcome of the audit might be, they felt threatened, and they wanted to protect themselves. That made sense to her."

I wasn't sure how to respond, so I waited to see what he would say next.

"She always sent me postcards," he said, turning to look at the spinner.

It was still tidy from my restock; was that only this morning? It seemed like a world away.

He ran a finger along the pockets, as though looking for something. He paused over a card of a fishing boat, then shook his head and continued his examination.

"This one," he said, picking up a shot of the tiny bay that gave the town its name. "This is the one she would have sent."

He turned back to me, his eyes clouded. "She knew I liked boats. It's the one she would have chosen. "

He carefully slid the card back into the rack, squaring up the corners as though trying to impose order on a world that had suddenly turned chaotic.

He was stalling. I was sure of it. There was something on his mind, something he had wanted to say from the moment he first walked in the door, but he couldn't bring himself to do it.

"She seemed like a nice person," I said. "I only just met her, but Karen and I both liked her. We hoped we could be friends while she was here."

"She hoped that, too," he answered without turning back to face me. "She texted me on Saturday morning, from Biloxi. Said you'd recommended the trip. She was having fun, she said, and thought she might go on over to New Orleans before heading back."

He hung his head and his voice dropped to a whisper. "That was the last time I heard from her."

He finally turned to look at me. His pain was clear on his face. "Miss Martine, Gloryanna, I just came from the police station. They said they had the results of the tests they ran, but I don't believe them. They're wrong. They have to be.

"They said she died of a self-inflicted drug overdose."

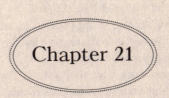

Chapter 21

"THEY ACTUALLY *SAID* IT WAS SELF-INFLICTED?"

"Not in so many words," he admitted. "They said she overdosed. No signs of foul play. It sounded to me like there wasn't going to be much of an investigation."

"Who did you talk to?" I asked.

"A detective, I think. His name was Sherman." He fished in his pocket and came up with a business card. "Gregory Sherman. Yeah, he's a detective. But he didn't seem especially interested in doing anything about Bridget."

"They're pretty busy this time of year," I said. "Maybe he was just in a hurry and didn't express himself very well."

"I don't know. I got the impression there are a lot of people around here that would like this audit to just go away. She said she had the same impression, said you and your friend were about the only people who didn't treat her like some kind of pariah.

"But just because Bridget is"—he struggled for a moment—"*gone*, it doesn't change anything. That's part of why I'm here. Bridget and I worked in the same department. She was a senior auditor—one of the best. I'm just a staff auditor. So far." He added that last bit with a touch of defiance.

"They'll send another senior person," he continued. "But there wasn't anyone else available on a holiday weekend, so they sent me. They knew I'd come anyway."

"They let you work with your sister?" I was surprised. I thought most big companies had lots of rules about family members working together.

"Half sister," he admitted with a shrug. "Our dad married my mom when Bridget was six or seven, I think. By the time I came along, she was ten and her mom had moved her to Chicago. We didn't see that much of each other when we were growing up.

"I didn't even know she was in the department when I started there. We weren't that close, really, though we were beginning to build a relationship."

I tried to imagine how anyone could not be close to their sibling. As an only child, I had longed desperately for a little brother or sister. In my early teens I had fantasized about an older brother. Especially an older brother with lots of cute friends. Instead I had Peter. Not a winner in the sibling-substitute sweepstakes.

But my folks never had any other children, and I never knew why. I had been too polite to ask my mother, too well behaved to question her about something so personal. After she was gone, I could have asked Linda. She might know. Heck, she probably *did* know; she and my mother had been good friends. But even if she would tell me, was I ready to know the answer, to know the intimate details of my mother's life?

I'd filled the family places in my life with friends: my foster parents, Guy and Linda; and Karen and Riley, the siblings I never had. And now I had Uncle Louis. Sort of.

Buddy's sigh brought me back to the present. "I guess there was more to my coming in here than just wanting to thank you," he admitted. "I think I wanted to talk to someone who knew her. Someone who would believe me when I said she wouldn't ever do drugs."

"But if you weren't that close, how could you be sure? Really?"

"There was an incident I heard about, right after I started at the bank. A couple of the junior accounting guys were getting high on the weekends, and word got back to the bank. They were gone within days. Turns out she was their supervisor, and she made it exceedingly clear that when she said she had a zero tolerance policy, she meant it."

I was still struggling with something he had mentioned earlier.

"How could you not know she worked in your department?"

He shrugged. "She was ten years older than me. I hadn't seen her in years, and I always figured she'd gotten married and changed her name. Bridget isn't that unusual a name. I knew there was a Bridget McKenna in the department, but I assumed it was her married name. She was out of the office a lot on travel assignments, and I'd been there several months before we actually met."

The bell over the door jingled and a trio of twentysomething women in tank tops and shorts wafted in on a cloud of coconut-scented sunscreen. Julie moved quickly to intercept them and offer her help.

Buddy, seeing the new arrivals, shifted gears. "Thanks for your time, Miss Martine. I really appreciate it. I'll be in town for a few more days, at least until we get another auditor down from Minneapolis." He drew a business card from his pocket and scribbled something on the back before handing it to me. "My cell number," he explained. "If you think of anything that might help, please give me a call. I know my sister didn't take her own life, accidentally or otherwise."

I remembered the trouble his sister had had finding a place to stay. Curious, I asked, "Where are you staying?"

"The other model home," he replied. He lowered his voice to a discreet whisper. "The police haven't released the house where, uh, it happened. But the bank owns both of the houses out there, and they arranged for me to get the keys to the other one."

He thanked me again for my time, and headed out the door.

A few minutes later, Julie rang up the purchases for the three young women and locked the door behind them.

"Thanks," I said to her as she came back across the shop.

"What was that all about?" she asked. "I tried to give you some space, but he seemed pretty intense."

"Bridget McKenna's half brother. The one the bank sent down here to take over for her. Temporarily."

"But what did he want here? I mean, why did he want to talk to you? And what did he want you to help with?"

"Nothing really. A detective, somebody named Gregory

Sherman—ever heard of him?—told him it was a drug over-dose, and gave him the impression they were blaming Bridget. He thought . . . I don't know what he thought. He wanted someone to listen to him mostly. Someone to believe Bridget wasn't responsible for her own death."

"And do you? Believe him, I mean?"

"I do, but not because anything he said changed my mind. I already agreed with him before he walked through the door."

But now I had to wonder if anyone else shared my opinion.

I was still debating the question when Jake called about dinner plans. "I have fixings for chicken tacos," I volunteered. "And there's plenty for two. Why don't you just come over here?"

"You don't want to cook chicken."

"It's already cooked. We just have to nuke it."

"Sounds like a plan then. Need anything more?"

"I've got sweet tea," I answered. That should be no sur-prise. There was always a jug of sweet tea in my refrigerator. "If you want something else to drink, you should bring it."

He chuckled. "I will be there with a six-pack of micro-brew as soon as I see what your friend Linda has cold."

I promised I'd leave the door open, said good night to Julie, and went to settle Bluebeard for the evening. He'd al-ready had watermelon for a treat, and several of the shop's customers had been allowed to feed him unsalted wheat crackers and shredded-wheat biscuits. I checked his food dish, added a couple apple slices, and gave him clean water.

Jake had just stepped through the front door when Blue-beard shook off his end-of-day lethargy and began squawking loudly. Jake hastily locked the door behind him and hurried to my side, where I was trying to calm the agitated bird.

Fixing Jake with a beady-eyed stare, Bluebeard ceased his squawking. The sudden silence was even more unnerving than the shrill noise had been.

Then he spoke, clearly and in Uncle Louis's voice.

"Find the postcards, buddy boy."

Chapter 22

I THOUGHT I WAS USED TO UNCLE LOUIS USING BLUE-beard to issue cryptic clues and veiled warnings. But this was the first time he'd tried to give orders. And as always, he said something that didn't make much sense.

"What postcards?" Jake asked.

But Bluebeard didn't reply. He ruffled his feathers as though shrugging off our puzzlement, and retreated to his cage.

"What postcards?" I repeated Jake's question, but I didn't get an answer either. Not that I really expected one.

What I did get was a string of curses, and a final announcement of "Trying to @^@$^%* sleep here!"

Bluebeard was quite clearly done talking.

Jake and I took the hint and retreated upstairs.

"Any idea what that was about?" Jake asked.

"Not a clue," I answered. "In fact, I cleaned up all the postcards this morning. Oh! And I ordered Bluebeard post-cards this afternoon! Julie's friend Mandy was here from the print shop."

I launched into an explanation of Mandy's visit, talking about the designs we'd chosen and what merchandise I'd finally settled on for my first order. Soon Bluebeard's outburst was forgotten in the excitement over my new venture.

"It's still a big gamble," I said. "And I'm a little scared at the amount of money I've committed to this. But Julie and Mandy are confident it will work."

Jake watched me pull ingredients from the refrigerator. "What can I do to help?"

I pointed to the domed plastic cover over the whole roasted chicken. "How about shredding the chicken?"

Jake nodded and took a pair of forks out of the drawer. He set to work removing the meat from the bones and using the forks to separate it into shreds. The man had some definite kitchen skills.

"Have you been watching the Cooking Channel?" I asked lightly. He had to have acquired the know-how somewhere.

"I used to, back in California. I did a fair amount of cooking for a crowd, once upon a time."

"Restaurant?"

"Naw." He tossed a handful of expertly shredded chicken in a ceramic bowl, ready for the microwave. "Just friends." His tone said the subject was closed for now.

I pulled on a pair of latex gloves to protect me from the peppers, and set to work on the salsa. With a sharp knife I slit open a couple jalapeños and carefully removed the seeds and membranes. Then I removed the stems from a handful of tomatoes, quartered and peeled an onion, and washed a bunch of cilantro.

I tossed it all in the food processor with garlic, salt, and pepper, and pulsed it a few times, just until the vegetables were chopped.

Jake's California roots weren't really a secret; I'd known all along he was from the West Coast, and I'd learned several months ago that he was from California specifically.

So far I had resisted the temptation to try digging into his history online, even though I knew with Karen's help I could probably find out anything I wanted to know. It was up to Jake to decide what he was willing to share, and I told myself I had to trust him just as I wanted him to trust me.

One thing I did know was how much he loved avocados. I started peeling and mashing the bright green flesh for guacamole and was rewarded with a broad smile.

"You better eat this," I joked. "Because this is one leftover Bluebeard can't have. Avocados are right up there with coffee on the bad list."

"I'll make that sacrifice," he said. "I wouldn't want him to get sick, after all."

We finished the dinner prep, heated the chicken in the microwave, and sat down at the table with our plates and beers.

"So how was your day?" Jake asked. "You said you had a story when you came back this morning. Oh, thanks for the change run, by the way. Good thing, too. I got two more big bills this afternoon."

I had to stop and think. This morning seemed a long time ago. "Well," I said, trying to reconstruct the day, "it started way too early."

I told him about the delays at the bank, and the grocery store, and the visit to Sly in between.

"I agree with him," Jake said, his voice somber. "That's an awful thing to say about anyone. And in your case, it's absolutely ridiculous."

"Thank you. But how do you know about anybody?" I asked. "How can you tell? I mean, I still don't want to believe that Bridget had anything to do with drugs, but how else do you explain what happened?"

He shook his head. "Who knows? Maybe she got involved with something over in Biloxi."

"Her brother did say she texted him from there," I said, thinking out loud.

"Her brother? When did you talk to her brother?"

"Half brother," I corrected. "He came into the store just before closing."

I repeated the story Bridget's brother had told me, emphasizing the part about the lab results. "They told him she died of an overdose, and there was no sign of foul play. What else could it be?" I still didn't want to think it was true, but I was having trouble coming up with any other explanation.

"I don't know, Glory."

I helped myself to another tortilla and carefully assembled a second taco. "I need to change the subject," I said. "This is just too depressing."

Jake nodded. But try as we might, every conversation seemed to circle back around and trip over the one topic we were trying to avoid, and we lapsed into silence.

"How's the website going?" Jake asked.

"Slowly. I'm making progress, but it takes time I usually don't have in the summer."

"For sure," Jake answered. "Did that last book help?"

In answer I got up and went to get my laptop. Setting it on the table between us, I navigated to the Southern Treasures page and showed him the latest additions.

"You should put up an announcement about the new T-shirts," he suggested.

"Good idea." I opened my to-do file and made a note.

As I was closing the file, my phone rang. Distracted, I didn't check the caller ID before I answered.

I wished I had.

"Glory?"

My cousin Peter's drawl leaned dangerously close to a whine, and I scowled at the phone.

"Yes, Peter."

Jake rolled his eyes. He knew how annoying Peter could be, how much I resented his intrusions into the running of Southern Treasures, and how crazy his suggestions were. Just because he had a lot of schooling didn't mean he understood a thing about running a retail business, and his visit on Sunday had just reinforced that. I guess he was a good engineer—he held a high-level job doing something that I didn't understand—but a master's degree in engineering had nothing to do with a souvenir shop.

"Glory, I was thinking."

That was a bad sign. It meant he was about to suggest some dang fool scheme again. It also meant I had to count to ten before I could speak, or risk using words I'd learned from Bluebeard.

"What, Peter?"

"Do you think we ought to consider branching out? Maybe finding another location?"

I held my tongue between my teeth for several seconds as I did a quick ten count, then took a deep breath.

"I don't think we're in a position to do that, Peter."

"But I've been hearing that the Gulf Coast is making an economic recovery, that tourists are back and spending like they used to, before Katrina and the oil spill. We should position ourselves to take advantage of that."

I tried to imagine where he was getting his information. I got to six before I blurted out, "Where did you hear that?"

"One of the guys at work. He showed me an article in *U.S. News* that said tourism spending is growing every year, and I keep hearing how the hotels down there are filling up every weekend. You told me the same thing when I was there on Sunday." His voice dropped into a lower register, as though he was trying to sound more authoritative. "The indicators are for improved cash flow in the second half of this year."

What? That sentence didn't even make sense.

"What indicators? Where did that information come from? Who's making these predictions?"

"Now, Glory," he said, his voice dripping with condescension. "It's all very complex economics. Very complex. I don't expect you to be able to—"

This time I didn't even try to count.

"Peter, I don't know who you are listening to, but for right now, you listen to this.

"I am on the ground here, and I see *exactly* how the economics are working in my town. I know how much money is being spent, where, and how. I take care of the sales and the expenses for Southern Treasures, and I send you your share of the profits every month. Take a look at those checks, and you tell me if there's enough there to consider opening another store."

I drew a ragged breath, fighting to control the adrenaline rush brought on by anger. "Have you looked, really looked, at those checks, Peter? Or do you just hand them to your wife to put in the bank?"

"Now, Glory—"

"Don't." The word came out quietly. "If you want to open another store, if you want to take on that expense and that risk, you can. Don't let me stop you. But don't expect to use the Southern Treasures name, and don't expect me to assume any responsibility for it. I have more than enough on my plate here, and like I told you Sunday, this is not the time to consider expansion."

I took another gulp of air, and tried to calm down. "Peter, you're my family, and I don't mean to yell at you. But you have to trust me on this. I am here twenty-four/seven, and I know what is best for Southern Treasures. Believe me when I say I want the shop to succeed; it's how I pay my bills. But you need to give me credit for knowing my business, just like I give you credit for knowing yours."

Okay, that last part was only kind of true. Right now I didn't give him credit for knowing a blasted thing.

Peter stammered a sort-of apology, promising to trust my judgment, and hung up.

I couldn't look at Jake, ashamed of my outburst. I had overreacted to Peter's suggestion and taken my frustration out on him.

It wasn't his fault that Bridget died, or that I was having trouble accepting the fact.

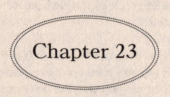

Chapter 23

I HAD TO DO SOMETHING. SHOUTING AT PETER WAS A clue I was far too stressed out, and my usual treatment for stress was activity.

I patted my pocket, checking for keys. "Want to go for a ride?" I asked Jake. "I promise not to drive like a crazy woman. Honest."

He shoved the last of the leftovers in the refrigerator, a task he'd started while I was on the phone. "Where we going?"

It was all the answer I needed.

"I want you to meet Bridget's brother." It was only part of the reason. I also wanted to take a look at the house where I'd been just a week ago.

The house where Bridget died.

We were already in the traffic of the main drag when I realized I hadn't called Bradford McKenna to tell him we were coming. I dug in my pocket for his card and handed it to Jake, along with my phone. "Can you dial this for me?"

I spoke briefly with Bridget's brother, and he said he'd be glad to have some company. Who wouldn't, stuck out there in an empty subdivision with no one else around? I wasn't exactly a city girl—Keyhole Bay wasn't exactly a city, just a small town—but just being out there for a couple hours had given me the heebie-jeebies. And that was when Bridget was still alive.

On the drive out to Bayvue, I distracted myself from thoughts of Bridget by filling Jake in on Peter's latest scheme. "I can barely keep up with one store. How am I supposed to take on a second one?"

"He has no idea how much work is involved," Jake agreed. "And you really would be better off to buy him out." He stopped, as though deep in thought. "Have you ever considered," he continued, "getting a different partner? One that actually understands what you're doing?"

"Sure. And I also wanted a pet unicorn. I think I'm just as likely to find one of those. I mean, who do you trust? Where do you even look?"

I turned off the highway onto the county road.

"Right here," Jake said quietly. "I might be looking for another investment, and Southern Treasures has a lot going for it. Including a really good manager."

The offer, and the compliment, stunned me. Jake wanted to invest in Southern Treasures? He was willing to help me buy out Peter?

"You, uh, well, um. It's a lot of money," I stammered. "Not that I mean to say you can't do it. I have no idea what your situation is, and, well, it's none of my business how much money you have and what you do with it."

I was handling this badly, and I couldn't seem to find a way out of the corner I'd put myself in.

I turned off the county road, driving between the brick gateposts, lonely sentinels with nothing to guard but bare land scraped clear of any sign of life.

I pulled up in front of the model home where a single light shone in the kitchen window. The house next door where Bridget had stayed loomed in the dark, a menacing presence in a deserted landscape.

It was like the setting for a slasher movie. I just hoped there wasn't a guy with a hockey mask lurking somewhere.

Before I got out of the truck, I turned to Jake. "Thank you for the vote of confidence. I appreciate it. Truly. But I don't want you taking any chances on account of me."

"Like I said, I may be looking for another investment." He held up his hand and ticked off his points on his fingers as he continued. "The bookstore is doing okay, I've discovered I like what I'm doing, I've got some money, and I think Southern Treasures is a good bet. So can we talk about me helping you buy out Peter?"

I nodded, then realized he might not be able to see the gesture clearly in the darkened truck cab. "We can talk," I said. "No promises. But we'll talk."

He shook my hand, a move that felt somehow more trusting and intimate at that point than a kiss. We had crossed some kind of invisible line, as though much more than a simple financial conversation was promised by our decision.

No porch light illuminated the front door. I leaned across,

opened the glove box, and took out a sturdy flashlight. I did a lot of treasure hunting in old barns and storage sheds without enough light to see what I was buying. I needed—and always had on hand—a good flashlight.

The bright beam lighted our way across the hard-packed dirt of the front yard.

The door opened, faint light spilling out. "Miss Martine, Glory, it's good to see you." Bradford invited us in.

"I haven't had time to make the place habitable," he said, leading us into the kitchen. A coffeemaker and toaster that matched the cheap ones I'd seen at Bridget's rested on an identical granite counter. The layout was different, but the atmosphere was the same: an open floor plan with lots of space, high-end appliances and cabinetry, everything finished in stone and natural wood.

That is, everything that was visible. Papers were scattered across most of the flat surfaces, and two laptops sat open on the far end of the counter.

I introduced the two men and they shook hands.

"Buddy to my friends," Bridget's brother reminded us. "So what can I do for you?" He looked at me, curiosity clear in his expression.

I hesitated. Why had I decided to come out here? What had I hoped to accomplish with this sudden excursion?

When in doubt, stick as close to the truth as possible.

"I don't really know," I admitted in what I hoped was a lighter tone than I felt. "It just felt like there was more you wanted to tell me this afternoon, and I cut you off."

"Not at all," he said. He bustled around, starting a pot of coffee, as though anxious for something to do. "Not at all," he repeated. "You had work to do. Actually I owe you an apology for the interruption."

"Oh no! It was sweet of you to even think of coming to thank me at a time like this. You have so many more important things on your mind right now."

Buddy's visit to Southern Treasures hadn't bothered me, but I had been a little freaked out by his intensity. Under the circumstances, though, I could understand. Memaw would have been proud of my graciousness. My mother probably wouldn't have believed me capable of it, but her early training had taken hold far deeper than she ever knew. I liked to think I had outgrown the surly teenager who refused to write thank-you notes.

"But yes, there was something more," Buddy admitted. "Bridget said she thought you might be a good source of background information."

"Don't sugarcoat it," I said. "You mean she thought I knew the local gossip."

He winced at the blunt description, but a tiny twinkle lit his eyes. "You sound like her," he said. "She was direct, said what she thought. You do that, too."

I blushed. "Sorry, I shouldn't have said that. It wasn't very nice of me."

"Actually, it's refreshing. It reminds me of Bridget. In a good way." His voice broke but he quickly regained control.

The coffeepot hissed, signaling the end of the brewing cycle. Without asking, Jake took three foam cups out of a package on the counter, filled them with steaming liquid, and handed one to each of us.

"Thanks," I said, touching his hand.

Buddy nodded his thanks, too, and continued. "Bridget did a lot of audits, and she specialized in small-town, family-owned institutions. A lot of times the personal background of the people involved told her more than the paperwork."

He sipped his coffee and winced at the near scalding temperature. "This wasn't her first rodeo, Miss—Glory. She had a regular routine when it came to her investigations. She did her formal job, and did it well. But she also tried to make friends with someone she could count on for reliable information about the community.

"She generally looked for a woman without a close connection to the bank. An independent. A woman, in her words, who was too smart for her own good. I'm afraid," Buddy said, "that three marriages left her with a pretty low opinion of men."

He glanced from me to Jake and back again as though assessing our relationship. I wondered what he concluded, since I wasn't sure myself.

"I'm not sure how to take that," I said slowly.

"I assure you, Glory, it's a compliment. Bridget said understanding the community was good for business, and her track record speaks for itself. But she never thought she knew everything. She wanted to be sure she got it right. Having someone she could trust helped."

He shrugged. "I'm probably putting it badly. And for that I apologize. But the bottom line was that she liked you and thought you were smart. That's a pretty big plus in my book."

Chapter 24

I SIPPED MY COFFEE AND TRIED TO SWALLOW PAST the lump in my throat. Bridget's good opinion of me shouldn't really matter. I had barely known her. Still, I was touched by her brother's words.

And more determined than ever to find out what really happened to her.

"What do we know?" I asked him. "Was she on some medication she could have mixed up, or taken wrong?"

Buddy reached for a large sealed envelope off one of the piles on the island counter. "I don't think so," he said. "The bank pulled some strings and got a copy of her medical records before I flew down here, in case the faxed copies didn't get to the medical examiner." He held up the envelope, wide tape with large red letters reading CONFIDENTIAL stretched across both sides. "But the doctor said he had everything he needed, and I honestly forgot I had these until I was going through the records tonight. I just don't know if I can make sense of them."

Jake reached for the envelope, but I got there first and took it from Buddy's hand. "She's dead," I said. "It can't hurt for us to look at these now, don't you think?"

Buddy put the envelope back on the counter and slowly pushed it toward me. "I have no idea what's in there, and I'm not sure I want to know. But if there's something in there that could help . . ." His voice trailed off, but his meaning was clear.

I picked up the envelope, carefully removed the tape, broke the seal, and pulled out the papers inside.

I skimmed the pages, grateful for modern technology. Instead of a cramped illegible doctor's scrawl, there were neat lines of computer printing detailing the notes from each medical interaction. There weren't very many.

Jake relented and moved to look over my shoulder. As I turned the pages, I could feel him leaning closer, his interest engaged in spite of himself.

As we turned the final page, he stepped back. "Nothing," he said with authority.

I shot him a questioning look, but I had to admit I agreed with him. "I didn't see anything either."

"So it wasn't an accident with a prescription," Buddy said. "Not that I expected it to be.

"And there's no indication in her records of any recreational drug use? Not that people don't lie about that," he added hastily. "But they usually don't lie to their doctor."

"No. Which means," I said, "she got something accidentally, maybe in her food or something."

"That isn't likely either," Buddy said. "The doctor told me it was an injection. It hit her fast, and she fell and banged her head."

"There's nothing accidental about an injection," Jake said. "You don't trip and fall on a needle."

"Where . . ." I stopped and swallowed hard, then tried again. "Where did they find her?"

"She was in the kitchen. She'd hit her head on the edge of the island. The detective told me the kitchen was a mess, but they could recommend someone to do the cleanup. Said they should be able to release the scene of the accident over the weekend and I could get started."

"I want to go look."

"Glory," Jake said warningly. "It's dark out, and there aren't any streetlights around, in case you hadn't noticed."

"I know. But I have a good flashlight, and there's another one still in the truck. I want to see where they found her."

I couldn't explain exactly why; I just knew I had to look. And none of Jake's arguments were going to change my mind.

"The house is locked," Buddy warned. "And there are seals on all the doors and windows."

"I won't go inside," I promised. "There are big windows in the back, just like this place. I won't touch anything, and I won't open any of the doors or windows." I remembered Memaw's saying I'd heard a few days ago. "I will look with my eyes," I said, "and not with my hands."

"If you're going, I'm going," Buddy said. "Let's go get that other flashlight."

Jake wasn't happy with my decision, but he insisted on coming with me. "I don't want you out there wandering around alone," he said as the three of us went out to the truck for my second flashlight. I resisted the temptation to remind him that Buddy had already said he was coming with me.

We worked our way around the side of the house, using the twin beams of the two flashlights to illuminate the occasional clumps of spindly grass and the sticker bushes that brushed against our legs.

In the dark, the flashlight beams sent shadows dancing across the barren yard. The light caught in the glass of the back doors and reflected into the inky black of the night.

I swept the beam across the yard and into the emptiness beyond, the light fading by the time it reached the tree line at the edge of the development. I had flashlights designed for seeing into tight corners of crowded buildings, not illuminating a wide landscape or the distant trees.

I caught the flash of eyes in the distance. There were lots of nocturnal animals in the panhandle. It could be a fox, or a possum, a coyote, or a raccoon. But whatever it was, it hurried away from the light.

We moved carefully, trying to avoid the potholes and divots left by the construction equipment. At the back of the house, an excavation marked the position of a planned patio, or perhaps a screened porch—what the developer would call a Florida room.

A snort of disgust escaped my lips before I was able to stop it.

"Glory?" Jake's voice was loud in the surrounding silence. He lowered it to a whisper and continued, "Are you okay?"

I played the flashlight beam around the hole in the ground. "Looks like they were planning to add another slab," I said, illuminating the initial construction of the forms for the concrete. "Probably screen it in and call it a Florida room. Like that makes it so much better than a screened porch, and they can charge three prices for it."

"I've never heard that expression before," Buddy said. "What does it mean?"

"It just means charging a lot," I answered. "Paying three times what something is worth."

Our conversation felt like nervous chatter designed to take our minds off what we were doing.

We stepped over the concrete forms and into the shallow hole where the patio was supposed to go. At least this small portion of the yard was reasonably level, as opposed to the lumps and holes we'd been walking through.

Ahead of us, yellow tape printed with the words CRIME SCENE looped across the glass doors and through the handles. Wide tape covered the gaps where the doors met the frames, and a large notice on the door informed us that we were not to enter the building or disturb the seal.

I had no intention of doing either one.

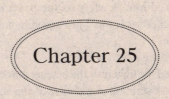

Chapter 25

ALL I WANTED TO DO WAS TAKE A LOOK.

I put my face to the glass next to the warning notice. I placed the flashlight lens close to the door, and slowly swung the beam over the kitchen.

The coffeemaker and toaster stood in the same place on the counter, and dishes were stacked neatly on the far side of the sink. Nothing appeared to be out of place.

I don't know what I expected. Chaos, maybe. Dishes and silverware strewn around the kitchen, the toaster ripped from the outlet and smashed on the floor. A shattered coffeepot.

Something.

Some sign that this was anything other than what the police had concluded. Some piece or part that I could point to and say, "There's your evidence."

Buddy lingered at the edge of the excavation, obviously

not wanting to get any closer to the spot where his sister had died.

Jake moved to the far side of the back wall, where he could use his flashlight to illuminate things from a different angle. I watched him slowly pass the beam over the same counters and cupboards I had just covered, but from several feet to the side.

I still didn't see what I wanted.

As he passed the light over the butcher block on the island, I noticed a dark stain on one corner of the counter. With a sickening lurch, my stomach recognized what my brain had registered: this was the place where Bridget had hit her head.

I recoiled, stepping back from the window and dropping my flashlight.

I remembered what Buddy had said about getting cleaners in after the police released the scene. That corner of the counter was only part of what was in that house, and I didn't want to see any more.

I battled with my stomach as I crawled after my flashlight. The last thing I wanted to do right now was lose my dinner all over the backyard.

I picked up the flashlight and aimed it toward the house next door, where the faint light still shone in the kitchen window.

"Let's go," I said. My voice sounded funny, pinched and tight, but at least I had regained control. For the moment.

I walked slowly across the shallow hole to where Buddy waited. Jake followed a couple steps behind me.

No one spoke as we retraced our steps to the front of the house and across the yards to Buddy's front door.

We shuffled into the house and went directly to the kitchen.

We retrieved our coffee cups and refreshed them from the pot. I shouldn't drink coffee this late, but something told me I wouldn't be sleeping much tonight anyway.

Buddy moved aimlessly around the room, fiddling with the papers. He picked up a stack of printouts, then set them back down on another stack without so much as a glance.

"What did Bridget say she wanted from me?" I asked Buddy, trying to get his focus back on our previous conversation. "You said she wanted to be sure she really understood the local community. What did she want to know?"

He moved another stack of papers, but didn't respond. I silently repeated every word I'd learned from Bluebeard, angry with myself for letting him go over there with us. I'd been so carried away with my own concerns I hadn't thought about how it might make Buddy feel.

"I'm sorry, Buddy," I said, taking his arm and forcing him to stop and look at me. "I should never have suggested we go over there. You didn't need to see any of that."

He shook his head, gazing out the dark windows with a faraway look. "I didn't really see anything." He brushed my hand away. "I'm sad that she's gone, and I really liked her, as much as I knew her. But she was just a friend, barely more than an acquaintance so far. And now she'll never be anything more than that." He stared into the dark, as though the answers he needed were hidden somewhere in the shadows. "That's the real loss," he said softly. "That I don't miss her more. Everyone deserves to be mourned."

He sighed deeply and squared his shoulders, bringing himself back from whatever dark place he had been.

He gestured to me and Jake to join him at the island counter, where he laid out several stacks of papers. "If you can help me through this," he said, his voice firmer than I'd ever heard it, "maybe we can figure out what she found. *I* know she didn't overdose, so what did *she* know that got her in trouble?"

"Aren't those records confidential?" Jake asked. "Maybe we shouldn't be looking at them."

"They are," Buddy conceded. "At least the customers' financial records are. But so were the medical records. A lot of this is Bridget's own assessments. Those are the bank's property, and I think I can trust the two of you to be discreet."

Discreet didn't begin to describe Jake Robinson. The man was a sphinx when it came to keeping secrets. He certainly kept plenty from me.

"Sounds like a good plan," I said.

Buddy flipped through the pages of notes. He began sorting them into several stacks. He moved with efficiency, deciding at a glance which pile a particular piece belonged in and putting it there without hesitation.

Watching him work, he hardly seemed like the same tentative and confused man who had come through my door that morning. He was clearly in his element, examining the information in front of him, making judgments and acting on them. He really was a lot like the sister he barely knew.

It only took him a minute to collect the pages he wanted. Shoving the rest of the stacks to the far side of the counter, he spread the pages in front of us.

"She's listed the primary players here." He indicated a short list of names, most of them Andersons. "This sheet has the major investors in Bayvue, and this one"—he pointed at the longest list—"is a list of Back Bay employees."

Bridget had printed each name in block letters, leaving several blank lines beneath each one. Some of them had additional information written beneath them in cramped but precise script. Others had only a printed word or two, and several were blank.

"Where do you want to start?" I asked.

Buddy scanned the lists. "Let's wait on the employees," he decided. "I'll have access to personnel files and employment records to fill them in." He pushed the employee list away and looked at the remaining two.

"Wait a minute." Jake pulled the employee list back from where Buddy had put it and placed it next to the investors list. Several of the names were on both lists.

"That doesn't seem right," Jake said. "Should the employees of the bank be investing in a development they were financing?"

"It's a small town," I said, coming to the defense of my friends whose names showed up on both lists. "You get these kinds of overlaps all the time."

"It still seems kind of sketchy to me," Jake said. "If they're involved in lending money to the development, they shouldn't be investors, too."

"Jake, these people are employees. Look." I pointed to Barbara's name. "She's a teller. She makes change, takes deposits, and cashes checks. She isn't involved in any loans."

"No," Buddy said slowly, pointing to a name on the list. "But he is."

It was Francis Simon, the recently fired manager of the bank. And right below his name on the investor list was Melanie Randall, the chief loan officer.

"And so is she," Jake said, pointing to her name. "She set up my line of credit when I opened Beach Books. She's definitely involved in making loans."

Buddy made a star next to the employee names on the investor list. There were several. "I'm sure Bridget already noticed the duplication," he said. "I'll have to find her notes on that." He looked up at Jake. "Good catch, though. A lot will depend on how, and how much, these people invested. We're not going to get too excited over a teller putting a few hundred dollars from her savings account into a multimillion-dollar construction project."

He looked back at the two lists, lying side by side on the counter. "But if there's someone with a sizable investment, or who went into unreasonable debt, that's somebody we'll look at a lot closer."

He pushed the employee list back across the counter, starting a new pile. He took a blank sheet of paper, wrote a giant "1" on it, and put it on top.

"How about the Board of Directors?" Buddy asked, pulling that sheet over where we could all see it. "She started making notes on them. Maybe you can tell me if her impressions are correct."

The names on the list were familiar. William and Felicia Anderson. His little sister, Pearl. Their parents, Willa and Richard. There were a couple other names that weren't familiar, and Bridget had noted they were partners of a law firm in Pensacola. But five of the seven names were Andersons. A big enough majority to do as they pleased, with other people's money.

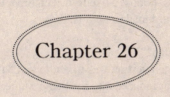

Chapter 26

OUTSIDE THE GLASS WALL OF THE KITCHEN, A DOG barked, startling all of us.

I jostled my coffee cup and barely managed to grab it and prevent it from spilling all over the papers on the counter. I carried the foam cup to the sink and carefully poured the cold contents down the drain. I clearly didn't need any more caffeine.

The dog continued barking. The sound was nearby, seeming to come from the darkened backyard.

Jake grabbed a flashlight and opened the French doors, playing the light across the bare dirt. His light caught the dog, a dark hound, standing next to a man sitting in the dirt.

The man on the ground shielded his eyes as the beam of light caught his face. He looked familiar as I moved closer to Jake, though I couldn't see him clearly.

"Cut it out," he whined. His words slurred, and I realized he was undoubtedly drunk.

I also recognized him as someone we had just been talking about: Andrew Marshall, the high-flying developer of Bayvue Estates. It looked like he'd been brought back down to Earth, and he'd made a hard landing.

"Andy?"

"Who's asking?"

I suppose the question was meant to be challenging, but his drunken slur reduced it to a pathetic whine.

"It's Glory, Andy. Glory Martine."

"Little Glory? Is that really you? What're you doin' all the way out here?"

Andy was a few years older than me, closer to Linda's age than mine. I suppose he did still think of me as a little girl, though I had passed that stage a long time ago.

"It's me," I answered. "Do you need a hand?"

"Naw." He waved his hand in front of his face. "I can manage. Just get that light out of my eyes."

Jake moved the beam aside, lighting up the dirt a few feet in front of Andy and his dog. In the shadow left behind, I saw Andy struggle to his feet and stagger toward the house, his hound dog sticking by his side.

Jake tensed, and I put my hand on his arm.

Andy stumbled over the concrete forms that defined the patio space, but he managed to stay upright. Judging by the miasma of unwashed clothes and spilled liquor that floated ahead of him, it was nothing short of a miracle.

He reached the back door, but didn't seem capable of

navigating the tall step up out of the excavation into the kitchen.

I struggled to reconcile the successful developer I knew with the man standing in front of me, swaying like he was on the deck of a ship. Andy Marshall took chances, but most of them paid off handsomely. He dressed well, visited his personal barber for a shave every day, indulged in the best food and drink, and collected rich man's toys. The man I faced was an emaciated drunk who hadn't had a shower or a shave in weeks.

I stepped down next to him. Jake and Buddy followed. I silently gave thanks for the evening breeze that allowed me to move slightly upwind of Andy. I tried not to think about what he would have smelled like in the confines of the kitchen. There wasn't a floor plan open enough to make it bearable.

Behind me I heard Buddy gasp as the stench hit him. He quickly closed the door behind him, trying not to let the stink invade the house.

"Andy, what are *you* doing out here, just you and Bear?" I asked.

"Just takin' a little stroll after dinner," he answered, as though that explained everything. He'd lost the genteel accent and precise diction he used with his customers, reverting to the cracker drawl of his childhood.

"But your house is way the other side of town." True, that meant it was only a few minutes' drive from where we stood, but I prayed he hadn't been driving in his condition.

"Not no more."

"Sure it is. You and Jen have a gorgeous house. I was just there."

That was an exaggeration. I'd been there six months earlier, for about five minutes. I'd let Felipe and Ernie talk me into contributing to some charity fund-raiser—I think it was for the "clean and sober" grad night—and we'd been invited to a cocktail party hosted by Jen Anderson, the committee chair.

One ginger ale and I'd been out the door. It was a beautiful house all right, but it wasn't my kind of party. I'd promised myself the next time I'd just send a check.

"Oh, Jen and the girls are still there. She swears she's gonna keep that house, though I don't see how. The bank's gonna take it, just like they took everything else I own."

It obviously wasn't the time to introduce Buddy. I glanced over and caught his eye, nodding slightly toward the darkened corner of the house. He caught my hint and faded back into the shadows, out of sight.

I reached for Jake's arm and pulled him a little closer to me, trying to keep Andy focused on the two of us.

"Andy, have you met Jake Robinson? He bought Beach Books a couple years ago." I held my breath and leaned in a little. "He's from California, but he's okay."

I laughed and leaned back toward Jake, sucking in a breath of marginally cleaner air.

"Glad to meet ya," Andy said, sticking out a grimy hand.

Jake didn't flinch. He took Andy's hand. "Same here," he said. "Any friend of Glory's, and all that."

Andy cocked his head and looked at me. "She is a purty little thing, isn't she? Always was."

"Andy, if Jen's still in the house, why are you out here? It's a long way from home."

"Not my home anymore," he whined. "Threw me out. Called me everything but a gentleman and said to get out and stay out."

He turned in an unsteady circle, his gaze taking in the entire development, hidden in the dark beyond the faint light spilling from the house. "This place took everything from me, Glory. Took my job, took my family, took every last cent I had in the world.

"All I got left's the trailer. Hauled it out in the woods so the bank won't find it." His voice grew bitter and angry. "They'd take it, too, if they could find it, the bastards."

His voice grew louder as he continued to rant about how the bank had taken everything. He cursed the Andersons and Francis Simon. He called Melanie Randall a couple names that even Bluebeard didn't use.

Jake put his arm around me and whispered in my ear, "I'll take care of this."

I shook my head. "Let it go. He's always been a bit of a hothead, but it never lasts long."

I hoped I was right.

Andy's tirade petered out into mutters and self-pity within a few minutes. Tears began to run down his face as he launched into a litany of excuses.

As hard as it was to watch him unravel, I could only imagine the pain he must feel.

"Can I give you a lift somewhere?" I asked as Andy sank into silence, an occasional sniffle the only sound he made.

He shook his head. "Me 'n' Bear, we're good. We got the

trailer out there, out where nobody will find us. We'll be just fine." His eyes glowed with anger for an instant. "We know how to take care of things."

The anger faded, and Andy gave a deep sigh. "C'mon, Bear," he said. The hound, who had waited patiently through his master's ranting, stood up and nudged Andy's hand.

The two of them turned their backs on us and faded into the dark.

"Nice seeing you, Glory," he called as he walked away. "You take care now, y'hear?"

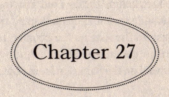

Chapter 27

BUDDY STAYED IN THE SHADOWS AS WE LISTENED TO Andy and Bear make their way to the edge of the woods. Bear barked again, a lonely, mournful sound, in the distance.

Jake pointed his flashlight in the direction they'd gone, but the light faded before it reached the tree line, and I couldn't see anyone.

I heard the door open and turned around. Buddy stood with the knob in one hand, waving us back inside.

Back in the kitchen with the lights on, I suddenly felt very exposed. The few low-watt bulbs hadn't seemed very bright before we went outside. But now I realized it was the only light around, and it felt like we were a target, shining in the dark.

Clearly, Buddy and Jake had the same feeling. Buddy shut down the laptops and closed them. He stacked the two computers with several bunches of paper, and put them next to the doorway.

"Maybe I'll work in the study. There are blinds on those windows." He sounded sheepish, as though embarrassed by his decision to hide behind the covered windows, but I didn't blame him. I wouldn't want to be on display either.

We went back to the lists on the counter, but we had all been unnerved by the encounter with Andy Marshall. We tried to concentrate on the names in front of us, but it was no use.

"I tell you what," I said to Buddy. "I have to work tomorrow; we both do." I gestured at Jake. "I wish I could help more, but I am going to have to get home."

"No problem," Buddy said. "I need to spend some time going over Bridget's notes. Maybe I can come up with some specific questions, things I need to verify."

He walked us to the door, apologizing all the while for taking up our evening with his problems, as though he'd forgotten it was us who had come to see him.

We were standing in the entry when his phone rang. He pulled it off his belt and looked at the display.

"I had no idea it was this late," he said. "I better get this. Time to say good night to the kids." He chuckled self-consciously. "My wife lets them call me before bed every night if I'm not home. Kind of a little family ritual."

We waved our good-byes and let ourselves out as he answered the phone. We heard him greet his wife, and promise her that everything was just fine.

As I dug out my keys and followed the beam of Jake's flashlight toward the truck, I sincerely hoped it was true.

We stowed the flashlights back in the glove box. "You might want to change those batteries," Jake said, closing the door. "It was getting kind of weak near the end there."

"I will. And thank you for everything you did tonight."

"I didn't do much."

"No, you did." I pulled away from the model homes, one dark, the other with a faint light coming from the back of the house. "You put up with my lousy mood, cleaned up my kitchen, and came with me out here.

"And you didn't overreact when Andy got a little crazy," I added. "A lot of people would have."

I couldn't see Jake's expression in the dark. "That was easy," he said. "You've known the people around here your whole life. You said to trust him, that he'd run down, and you were right."

I pulled onto the empty county road, our headlights the only bright spots visible. "I hope he doesn't come back," I said. "He seemed pretty angry at the bank. What if he decided to do something stupid?"

"Do you really think he would?" Jake asked.

I thought about it for a minute as we neared the highway. I stopped at the intersection, waiting for traffic to clear so I could turn.

"I wouldn't think so," I answered. "But I didn't think Bridget would take drugs. So what do I know?"

The thought that I had been wrong about Bridget bothered me. But what other explanation was there? Jake was right. She didn't accidentally fall on a hypodermic full of drugs.

What bothered me even more were all the unanswered questions.

Christy Fifield

"I wish we knew more about the medical examiner's report, like what drug actually killed her. And if she was using, were there other needle marks? And if she wasn't, then how else would they get in her system? You don't just sit there and let somebody shoot you full of something that kills you."

"I agree," Jake said.

"Then how?" I persisted. "Either she did it herself, or someone did it to her. And if someone tried to inject her and she didn't want them to, she would have fought with them."

"And the police said no signs of foul play, right?"

"Right," I said. "So we're right back where we started."

I turned off the highway and made my way along the back streets to the lot where Jake had parked his car. It was the least I could do after dragging him out to Bayvue.

"Will you be okay?" he asked before climbing out of the truck.

I assured him I would, and kissed him good night. I bit my lip as he closed the door, fighting the impulse to invite him back to my place.

I drove home thinking about Jake, and about Bridget. Buddy said she'd been married three times, but he didn't mention children. And he was the person taking care of everything—a half brother she barely knew. I remembered thinking she seemed lonely, and I wondered if there had been anyone else in her life, anyone she was close to.

I was afraid I already knew the answer.

There wasn't.

I unlocked the back door and reset the alarm. Through the doorway I could see the streetlights casting soft shadows in the front of the store, but I didn't see the night-lights I usually left burning.

I'd better go check them.

But when I stepped into the front, I discovered that the problem wasn't just the night-lights.

Bluebeard had gone on one of his rampages. Either that or I'd been vandalized.

No broken windows. No tripped alarms. The register stood open and empty, just as I'd left it.

Nope. This was all on Bluebeard.

I turned on the overhead lights to examine the shop and assess the damage. Piles of T-shirts littered the floor, postcards spilled from the spinner, and plastic water bottles had fallen from the shelves and rolled away into all the nooks and crannies.

As the lights revealed the extent of the mess and the work I had ahead of me, Bluebeard stuck his head out of his cage.

"Find the postcards," he said.

He glared up at the overhead fixtures, with all the fluorescent tubes burning brightly. "#%&$%#$^ lights! Trying to $#%#&# sleep!"

He stomped back into his cage and refused to come out or to say anything more. He didn't respond when I asked him about the postcards, and he even ignored the offer of a banana. He was done talking for the night, and there was nothing I could do to change that.

I started picking up the shirts, inspecting them for dust or tears, but Julie had swept the floors at the end of the day and all the shirts were clean and intact. I had to marvel at how

Bluebeard had managed to completely destroy the display, strew merchandise around the shop, and create havoc—all without actually damaging any of the inventory.

I told myself it was part of his charm, and set to work cleaning up the mess he'd made.

I piled shirts on the front counter to be folded and tracked down the water bottles. As I placed them back on the shelves, I straightened the rows. It reminded me of helping Guy stock shelves at the Grog Shop, and made me smile. I'd been training to take over Southern Treasures since I was a kid.

I gathered up the postcards and put them in a box. They would have to be sorted, *again*, and put back in the proper slots on the spinner rack. That much, at least, could wait until morning.

I sorted the shirts by design, turning the big pile into several smaller ones. It was tedious work, and my mind wandered as I set about refolding each shirt and putting the sizes in order.

I thought about Buddy, talking to his kids every night before bed. I'd heard his warm, happy tone when he answered his wife's call. He had people in his life, people who would know if something was wrong. People who would notice and care.

I remembered what he had said about Bridget, that the saddest part was that he didn't miss her more. That everyone deserved to be mourned.

Was that why I'd thought about inviting Jake back here?

I pushed the thought aside. The answer was simpler than that, if I was honest about it. Jake was gorgeous and smart, a rare combination in my experience. Of course I was attracted to him. Any woman with two eyes and a brain would be.

Simple.

I finished folding shirts and carried the tidy stacks to the shelves, filling in the bare spaces where Bluebeard had emptied the display.

As I reached to slide a stack of back-stock shirts into the bottom shelf, something caught my eye.

I reached into the space between the stacks and felt around. My fingers closed around a piece of stiff paper, and I pulled it out into the light, where I could examine it.

The address side of the postcard had just a city and state, like somebody had started to write the address and had been distracted. Edina, MN, and the message side had only part of one word, as though the writer had been interrupted before she could finish. I had no idea what she meant to write.

The handwriting, though, was perfectly clear.

And it matched Bridget McKenna's precise block printing on the lists I'd looked at earlier in the evening.

Chapter 28

THE POSTCARD MESS WAS WAITING FOR ME WHEN I came downstairs the next morning with my coffee. I brought Bluebeard's breakfast down, but I wasn't quite ready to forgive him for trashing the shop while I was gone.

"Was that really necessary?" I grumbled as I cleaned his dish and changed his water.

"Find the postcards," he said, as though that explained everything. As far as I was concerned, it explained nothing. I'd found one postcard that had fallen behind a T-shirt display, and despite being possibly written by Bridget, it didn't have anything useful on it.

"You were just being cranky," I told him. "You think you have the right to trash the place and waste my time cleaning up after you."

He didn't answer me, just turned his back and pouted.

I swear, sometimes that bird was more trouble than a two-year-old. Of course I'd never had a two-year-old, but I'd heard stories about the Terrible Twos.

Those kids had nothing on a parrot in a foul mood.

Bluebeard was still ignoring me when Julie and Rose Ann came in. Someday Rose Ann would be a Terrible Two, but right now she was only a few months old.

She looked adorable in a ruffled sunsuit and a tiny bonnet, with a light flannel blanket covering her bare arms and legs.

I worried aloud that she might be cold without a sweater.

"It's seventy degrees outside." Julie laughed. "And it'll be ninety-five by noon. She's fine." She carried Rose Ann and her diaper bag through to the back. "She's had breakfast already," Julie called from the nursery area. "Let me put her down for a nap and I'll be right out."

It took her about ten minutes to get Rose Ann settled, while I started sorting the postcards that I'd left on the counter the night before.

"Didn't you just do that?" Julie asked, slipping behind the counter and taking a handful of the jumbled cards.

"Yes, I did. But *someone* decided they had to mess up the rack again last night."

"I see," she said. She quickly shuffled cards onto the stacks I'd started and took another handful. "And do I need to guess who that might have been?"

"I think you know."

I didn't tell her what he'd said, or what I'd found. Julie might have her suspicions about Bluebeard, although we had never actually discussed Uncle Louis. I didn't know how much longer I could put off telling her, but today wasn't the day for that conversation.

We got enough of the cards sorted to refill the rack before it was time to unlock the front doors. I stashed the box of unsorted cards under the counter. If there was time later in the day, I would finish the task. If not, it could wait until after closing.

The morning started with a steady stream of customers, and they continued coming well into the afternoon. Somewhere around noon I managed to slip upstairs and throw together a ham sandwich, but Julie called from downstairs before I took the first bite.

"There's someone here who wants to talk to you," she said over the intercom. "Can you come down, please?"

Her manner was in such sharp contrast to her usual friendly chatter that I didn't stop to ask questions. I slipped the sandwich into a plastic bag and tossed it into the refrigerator.

The shop was quiet when I got downstairs, with a few tourists milling around the souvenir racks.

A woman waited at the counter, fiddling with her cell phone and glancing up at the clock every few seconds. Her curly, dishwater blond hair had turned into a frizzy halo in the humidity, and a deep tan branded her as a local who spent a lot of time in the sun.

It took me a minute to place her. She worked someplace with a uniform, but in jeans and double-layered white tank tops, she wasn't familiar. I was used to seeing her in a lab coat. At first I thought she might be from my dentist's office, but then something clicked. The pharmacy. Lacey Simon.

"Lacey," I said, approaching the counter with my hand out.

She took my hand and leaned in with an air kiss. It wasn't my style, but I'd learned long ago to tolerate the familiarity.

"Good to see you. How are you and Francis doing?"

Not that I really needed to ask. From her appearance, it was clear they weren't doing well.

Lacey had a reputation as a health nut, finishing first in every local walk-a-thon and leading beach runs for visiting snowbirds during the winter.

No wonder I hadn't recognized her. Dark bags under her eyes spoke of sleepless nights, and the muffin top that spilled over the waist of her jeans and strained at her shirt told me she hadn't been eating right. Or exercising.

"Can I talk to you?" she asked, looking around the store at the scattering of customers. Clearly she meant privately.

"Sure," I said. "Come on back."

I led her into my storage area, putting a finger to my lips as we passed the slumbering Rose Ann. Lacey glanced at the baby in her crib and attempted a smile, but it didn't reach her eyes.

We moved past the partition that marked Rose Ann's nursery, and stopped a few feet beyond. "She's a sound sleeper," I said softly. "But I'd still hate to disturb her."

Lacey nodded her understanding. "Sure thing," she whispered.

"So what can I do for you, Lacey?"

"I, uh . . ." She gave an embarrassed laugh and tried again. "I need to, well, to sell some stuff. We're moving to a smaller place, and I need to get rid of some of the clutter."

I didn't let on that I already knew she was losing the

house. Let her keep some shred of dignity for as long as possible. "What kind of stuff?" I asked.

"Some knickknacks. A few of the larger pieces of furniture." She swallowed hard and I could see her pulse pounding in the hollow of her throat. "I've got some antique quilts that I'm ready to let go," she continued, "and some Fiesta ware. Oh, and a big collection of Bakelite, including some jewelry."

I knew I would take the Fiesta ware, if I could get it at a reasonable price, but I struggled with the idea of benefitting from Lacey's troubles. On the other hand, I couldn't overpay for merchandise I was going to resell; if I wanted to stay in business, I needed to turn a profit.

"I might be interested in some of that. But this is a small shop; I don't have room for furniture, especially if it's very big."

She rolled her eyes. "The dining room set seats a dozen," she said. "And there's a grandfather clock that's about eight feet tall."

"Have you thought about an auction house? I can help you find a reputable one."

She shook her head. "They take forever. Weeks to set things up and advertise, and then a month or more before they actually *do* anything. And I don't have enough to justify doing a private sale, so I'd have to wait until they got enough sellers together to make it worthwhile.

"Besides, they charge a fortune, and they add more fees and charges for every little thing. It's worse than the airlines."

Since I hadn't flown anywhere in many years, I had no idea how bad the airlines were, but the rest of her arguments were valid. An auction house couldn't afford to stage a sale for a few pieces of furniture. Not unless they were from Versailles, or Buckingham Palace. She would have to wait and be one of a group of sellers, and I knew why she was in a hurry. She had to move next month, and she didn't have the luxury of waiting.

"I can't handle the big stuff," I repeated. "But Felipe Vargas, over at Carousel Antiques, specializes in that kind of thing. He loves dining room sets. Does yours have a china hutch? Felipe's a sucker for china hutches."

Lacey lifted the corners of her mouth in another attempt at a smile, only slightly more successful than the last one. "It does. It's monstrous, takes up an entire wall of the dining room. And there's a sideboard that goes with it."

I tried to imagine how big her dining room must be to hold the massive pieces she described. Bigger than my entire apartment, I'd bet. They didn't support a place like that on the salary of a bank manager and a pharmacy tech. Not unless the pharmacy paid a lot better than I thought.

Or Francis had some income on the side. Like investing heavily in real estate developments. If he'd been riding Andrew Marshall's coattails, he could have afforded a great house. Right up until he couldn't.

His name had been on the investor list, after all.

All of which led to a desperate attempt to liquidate what they could, before their creditors came calling.

"Let me call Felipe and see if he's available. And come back with the Fiesta ware and the quilts and let's see if we can work something out."

I called Felipe. I filled him in, choosing my words carefully. He said to send her over, and I saw the relief in her eyes when I told her he was interested in the furniture. Desperation like hers was not pretty.

I felt like a fraud accepting Lacey's thanks. I'd buy the quilts and kitchenware at a fair price, and I knew Felipe would take the furniture, but we wouldn't do her any favors.

Deep down I didn't think she, or Francis, deserved any. They'd done plenty for themselves.

I watched Lacey leave, trying to hold her head up and pretend her life was still somewhere near normal. I knew the truth was far different that the image she wanted to preserve.

The phone in my hand buzzed, and I pushed the answer button without looking. Probably Felipe calling back after he figured Lacey was gone.

"Good afternoon, Southern Treasures. How can I help you?" I almost said, "Hi, Felipe," but I stopped myself at the last second.

"Miss Gloryanna, is that you?" The voice wasn't Felipe, and I was glad I had used our standard greeting. It sounded a lot like Peter's nasally whine, but it wasn't him, either. Thank heavens.

"This is Gloryanna," I replied. "How can I help you?"

"It's Francis Simon. I, uh, well, I was looking for Lacey." He sounded almost scared, like a kid looking for his missing mom. "She said she was coming by your place, and I, um, need to talk to her. Is she still there?"

"I'm sorry, Francis," I said. "She just left. I think she's going down to Carousel, to talk to Felipe. Maybe you can catch her there. Do you need the number?"

He declined my offer, mumbling that he was sure he had the number, and hung up. As I put the phone back in its base, I wondered why he hadn't called Lacey on her cell phone. Were things so bad she didn't even have a working phone?

Chapter 29

I DIDN'T GET BACK TO SORTING THE POSTCARD MESS until late in the afternoon. Bluebeard was still pouting in the corner, and I told myself I really didn't care. Whatever he was trying to tell me, he didn't need to trash the shop and make extra work for me in the process.

I didn't want the stacks spread across the counter, so I sat in the tall chair at the register and flipped through the jumble in the box, pulling out one design at a time. It was slow-going, but at least I was able to work in between customers without cluttering up the counter.

The bell rang over the front door and I looked up from my sorting. Buddy McKenna, a zippered leather portfolio tucked under his arm, walked in. He hesitated as though he was intruding, then made a slow circuit of the store.

He took his time, examining each T-shirt and souvenir, and he went back to the postcard spinner several times.

When he finally approached the counter, he was carrying a handful of trinkets and a couple colorful T-shirts.

"I haven't got this packing thing down quite yet," he said with a nod to the T-shirts. Just like his sister.

"The department manager called a little bit ago," he continued as I rang up his purchases. "He verified that he wouldn't be able to get anyone down here until the middle of next week. Asked me to stay on and continue Bridget's work."

"That sounds like a compliment," I said.

"Backhanded, I'm afraid. Like I said, they still plan to send a senior auditor next week. But yeah, still something of a compliment, I guess."

He paid for his purchases, and lingered at the counter. He laid his portfolio down and put his hand on top of it. "I wondered if you might have some time this afternoon. To go over the notes we talked about. I found some things I'd like you to look at."

I glanced up at the clock. Nearly closing time. The postcards could wait. I was intensely curious about what Bridget might have uncovered, and I thought it would be interesting to hear her impressions of Keyhole Bay and its inhabitants. The prospect of seeing my hometown through the eyes of an outsider enticed me. Especially an outsider who didn't expect anyone in town to read what she thought.

"I close in a few minutes. How about I meet you next door at Lighthouse?"

Buddy accepted my suggestion, and we agreed to meet for coffee as soon as I could get closed up. He was about to say something else when we were interrupted by a wail from the back room. He gave me a startled look and turned in the direction of the noise.

"Rose Ann," I said. I told him about setting up the nursery and having the baby in the shop when her grandma wasn't available. "Anita'd rather have the baby with her, of course. But she can't keep her every day, so we found a way for Rose Ann to come to work with her mom.

"I know it won't last forever, but it works for now."

"It's a great idea. I wish the bank had something similar; it would make life easier for my wife and me.

"How about you, Glory?" he asked. "Any kids?"

I shook my head. "Not me," I answered. "Just a business that takes all my time, and a badly behaved parrot."

From his perch on the other side of the shop, Bluebeard squawked a mild curse, then settled into a litany of muttered complaints.

"Language, Bluebeard."

The muttering became quieter, but I knew what he was saying, even if Buddy couldn't understand it.

"He's having a bad day," I said. "He's sort of like a cranky baby sometimes. Probably just needs a nap."

Buddy laughed politely at my lame joke, and said he'd wait for me at Lighthouse. I promised to meet him as soon as I could.

A few minutes later I flipped the sign on the door from "Open" to "Closed" and went next door. As soon as Chloe spotted me, she started a vanilla latte. "Hot or iced?" she asked when I reached the counter.

"Hot, I think."

A minute later she handed me a cup in a paper sleeve. I reached in my pocket but she refused my payment. "Your friend already took care of it."

Buddy had a table against the wall, where he had unloaded the contents of his portfolio, and he sat studying the pages spread in front of him.

I took the seat across from him and sipped my drink. "Thank you," I said.

"My pleasure. But the bank's paying for this one. It's part of the job."

"Either way, I'm grateful." The caffeine and sugar were giving me a pleasant buzz after a long day in the shop. And it was only July. There were several weeks of summer yet to go.

"So what have you got for me?" I asked Buddy. "How can I help?"

"Well, I went back to the lists from last night, and looked at all of Bridget's notes. I found a couple files on her laptop, too. Some of it is confidential, but there are some things that I'd like you to confirm if you can."

He looked at the top page and ran his finger along the list. "Jennifer Marshall, for example. You mentioned her when you were talking to her husband. Does she really have the resources to hang on to their house?"

I thought for a minute before I answered. Memaw would be horrified to hear me gossip about my neighbors with a Yankee. On the other hand, I really didn't know anything I could tell him that wasn't common knowledge. Besides, I had promised to help him, and it was for a good cause. We both wanted Bridget's killer found.

"Good question," I said. "I'm really not sure. When Andy said the bank was going to take it—"

"Thanks, by the way," Buddy interrupted, "for not giving me away to Marshall. I don't know if he's violent, but I really didn't want to find out."

"Got in a few fights when he was a kid, from what I'm told. Nothing serious." I shrugged. "Anyway, that's all ancient history. He's mostly the kind of guy who blows up and gets over it pretty quick. Like he did last night."

"Still, I appreciate that you didn't tell him who I was."

"You're welcome." I went back to his original question. "Jen's folks have money, and I believe she had an inheritance from her grandparents, but I don't know how much. You're more likely to be able to find that out for yourself, in the bank records.

"People around here don't talk about money a whole lot. It's just not something you share with everyone. Like—" I stopped myself before I said what I was thinking, searching instead for an overly polite euphemism. "Like, you know, your private life."

Buddy blinked in confusion a couple times, then a faint blush crept up his pale face. He got my meaning.

"And I don't know if she still has it," I continued. "Her grandmother passed away right after their second daughter was born, and that's been probably ten years."

I stopped and took another sip of coffee, letting the sweetness fill my mouth and slide down my throat.

"She and Andy may have spent it. On the business, or the girls, or a vacation. Or on that house."

"You said you were just out there. What's it like?"

I explained how I'd come to be in Jen Marshall's house, however briefly. "It was lovely, in a new-money kind of way. Jen came from money, but Andy didn't. You saw him."

"I saw a man who'd lost everything," Buddy said. "He looked like he'd started drinking on New Year's Eve and hadn't stopped. But with the pressure he's been under, well"—he shrugged—"I try not to judge too harshly."

"Memaw used to say, 'Don't marry a boy from a dirt road,' and Andrew Marshall could have been exactly the kind of boy she was talking about. No education, no prospects, and a taste for hard liquor. Except Andrew was stubborn and he worked hard. He's one of those up-by-his-bootstraps success stories."

"And he married into money," Buddy added.

"Yeah. He was the local boy who made good and swept Daddy's Little Princess off her feet. I remember their wedding, even though I was just a kid. It took the entire front page of the 'Society' section in the *News and Times*. They called it the wedding of the year."

"Sounds like a proper Horatio Alger story," Buddy said.

"It was. Andy purely wore himself out, the number of hours he'd work. He was used to living poor, and he managed to put a lot by to start his own construction company.

"I think Bayvue was supposed to be his big score, the one that finally set him up for life."

"I'm not telling you anything you don't already know when I say he was overextended," Buddy said. "He'd leveraged everything he had to buy the land and start construction. And he sank every penny into what's out there right now. Which isn't that much."

It didn't surprise me. "I'd heard rumors for years about how Andy Marshall kept plowing money back into Marshall Development. Each time he pulled out a win, he'd turn around and pour it all into the next project, culminating in Bayvue Estates."

"That ties in with what Bridget found," Buddy said. He made an X next to Marshall's name on his list. "I don't think he defrauded the bank exactly," he explained. "Poor judgment, yes. But I don't think there was anything criminal in his handling of the loans."

We talked about the Andersons. Bridget had pegged them accurately as clueless and entitled. I told him about Felicia's visit to Carousel Antiques right after Bridget's death.

"My friend Felipe said she acted as though she was immune to what was going on. Like she'd get her way, like she always does. If Bridget described her as entitled, that's pretty accurate. And Billy is the same way."

I thought about the difference between the two couples. "Jen and Andy took their money seriously," I said. "Jen always supported local charities, and Andy supported Jen. They would open their house for every good cause that came along.

"Billy and Felicia had a party for their employees once a year, at Christmas. They served a lavish buffet, and handed out holiday bonus checks. But the checks came from the bank, not the Andersons."

Buddy made a note under Billy Anderson's name, and slid

his finger along the list. "Pearl Anderson. It's still Anderson on all our records. She is single, right?"

I nodded. "I don't know much about her. She's a couple years younger than me, but she didn't go to school here. Her parents sent her away to some exclusive boarding school, and she was only home for short periods. She travels a lot, like a lady of leisure out of a nineteenth-century novel, but she shows up for every meeting of the board and—according to people who work at the bank—votes the way her brother and father tell her to."

"Bridget seemed to think she might be, um, challenged in some way. Had you heard anything like that?"

I considered the question. "The family does seem to keep her out of the public eye. Just never thought about why. That would explain a whole lot."

Buddy put a question mark next to Pearl's name.

"Sorry I wasn't more help on that one."

He drained his coffee cup and set it aside. "I can't expect you to do *all* my work for me," he said lightly. "Especially when I'm only paying you in coffee."

A shadow fell across the table and I looked up to find that Jake had come in while we were talking. Buddy jumped to his feet, greeting Jake warmly.

"Good to see you, and thanks for your help last night."

"Thanks for letting me tag along," Jake replied.

"Please, sit down. Join us." Buddy pulled another chair over and placed it next to me. "Can I get you something?"

Jake shook his head. "I was just heading home and I spotted Glory sitting here. Thought I'd come across and say hello before I left."

I patted the chair and Jake sat down, though he didn't relax. He looked tired and he was probably anxious to get home after I'd dragged him out last night.

We talked for another few minutes, but I realized Chloe was hovering nearby, clearly ready to close up herself.

"We better get going," I said. "I'd be glad to talk some more, Buddy. Why don't you give me a call if you need more information?"

I scribbled my cell number on my business card and handed it to him. "Holler if you need me."

Buddy thanked me and excused himself, saying he had a lot more work to do tonight. Jake and I followed him out, and said good night as he walked away toward the city parking lot.

"I better get going, too," Jake said. "I'd love to take you to dinner, if it wasn't a Saturday night." He laughed. "See? I'll turn into a local yet."

I smiled up at him. "And I'd love to go. But not on a Saturday night. Besides, I am beat and tomorrow's going to be another long day. I think I'll go upstairs, have a bowl of cereal, and collapse."

"Cereal? For dinner?"

"That's the joy of being a grown-up," I said, rising up on my tiptoes to give him a quick kiss. "If I want cereal for dinner, nobody can tell me not to."

Chapter 30

JAKE PAUSED AT THE CROSSWALK, WAITING FOR traffic to clear. "How about tomorrow night? I'll cook."

"Deal." Never turn down a meal when someone else volunteers to cook.

I let myself in the shop, prepared to spend the next hour getting ready for the Sunday summer rush. But Julie had already straightened and restocked. The shelves were dusted and the floors swept.

All I had to do was take myself upstairs and relax.

Which I did.

Late Sunday afternoon Jake called me. "I'm having car trouble," he said. "I called Sly, and he offered to come by the house in about an hour. But I didn't want to upset our dinner plans."

"Tell him to come ahead. I know what a pain it is to be

without a car." Jake knew, too. I'd had to borrow his car a couple times when my old car had been out of commission.

"It might be a good thing to cook enough to share," I said. "It'd be the polite thing to offer him dinner."

"You sure this is okay?" he asked again.

"It's fine. I'll see you in an hour."

When I pulled up in front of Jake's, there was a vintage Thunderbird already parked at the curb. The chrome gleamed in the late afternoon sunshine, and the turquoise paint was buffed until it gleamed. No need to wonder whose car it was.

I started up the walk, but Jake called to me from the carport. I walked around the corner of the house and spotted Jake and Sly up to their elbows in the engine of Jake's car.

"Sly thinks it's probably just a spark plug," Jake said. "I'll take it over later this week."

"Hey, Miss Glory," Sly said, smiling broadly. "Mr. Jake says he's fixing to feed us." He wiped his hands on a shop towel and tossed it in his toolbox.

I started to answer, but the ringing of my cell phone interrupted me. I pulled out the phone and checked the number before I answered. No sense having another argument with Peter when I could let it go to voice mail.

"Karen," I said. "I was beginning to wonder where she is. Excuse me for a minute."

I hit the "Answer" key and said hello.

"Where have you been?" I asked her. "I haven't talked to you in forever!"

"It's been three days," she said. "Don't exaggerate. And a

holiday weekend besides. Figured you'd be too exhausted to do anything but sleep."

She had me there.

"Anyway, I thought I'd check in, see what you were up to."

Jake moved close to me and signaled for my attention. I muted the phone. "Yes?"

"There's plenty of food," he said. "Tell her to join us."

"Sure?"

"Why not?" He grinned at me. "Let's make it a party!"

I went back to Karen. "Hey, I'm at Jake's, and Sly's here. We were just getting ready to eat. Why don't you join us?"

It was my turn to wait while she turned to someone else. I heard a soft conversation in the background, then she came back to the phone. "Riley's here, too. Does the invitation include both of us?"

I looked at Jake, who was standing close enough to hear what she said. He nodded and I relayed the expanded invitation.

"All right," she said. "Give me the address."

Sly and Jake went to wash up, and Jake said he needed to check on dinner. I waited in the carport, watching for Karen and Riley.

I did wonder where Karen had been. I hadn't talked to her since our dinner on the Fourth, and as I thought about it, I realized I hadn't heard her on the radio all weekend. She hadn't said anything about being gone, but it seemed like the logical explanation.

In just a couple minutes, Riley's pickup rolled up across the street from Sly's T-Bird and the two of them climbed out. I greeted them with hugs and took them into the kitchen through the side door.

Inside, the tang of tomato and the musky fragrance of oregano mingled with onion and garlic into a heady promise of Italian delights.

Jake stood at the counter, stirring a dark red sauce in the Crock-Pot. "Spaghetti," he said unnecessarily. The smell had already given it away.

"Smells divine," Karen said. She spoke for us all.

Dinner turned into the usual group effort. I made garlic bread, Sly put together a salad, and Jake boiled the pasta.

Karen and Riley volunteered to set the table, but Jake suggested we eat on the screened patio. He showed them the way, and the two of them disappeared with a stack of plates and silverware.

They came back several times for things like glasses and napkins. Both of them. As though they couldn't stay apart for long enough to walk from one room to another. And each time they seemed deep in a private conversation. They hardly noticed that the rest of us were there.

Jake drained the pasta and tossed it with a small scoop of the sauce to keep it from sticking. I sliced garlic bread and piled it on a platter, and Sly tossed the salad with a dressing of olive oil, wine vinegar, and assorted herbs.

Riley carried the crock of sauce, and the food procession made its way down the hall and out to the porch.

Even without the usual Thursday group, the conversation followed our normal pattern: We spent the first half of the meal quizzing Jake about his sauce and sharing our own personal takes on the art of spaghetti. Everyone had their own recipe, and we all had our own take on what was essential.

When we had exhausted that topic, Jake asked me about

my meeting with Buddy McKenna. "What did he want to know?"

"The kind of thing we talked about on Friday night," I said. "Did I agree with what Bridget said in her notes. Did I have something to add that wasn't there. He was very careful not to tell me anything he didn't think I already knew, but he did confirm that Andy Marshall had sunk everything into Bayvue, and then gone into debt so deep he couldn't get out."

I told Jake what Buddy had said about Andy's behavior, and about not judging too harshly.

"Wait a minute," Karen said. "Let's back up a little, shall we? When did you see Andy Marshall? And for that matter, when did you spend all this time with Mr. McKenna?"

Jake and I took turns filling the three of them in on the adventures of the weekend. Riley looked especially upset as we described Andy's appearance and behavior.

"He was a few years ahead of us, wasn't he?" I said. "How did you know him?"

"I didn't know him very well, but my older brother did. Well enough to get in a couple fights with him," Riley said. "They played football together, and didn't always see eye-to-eye on things. Andy was rough around the edges, and he was a fierce competitor. Hated to lose. Just purely hated it. Once in a while they disagreed about tactics; what was okay and what wasn't."

"I remember one time," Karen said. "Tom had a knot on his head for a week. Was that from Andy?"

"Sure was. Andy didn't think Tom had hit an opposing lineman hard enough, and he showed Tom exactly what he thought he should have done. Tom said his ears rang for days."

"Sounds like a dangerous guy," Jake said, his brow furrowing in concern. He turned to me. "You sure Buddy's safe out there with that guy stumbling around?"

"Andy's broken," Sly cut in. "He's done lost everything he worked for, and it broke something inside him. Seen it happen before. Makes a man weak, or it makes him mean." He turned to look at me. "Which do you think he is, Glory?"

I shook my head. "I couldn't say, Sly. But I don't think I saw mean in that man out there."

"I sure hope I'm right," I added softly.

"So anyway, after our talk on Friday night, Buddy stopped by the store on Saturday and wanted to ask me some questions. I met him at Lighthouse and had a cup of coffee, Jake dropped by and joined us for a few minutes, and that was the end of it.

"Which, by the way, you would have heard about if you'd been around this weekend." I glared at Karen and Riley. "Now give. Just where were the two of you the last three days? 'Cause I am convinced you weren't in town."

Karen reached for Riley's hand and held it so tightly her knuckles turned white. "We went away for the weekend."

Clearly there was more to the story. "And?" I prodded.

She looked around the table. "You all have to swear you will not repeat a word of this. Not a word.

"Swear."

We nodded but that wasn't enough for her. "Say it!"

Sly, Jake, and I each promised, but she had me really worried. I had asked Linda what to do about Karen and Riley and she'd told me to just be supportive, but now I wondered exactly what I was supporting.

"We went to a couples retreat."

"A retreat? You mean like a church camp or something?"

Karen shook her head. "No. It was just something our counselor recommended. A few days away, concentrating on the two of us."

"Your counselor? Since when do you have a counselor? And why do you need a counselor anyway? You're divorced!"

"Because," Riley explained, "if we're going to get married again, we want to do it right this time."

My gaze shot to Karen's left hand. Bare. So it hadn't happened yet. Maybe.

I thought I'd lost my mind. "You're getting married again, and you're seeing a counselor to help you do it right, *and* you went to a retreat—and you haven't mentioned a word about this to me? Did I hear all that right?"

"It's only been the last couple weeks," Karen said. "And you've been so worried about Riley and me getting back together that I didn't want to say anything until we were sure."

"So it isn't really *if* you get married again, it's *when.*"

Karen nodded.

Jake got up from his chair and walked around the table. He shook Riley's hand, a huge grin on his face. "Congratulations, man! That's great news."

Riley grinned back. "Yeah, I think it is."

Jake reached down to hug Karen. "You'll be great," he said. "Just great."

By that time I was out of my seat and around the table. I threw my arms around Riley, unsure whether to laugh or cry. "Do it right this time. Or there will be hell to pay."

Karen stood up and I wrapped my arms around her. "If

this is what you want, then I'm happy for you," I said, and I meant it. I never doubted for a minute that they loved each other. They just needed to learn how to live together. And maybe they had matured enough to make it work.

"Have you told your families yet?" I asked when we had settled in lounge chairs with refilled glasses a few minutes later. "Does Bobby know?"

"Nobody knows," Riley said. "They didn't even know we were spending the weekend together. Like Karen said, we didn't want to say anything until we were sure."

"And if you'll notice," Karen added, "you were the first person we called when we got back."

"I'm so sorry," I said. "I should have thought of that before I shot my mouth off."

"That wasn't exactly how we planned to tell you," Karen said. "I had a little speech all prepared, but then we got to talking about everything that happened and it just came out."

"Well, I, for one, am honored to have been part of this," Sly announced. "I think anyone getting married is reason enough for celebration." He raised his sweet tea in a toast. "Here's to many years of happiness."

"How about you, Sly?" Riley asked. "You never married?"

"Nope." He shook his head, his expression far away. "I came close once. Really loved that little gal, but my mama pitched such a fit I couldn't do it.

"I went to Mr. Louis about it," he went on, his voice soft and low, as full of longing as if it had been yesterday instead of decades ago.

"He told me he'd help me if I was determined to do it, but we both knew it wouldn't happen. I wasn't brave enough to go against my mama's wishes and break the law, so I joined the Army and went away for a while."

"Break the law?" Jake said. "How?"

"I know," I said. "Your girl, she was white, wasn't she, Sly? That's why you couldn't marry her."

"That's right, Miss Glory. It was a different world back then."

"It was before either of us was born," I told Jake. "But I heard about it. It took a long time for things to change, but eventually they did."

I looked over at Sly. "It was just too late for some."

Sly nodded. "Your uncle Louis, he understood. Offered to drive us up to Chicago or New York, one of them places, if we really wanted to go. Coulda got hisself in trouble for it, but he was willing. He was a real good man, Miss Glory."

"Do you mind my asking about this?"

Sly shook his head. "Ancient history, Miss Glory. Can't hurt me now."

"Why you? I mean, sure, he was a good man. And he didn't seem to have much patience for a lot of what went on back then. But why did he help you and not someone else?"

"Mr. Louis was a friend of my mama's," he said. "She worked cleaning houses with her little sister. They worked for Mr. Louis's daddy when Mr. Louis was a young man, and he took a shine to my aunt Sissy. You can bet his mama put an end to that right quick. Sissy got shipped over to cousins in Slidell, and Louis ran off and joined the Army.

"Sorta like me."

"I had no idea," I said, my head spinning.

"Course, all that happened before I was born," Sly said. "So I only know what my mama and daddy told me later on. They used to carry news about Sissy to Mr. Louis, right up to the day he died. I think helpin' me was his way of sayin' thanks."

Chapter 31

SLY'S STORY EXPLAINED A LOT ABOUT UNCLE LOUIS. He must have been one stubborn son of a gun to come back to Keyhole Bay after his stint in the Army.

"I don't know if I'd've ever come back here," Riley said. "Even if my mama and daddy were here. I'd've hightailed it west so fast you wouldn't have seen me go."

"West?" Jake asked. "I've been there. Not that much different from here, unless you're in one of the big cities. Otherwise it's the same; good people and bad, rich and poor, happy and miserable. From what I've seen, people are the same wherever you go."

"True, that." Sly nodded his agreement. "I saw a lot of places courtesy of my uncle. Uncle Sam. Good people and bad, wherever you go. Whatever you go looking for, that's what you're gonna find. And I found good people, generous and helpful people, everywhere I went."

I got up from my chair and walked over to Sly, and knelt down next to him. Tentatively, I reached out and put my arm around his shoulders, and gave him a one-armed hug. "That's because you're a good and generous man, Sly. Like goes to like, as Memaw would say."

Sly reached out with one callused hand and ran his fingers along my cheek. "Louis would be proud of you. I think he *is* proud of you. You're a good girl, Miss Glory."

"Thanks." I stood up and blinked back the tears that threatened to spill over. Sly had given me a fresh look at the only family I had in Keyhole Bay, and I was grateful. Uncle Louis and Bluebeard could be mighty annoying, but I was still glad to have them in my life.

"Speaking of Uncle Louis," I said to my friends, "have I told you about his latest antics?"

I launched into the story of the postcards, lightening the somber mood with the tale of his mess and of the epic pout that followed. "He was still pouting the next day," I said, "when Buddy McKenna came in. I think that was some kind of record, even for Bluebeard."

It was good to be among friends, people who knew about Uncle Louis, and be able to speak freely. I had kept the secret of my ghostly roommate for a long time, unwilling to admit it, even to myself. But now everyone in the room knew about Louis, and accepted his presence in my life.

Soon Karen and Riley announced that they had to leave. They thanked Jake for dinner, and a few minutes later we heard Riley's truck pull away.

Sly hugged me good-bye, a real hug. Somehow it felt right this time. Sly's connection with Uncle Louis made it feel like we were family, and I was happy to add another person to my little family circle.

"I'll see you later in the week," he said to Jake, "and I'll see you tomorrow."

"Lunchtime," I agreed. "And I'll be sure to bring a treat for Bobo."

We watched the T-Bird pull away, and Jake and I were left alone.

"Time for me to go, too."

"You're welcome to stay a little longer," Jake said. But when I didn't accept the invitation, he walked me to my truck and said good night.

"I'll stop by in the morning," he said, "and see if Bluebeard is still pouting."

"Probably will be."

I started the engine and drove the few blocks back home. I parked in the back and let myself in, checking the locks and alarms twice. All the talk about Andy Marshall had left me uneasy, and I still wasn't ready to accept the police's explanation of Bridget's death.

I peered through the dim light in the shop, but everything was in its proper place, and Bluebeard didn't even complain about me disturbing his sleep.

I was about to head upstairs when I noticed the box of postcards still behind the counter. I picked up the box and carried it upstairs with me. I could turn on the TV and finish resorting the cards before bed, and then I wouldn't have to look at the mess in the morning.

I found a sappy romantic comedy on a local channel and set to work on the postcards.

I was halfway through when I found another card with Bridget's precise printing. Like the first one, this one also said Edina, MN, on the address side. But where the first one had only a few letters in the message space, this one had two complete words.

Let's talk.

Who did she want to talk to, I wondered. There was only one person who might be able to tell me, but good manners told me it was far too late to call anyone, and especially someone I only knew casually.

Good manners, however, didn't prevent me from sending e-mail. Buddy might not get my message until tomorrow, but it could wait that long.

I grabbed my laptop and opened the e-mail program. Using the address on Buddy's business card, I typed in my question:

Who did Bridget know in Edina, Minnesota?

I set the computer aside and got up for a glass of sweet tea before I went back to my sorting.

To my surprise, the computer chimed with an incoming message just a few minutes later.

Just my dad, as far as I know. Why?

I debated how to answer him. If Bridget was actually sending a postcard to her father, offering to talk to him, then maybe she was trying to mend their broken relationship. Perhaps working with Buddy had somehow convinced her to reach out to her father, even if it was only a postcard.

But that wasn't something for an e-mail in the middle of the night. It was a message loaded with emotional baggage, and I wasn't going to trust it to pixels on a glowing screen.

Nothing critical. Just something she said. I'll tell you about it the next time I see you. Good night!

I closed the e-mail program and shut down the computer. If Buddy answered my e-mail, if he asked any more questions, I could honestly say I hadn't seen the message.

I thought about how I'd found Bridget's message while I finished sorting the postcards and got ready for bed.

Of all the things Bluebeard had said, all the clues he'd dropped, why this one?

I put the box of postcards, now carefully sorted again, at the top of the stairs so I would remember to take them back downstairs. The one with Bridget's message I left in the middle of the coffee table. I'd try to remember to give it to Buddy next time he was in the shop.

Chapter 32

I FLOATED IN THAT HALF-DREAMING STATE BETWEEN the first soft beeps of the alarm clock and the "I have to be downstairs in fifteen minutes" freakout, savoring the last few minutes of peace and quiet before the onslaught that was a summer Monday.

The early morning warmth made me kick off the light blanket, but the slow whirring of a box fan kept the bedroom reasonably cool for now.

Although I didn't have to get up for another few minutes, my brain had already kicked into gear. Julie would be here with Rose Ann, so I could get out of the shop for a little while. There was a short list of absolutely necessary errands, and I considered how best to make use of my time.

The bank was a high priority after a holiday weekend. And groceries. No one who lived in Keyhole Bay went near the market on a summer weekend. My Friday morning visit had been problematic; Saturdays were impossible, and by Sunday the shelves were picked clean.

I remembered my date with Sly. I had promised to bring the truck for an oil change, and I'd said I would bring lunch. Which meant I either had to make something, or stop for takeout. But if I didn't get groceries, there weren't a lot of options in the making-something department.

Takeout it was.

I didn't like carrying around cash, so I'd go to the bank first, pick up lunch, get the truck taken care of, and swing by the store on my way back. That way I didn't have to leave too early, and Frank and Cheryl should have restocked by early afternoon, which would make my shopping easier, too.

I lingered in bed a moment longer, pretending to think about what to wear. I knew I was stalling; my work wardrobe was jeans and sneakers. In the winter I wore T-shirts or polos, in the summer I wore T-shirts or tank tops. I could probably qualify for one of those wardrobe makeover shows.

I forced myself out of bed and into the shower. I was toweling dry when I heard my phone beep with an incoming text. I finished dressing and retrieved the phone on my way downstairs with my coffee.

"Coffee?" Bluebeard said the instant I appeared at the bottom of the stairs.

"No coffee," I answered. Why did he even bother asking? He got the same answer every day. I gave him some apple slices and part of a banana instead, and changed his water.

Slipping back behind the counter, I checked the phone messages. There was only one text, from a number I didn't recognize. I almost deleted the message unopened, but there was something vaguely familiar about the area code.

I turned on the computer and did a quick search. Area code 952 covered an area south and west of Minneapolis. That was why it looked familiar: I'd seen it on Bradford McKenna's business card.

Reassured, I opened the message. Sure enough, it was from Bridget's brother.

Found something I need to show you. Meet me at Bridget's.
Buddy

I glanced at the clock. Julie would be here in half an hour, but I didn't want to wait. I could get out to Bayvue and back before we opened, if I left right now.

I texted back, *On my way*, scribbled a note to Julie, and left it on the counter in case I wasn't back when she got here.

"Mind the store," I hollered to Bluebeard as I headed out the back, stuffing my wallet in my pocket. "I'm gonna go see what Buddy wants."

I was in the truck and on the road before it struck me. Buddy. Sure, Jake called Bluebeard "buddy," but I'd never heard the parrot use the word in reply.

Not until Buddy McKenna came to town.

Maybe Bluebeard wasn't talking to Jake. Maybe he was talking about Bradford McKenna, the "Buddy" I was on my way to see.

The traffic was still light this early in the day, and I was able to take the highway out to the county road and turn north toward Bayvue Estates. In a couple minutes the brick gateposts appeared on my right, and I turned in to the abandoned development.

I hadn't seen another vehicle since the smattering of traffic on the main drag, and the empty roads made the vacant lots and unpaved streets seem all the more deserted.

It felt like the main street of some Western movie, just before the big showdown, with brittle palm fronds in the dusty road instead of tumbleweeds. I almost expected to hear the lonesome whistle of a distant steam engine.

But this was the twenty-first century, I was in Florida, not the Wild West, and I wasn't heading for any kind of confrontation, just trying to help out the family of a friend.

I parked my truck in front of the house where Bridget had stayed and stuffed the keys in my pocket. I stepped carefully around the jagged edge of the concrete walk where the crew had apparently just stopped pouring and let the wet cement puddle and dry in a lump.

The front door was ajar when I reached the porch, and I pushed it open. "Buddy?" I called out. "You in here?"

A muffled voice answered, "Upstairs. C'mon up."

I walked through the entry hall and started up the stairs. "What'd you find?"

"Up here," he answered.

At the top of the stairs I turned down the hall past the sagging cabinet door. I pushed it closed, even though I knew it would just fall open again.

"Where are you?"

"Here," the voice, high-pitched with excitement, came from the back bedroom. The one with the unfinished closet.

But I didn't find Buddy McKenna in the bedroom.

Instead I found myself face-to-face with Lacey Simon. And she didn't look happy.

"Lacey? What are you doing here?"

"Trying to talk some sense into this, this Yankee!" She spat the last word. "But it doesn't seem to be working."

Who was she talking about? There didn't appear to be anyone else in the room. But just then a groan from the closet drew my attention. There on the floor was Buddy McKenna, blood pooling under his head.

I turned to run but Lacey was ahead of me, blocking the door, a length of cedar plank in her hand.

"Francis was too squeamish to take care of his own mess," she said. "But someone's got to clean up after him and his damned fool friends. It was good of you to come so quickly when I asked you to."

The outline of a cell phone bulged in the pocket of her shirt, and I guessed it was Buddy's. My stomach knotted as I realized *anyone* could send a text message.

I saw her swing and tried to duck, but it was too late.

The timber caught me in the temple and I collapsed on the floor.

I looked up at Lacey. I wanted to ask her why, but I couldn't decide which Lacey to talk to. There were at least three angry women looming over me.

And all three held needles.

Even my addled brain knew what came next.

A prick against my skin.

Heat sliding through my veins.

Darkness.

Eternity.

Chapter 33

"YOU JUST COULDN'T LEAVE IT ALONE, COULD YOU?"
the Laceys said, each of them waving her needle. "We all told
Boomer it had to be an accident, had to be her own fault."

They filled the needles from identical bottles of clear liquid, pulling the fluid into the syringes. Tapping the side of
the tube. "But you couldn't accept that and move on.

"I saw you, you know. Right after I was in your store.
Couldn't wait to go running to your new best friend and tell
him all about my business. We just needed a couple days, but
the two of you wouldn't let us have it, would you? If you'd
just waited a little bit, 'til I sold our stuff, we'd have been
long gone. But oh no, not you. Not little Miss Busybody.

"So now I have to clean up another mess."

The needles came closer, and I tried to squirm out of the
way.

I felt a hand grip my arm, roughly shoving my T-shirt

sleeve toward my shoulder. A rubbery strap slid around my arm and pinched it tight. My fingers went numb, and I felt something poking the soft flesh on the inside of my elbow.

For an instant the three needles merged into one, its tip pressed against my vein.

Fueled by panic, adrenaline surged through me. I wrenched my arm away from the needle and heard a tiny snap, followed by a string of curses that would have made Bluebeard blush.

"I can't find another needle," the Laceys muttered, digging through identical black bags. "Maybe in the car . . ."

The echoing voices drifted toward the door. "Don't go anywhere," they said. "I'll be right back."

Go anywhere? It took all my strength and concentration to remember to breathe. How could I go anywhere?

But if I didn't, she would be back. With another needle, and another vial.

I tried to raise myself up on my elbow, but my arm didn't want to cooperate. Sharp pain stabbed me in the joint and I had to lay back down.

I straightened my arm and found pieces of the needles sticking out of the veins, the ends broken off an inch above my skin. Blood seeped from the veins that bulged around the broken needles.

I closed one eye, hoping I could figure out which needle was the real one. The three needles blended into two, but not one coherent image.

I dragged my other arm across my body, clumsy fingers grasping for the sharp points.

In the distance I heard a car engine start. Lacey was leaving. I could just take a little nap, then I could try again.

From the closet, Buddy groaned. I remembered the pool of blood. I might have time for a nap, but did he?

The double images refused to come together, and I closed my eyes against the nausea-inducing sight. If I couldn't see, I would have to rely on my other senses.

I ran my hand up my arm, reaching for the strap. I found a rubber tube, like the nurses used at the blood bank. I tugged on the short end, and was rewarded with a sudden loosening of the pressure on my arm.

The warmth of returning circulation flooded my arm. But there was still a needle to deal with. I ran my hand back down toward my elbow, feeling the slick of blood that covered my arm.

I was bleeding. A lot. Just like Buddy.

I shoved the terror into the back of my brain and slammed a lid on it. No time for panic.

My fingers slipped in the blood. Pain shot through my arm as my hand brushed against the needle, pushing it sideways. Instinctively, I drew my hand away, releasing the pressure on the needle.

Slowly, gingerly, I reached again. I inched my fingers closer, trying to find the needle without causing more pain.

At last I felt the fine metal against my fingertip. I squeezed my eyes tighter, and held my breath.

My hand trembled, and I clamped it into a fist to control the nervous tremor, then reached for the needle again.

The slender shaft was slick and difficult to grasp. I tried to pull on it, but my fingers slipped off. A second time, same result.

The pain didn't matter. I had to pull the needle out of my arm, if I wanted any chance of getting away from the Laceys.

I tugged at the bottom of my T-shirt, wiping off my arm. The needle dug into me, and I bit my lip to stifle the scream that rose in my throat.

On the third try I managed to keep hold of the needle, and I finally pulled it out. The sharp pain gave way to a dull ache and a heaviness in my arm, but the needle was no longer piercing my skin.

I rolled over, using my good arm to push myself to my knees. As I did, something dug into my thigh. I still had my cell phone in my pocket.

I grabbed for it, but I couldn't focus on the keys. I tried punching numbers, but all I got was a sharp tone that pierced my skull and a voice telling me to hang up and dial again.

I managed to stop the voice after some random button pushing, and began crawling toward Buddy. I didn't know how long we had before the Laceys came back, but I was sure it wouldn't be long enough.

Buddy's breathing was ragged, but at least he was still drawing breath.

That was the good news.

The bad news was that he didn't respond when I spoke to him.

I leaned closer, putting my mouth against his ear, and called his name. He moaned and shifted slightly.

"Buddy! You have to wake up!"

Nothing.

I had to leave him here. I couldn't wait any longer.

I managed to get to my feet, and staggered toward what I hoped was the door. I missed the doorway the first time, but made it into the hall on my second try.

I inched along, holding on to the wall for support. I had no idea how I'd get down the stairs, but I had to keep moving.

I heard running footsteps on the stairs. Lacey, several Laceys, appeared on the landing.

With an angry shout, they launched themselves in my direction. The cabinet door sagged open, hanging between us. I grabbed the door, leaned my weight against it, and leaped at the Laceys.

The door connected with a satisfying crunch, and bodies crumpled at my feet.

I didn't stop to try and sort things out.

I ran for the stairs, grabbing for the railing with my good hand. I touched a solid piece of wood, sloping away into the jumble of stairs that swam in front of my eyes.

I held on tight and let gravity pull me down, stumbling and bumping my way to the bottom.

The open front door was a blaze of light against the cool interior of the entry. I aimed for the light and kept moving, trusting I would find my way outside.

I staggered onto the porch and down the walk. I tripped over the jagged cement jumble I had avoided so easily before. I went down, banging my knee painfully against the concrete walk.

My truck, several trucks, sat at the curb, but there was no way I could drive. Even if I could manage to get in, and get the key in the ignition, I wouldn't make it to the county road before I drove into the ditch.

I had to stay on foot.

The bare lots around me offered no place to hide. I struck out across the unpaved street, heading for the swamp at the edge of the development.

Someone would miss me, and help would come.

Julie knew where I was. Somebody would find me. I just had to stay safe until help arrived.

But Buddy couldn't wait.

And I couldn't abandon him.

Chapter 34

I MADE IT TO THE TREE LINE, AND HUNKERED DOWN behind a cypress tree. From my vantage point I watched the front of the house for a couple minutes. The door kept multiplying and then merging back into a single image, sometimes even holding together for several seconds.

Fatigue washed over me, buckling my knees. I tried to focus on the house, the door, but Lacey did not appear, and I worried what she might do to Buddy.

I had to keep moving.

I'd grown up here. I knew the area. All I had to do was stay behind the trees and head toward the county road.

Even if no one came along that road, it was only a couple miles to the highway. I was sure to find someone who could call for help once I reached the heavily traveled main road.

I staggered from one tree to the next, holding on to maintain my balance. I was still seeing double most of the time, and it slowed my progress as I dodged trees and roots that weren't there.

I tripped over a long branch hidden in the tall grass, and fell heavily against a tree, scraping the side of my face.

My left arm ached with a weariness that frightened me. I'd broken Lacey's needle, but not before she'd managed to inject part of the drug dose.

It wasn't a happy thought.

Using my good right arm, I dragged the branch out of the grass and used it to reach in front of me. I swung it from side to side, the way I'd seen blind people use their canes.

I didn't know exactly why they did that, but I guessed it would alert them to obstacles in their path. I hoped it would do the same for me.

I walked slowly, waving my makeshift cane, for what felt like hours. Each time I heard a noise, I stopped and listened, wondering when Lacey would catch up to me. How long before I felt that viselike grip on my arm, and the sting of the needle? How much time did I have left?

Even more worrisome, how much time did Buddy have?

At last, after an eternity of staggering through the trees, I came to the intersection with the main highway. I hadn't seen or heard a single car on the county road, and there wasn't a car on the highway either.

I wanted to turn toward town, but in order to do so, I had to leave the protection of the trees. Terror rooted me in place, refusing to let me move forward.

I gripped my stick in both hands, and forced myself out from the tree line. I limped toward the road, leaning on my makeshift cane.

A car came toward me. I fought the impulse to run and hide, fearful of who might be behind the wheel.

It wasn't until after the car sped past without even hesitating that I realized what they must have seen. A woman with a scraped-up face walking along a deserted road in a bloody T-shirt, waving a giant stick.

I tried to tell myself I would have stopped to see if she needed help, but the truth was darker and more unpleasant. I wouldn't have stopped, would have been afraid to stop.

But I would have called the police, and maybe they would, too. That would be enough.

The thought of calling the police worked its way through my addled brain, and I reached for my cell phone. Maybe I could focus enough to use it.

But my phone wasn't in my pocket. I checked every pocket, even those far too small to hold my phone, then checked them all again. But no matter how many times I patted and prodded every opening, there was no phone.

When had I seen it last? I knew it wasn't important; all that mattered was that I didn't have it. But it was a puzzle I couldn't leave alone, in the same way you can't ignore a stray thread on a shirt.

I started walking along the road in the direction of Keyhole Bay. Even if no one was willing to stop, I had to keep moving toward town, toward help.

Toward someone who could rescue Buddy.

As I walked, I puzzled over the phone. I'd had it when I left the store; slipped it into my pocket just before I got in the truck.

I remembered a voice, telling me to hang up and dial

again. When was that? Had I tried to make a call while I was driving?

I watched two more cars zoom past, and hoped one of them would call the police.

Where the hell was my phone?

The voice had come after a piercing noise, a noise that shot through my brain like a hot needle.

Needle! I'd used the phone after I took the needle out of my arm. In the upstairs bedroom where Lacey had attacked me.

I knew where I'd seen the phone last, but that knowledge did me no good. If it was in that room, Lacey had it now, and I wasn't going back to look for it. All I could do was keep moving forward.

Perspiration stung my scalp, fat drops rolling down my neck. My T-shirt clung damply to my body, sweat mixing with drying blood and dirt from the swamp. I pulled on the neck of the shirt and wiped my face. I winced at the touch of the cloth against my scrapes. The feeling of momentary relief was quickly displaced by a fresh sheen of sweat.

I walked slowly, concentrating on just putting one foot in front of the other. Time didn't seem to make any sense. I didn't know whether I'd been walking for an hour or a week. It could have been either one.

Far ahead I could see buildings. I knew they were the motels and fast-food restaurants that dotted the fringes of Keyhole Bay, though I couldn't identify them at this distance. I had no clue how much farther I had to go. Half a mile? A mile? Two miles?

Could I even see two miles away? I didn't know, but the thought provided a welcome distraction. Anything was better than thinking about what could be happening in the empty model home in Bayvue Estates.

Double and triple images danced in the distance, and I abandoned the effort to make them merge. It hurt too much to force my eyes into focus, so I let my eyelids droop and my vision blur. The pain receded slightly.

I heard a car slow alongside me. Panic sent adrenaline surging through my exhausted body. Fight or flight, and I was too weak to fight.

I dropped my stick and tried to run, tried to focus on the field beside me. To find a path away from the attack I knew was coming.

But without the support of my stick, my legs refused to cooperate. My knees buckled, and I fell.

Hard.

I crawled, dragging myself along with my good arm. It didn't matter where I was going. I just had to get away.

"Glory!" I heard someone shouting my name.

I glanced over my shoulder, still trying to crawl away. The figure of a man, of several men, loomed over me. A hand reached down and clamped around my arm, pulling me to my feet.

A chill shot through me, and the world went black.

Chapter 35

"GLORY!"

I heard my name again, from a long ways away. Somebody was shaking me, telling me to wake up.

I didn't want to.

"Go 'way," I said, swatting at whoever was jostling me. "Want to sleep."

"I can't understand you," a man said. His voice was familiar, but I couldn't place it.

"Go 'way," I repeated as forcefully as I could.

"Glory, look at me!" It was a command, and somewhere deep inside, an obedient child forced my eyes open in response.

A broad, khaki-covered chest floated in front of my eyes, dozens of dark buttons dancing across the layers of fabric. I looked up from the chest to the face, closing one eye in an effort to bring his features into focus.

"It's Boomer, Glory. You know me."

Relief flooded my eyes with sudden tears.

Boomer was here. I was saved.

"Buddy," I said. My tongue felt funny in my mouth, and I tried again. "Buddy."

Boomer's face shifted and for a few seconds he had a single mouth, the corners turned up in a faint smile.

"Yep, I guess I am your buddy about now." He slid an arm underneath me, and raised my head slightly. "Can you sit up? We need to get you out of here."

He pulled me up. I grabbed at him, my fingers digging into his starched khaki shirt.

"Buddy!" I yelled. "Have to save Buddy!"

Boomer shook his heads. Head. I knew there was only one, in spite of what looked like two or three Boomers helping me to my feet. "That's a nasty bump you got there," he said. "How did you hurt your head?"

I raised my hand to my head, feeling for the bump he said was there. I didn't remember hitting my head on anything. I'd fallen and banged my knees, and my arm felt funny. But I couldn't remember exactly why; and I didn't remember hitting my head.

I leaned heavily on Boomer. He had one arm around my waist, and my feet barely touched the ground as we walked back toward the sounds of traffic on the highway.

Boomer put me in the passenger side of his cruiser and went around to slide under the wheel. He pulled out, headed back to town.

"Stop!"

This time he understood. He pulled abruptly back onto the shoulder, the car rocking to a sudden stop.

"Glory, we need to get you to a doctor," Boomer said, turning his head to look at me.

I squeezed my eyes shut and concentrated on forming the words he had to hear. "Must. Go. To. Bayvue."

I opened my eyes, silently begging him to hear the words I was trying to say.

He nodded, two heads bobbing his understanding. "Why?"

"Buddy. Danger. Needle." I had to work to produce each word as clearly as I could, to make my lips and tongue and teeth cooperate to form the precise sounds. "Hurt."

"But you need a doctor." He turned away, watching traffic.

"Go. Now. May. Be. Dead."

His head whipped back around. "Dead?" he asked.

"Maybe."

A siren, louder than I'd ever heard, stabbed into my skull. Colored lights flashed around me, and the car shot into traffic. The rear end squealed around in a high-speed U-turn, sending gravel showering across the road.

I was forced back into my seat as Boomer accelerated toward the county road. Whatever he'd heard, it had convinced him. Now all I could do was hang on and hope we got there in time.

Boomer flipped a switch on the dashboard, stabbed the brakes, and swung in a controlled slide around the corner onto the county road.

As he straightened out, he began yelling. "Need backup at Bayvue Estates. Code Three. Possible drug overdose. Request emergency rescue unit meet me there."

For an instant he swiveled his head toward me then immediately back to the empty road ahead of him. "And send an ambulance. I have one casualty, unknown how many more are at the scene."

Boomer cut the lights and siren as the brick gateposts appeared on our right. I thought we were going to fly right past them, but he swung wide and fishtailed into the deserted development.

I spotted my truck, still parked on the street. As we drew closer, the multiple images merged into one and held. I moved my head and they split apart again. But they had been one truck for several seconds.

I turned to look at the second house and held my head steady while my brain slowly pulled the image into focus. Buddy's rental car sat in the driveway alone.

Lacey's car was nowhere in sight, but I didn't remember seeing it when I arrived. Was it hidden, or had she actually left?

Boomer threw his door open.

Moving slowly, I unbuckled the seat belt Boomer had put around me, and opened the door.

"Stay there," Boomer ordered, reaching past me to pull the door closed. "I'll check it out."

"Wait."

He hesitated.

"Lacey might be here." The words came out slowly, but Boomer watched me as I spoke. "She had a needle." I gestured to the bruise on the inside of my elbow where the needle had broken off. "She tried to give me a shot."

Boomer closed his door and looked at me as though I was finally making sense. My efforts were paying off.

"Was there anyone else in the house?"

"Buddy McKenna," I said. "He was bleeding."

"McKenna? The McKenna woman's brother? That's who you were talking about." I half expected to see a lightbulb go off over Boomer's head. "He was here?"

"Upstairs. Closet in the back bedroom." A deep sadness welled up in me as I thought of Buddy left alone in that closet. "I couldn't wake him up."

"I know how that feels," Boomer muttered as he opened his door again. He slid out, crouching behind the open door.

He stayed there for a minute or two, then darted quickly toward the house, flattening himself against the front wall. I saw him turn his head, and heard his voice speaking softly through the radio in the car.

"There's a second victim reported to be upstairs," he said. "I'm going to check."

I could hear sirens coming in our direction, growing louder.

"Backup is on the way," the dispatcher said from the radio. "Hang on, you'll have help in two minutes."

I could see Boomer moving toward the front door, crouching down below the windowsills and sliding along the front of the house.

He reached the door just as the first car slid to a stop behind the cruiser where I waited. An officer in a protective vest, his gun drawn, jumped from the front seat and sprinted across the bare clay of the yard.

Together, the two men entered the house. Boomer provided cover for the armored officer, then followed him inside.

Another car pulled in ahead of Boomer's and two more officers spilled out. The radio crackled with questions and terse answers as the two men inside made their way through the house.

Repeated calls of "Clear" marked their progress as they checked for signs of life.

As Boomer radioed that they were starting up the stairs, a rescue unit slammed to a stop in the middle of the road. Two paramedics piled out and began pulling equipment cases from the back of the truck.

"Pool of blood in the upstairs hall, and blood on a cabinet door," Boomer reported. "But no one here."

I felt a grim satisfaction at their discovery. I remembered a solid thud of the cupboard door as it hit Lacey. I felt certain the blood was hers.

Payback.

I listened as they made their way through the bedrooms, calling out each time they verified a room was empty. They cleared the master suite, and the second bedroom, without seeing anyone. All that was left was the back bedroom.

The place I had last seen Buddy.

A familiar car lurched to a stop next to the cruiser, blue and red lights strobing from a portable flasher. A tall figure burst from the door.

Jake.

He threw open the cruiser door and pulled me into a tight hug.

"Are you okay?" he asked. "I got here as quick as I could."

"Yes," I answered, my face buried against his chest. "I'll be fine, just as soon as I stop seeing double."

Jake pulled back and immediately started inspecting my head. He found the lump on my left temple, gently pushing aside my hair and inspecting the injury.

"You need to see a doctor," he said. "Why did Boomer bring you back out here instead of taking you directly to the hospital?"

"I told him to."

"And he did what you told him, not what he should?" Anger tightened Jake's voice.

I started to explain, when Boomer interrupted me. "Second victim," he said over the radio. "Head wound. Possible drug overdose. I need the paramedics up here now!"

Jake released me. "Sure you're okay?"

I nodded.

He sprinted across the front yard and disappeared into the open front door. Seconds later I heard his voice on the radio. Calm and confident sounding, he repeated information from the paramedics to the hospital emergency room and the incoming ambulance.

But he didn't sound like a volunteer repeating the words of others; he sounded like someone in charge. Someone who knew and understood exactly what was going on. Someone with more training and experience than Keyhole Bay could ever provide.

The kind of person who read the things I'd seen on his bookshelf.

But there would be time to speculate on that later. Right now I wanted to know about Buddy.

The house was clear. Boomer had assured everyone of that in his last transmission. No reason I had to stay in the car.

I opened the door and got out. For the first few seconds the ground tilted and swung around me as I clutched the door frame to steady myself. But eventually the world righted itself and I was able to let go of the car.

Stepping with exaggerated care, I made my way to the front door and went inside. The staircase stretched in front of me, triggering memories of my last trip down it, clinging to the handrail and half crawling, half falling to the bottom.

I tried to grip the rail with my left hand, but my arm still didn't cooperate properly. Instead I leaned my good right arm against the wall and inched my way up.

I was still a couple steps from the top when Boomer found me.

"I told you to stay put," he said, taking my hand and helping me up the last two steps. "Don't you ever do what you're told?"

"I waited," I said. My words came quicker now, but I still had to concentrate. "Until you said the house was clear."

"That doesn't mean it was safe for you to go walking around," he answered. He turned my back to the wall and gently pushed my shoulders down, forcing me to sit at the top of the stairs.

"Is Buddy . . ."

"They're still working on him," Boomer answered the question I couldn't finish. "They'll get him stabilized before they take him to the hospital. But the paramedics seem to think he's going to make it."

That was the good news.

"And Lacey?"

Boomer shook his head. "No sign of her. But we have four states on the lookout for her car. She won't get far."

I nodded and closed my eyes. "Can I sleep now?" I asked.

"Fifteen minutes," Boomer said. "You almost certainly have a concussion. I'll see if I can find you some ice. And you have to wake up every fifteen minutes until the doctor says different."

I heard his rapid footsteps go down the stairs as I faded.

Chapter 36

SUDDEN COLD AGAINST MY SCALP JOLTED ME BACK TO awareness. Boomer held a towel to my temple, the ice inside it already beginning to melt in the afternoon heat.

Drops of cool water slid down my cheek and splattered onto my grimy T-shirt. I looked down and realized I couldn't tell what color the shirt had been when I put it on that morning.

Two men in navy slacks and crisp white shirts hurried past me with a stretcher.

They disappeared into a door at the end of the hall.

Much later they wheeled the stretcher out of the room. This time there was a body strapped to it, tubes and wires running from under the draped sheet to beeping monitors and bags of clear fluid.

As they neared the top of the stairs, I forced my way to my feet. I had to see for myself.

Buddy's face was nearly as pale as the stark white sheet. His eyes were closed, and he made a nasty gurgling sound with each breath. But he was breathing, and his eyelids fluttered as the paramedics rolled him down the hall.

They reached the stairs and stopped to maneuver the stretcher into position to carry it down. Buddy's eyes opened slightly, and he caught sight of me.

The tube in his throat prevented him from speaking, but his expression of relief matched the emotion that passed over me.

We were both alive. Something I wouldn't have bet on a few hours earlier. I hoped someday he could tell me what had happened in those hours. But for now we both needed medical attention.

The ambulance crew folded up the legs of the stretcher and made their way down the stairs. At the bottom I heard the legs click into place once again and the wheels clattered across the entry and out the door. A minute later the siren gave a chirp and the ambulance rolled away.

Jake emerged from the back bedroom with the paramedics, helping them lug their equipment back to the truck.

As I looked in his direction, I caught sight of the sagging cabinet door. A blossom of brownish dried blood marked the side facing the stairs.

"I did that," I said to Boomer, pointing at the door. "She was coming at me, and I hit her in the face with the door."

"I'd be willing to bet you broke her nose," he said, "judging by the looks of it, and that puddle on the floor. I'll be sure to add that to the bulletin.

"If she goes for medical help, we might find her that way."

The three men reached us and stopped. Boomer took the equipment case away from Jake. "I'll take this," he said. "You take care of her and I'll meet you at the emergency room."

He held out his hand. "Give me your keys," he said. "I'll see to it that someone brings your truck back into town."

The truck. "What time is it?"

Jake glanced at his watch. "Half-past twelve. Why?"

"Sly's waiting for me. He was supposed to change the oil on the truck today." I knew better than to even ask. There was no way Boomer would let me drive until I saw the doctor.

I dragged the keys out of my pocket and reluctantly placed them in his upturned palm.

"We'll take it to Mr. Sylvester," Boomer assured me. "But I suggest you call him so he doesn't worry."

"I would, but I lost my phone somewhere."

"Oh, yeah." Jake dug in his pocket and handed me my phone. Bloody fingerprints on the screen made clear when I had last tried to use it, and a shudder ran up my spine.

Jake grabbed it and stuffed it back in his pocket. "Never mind," he said. "You can use my phone when we get to the car."

He wrapped his arm around my waist and helped me down the stairs and out to his car. He retrieved his phone from the console, punched a couple buttons, and handed it to me. It was already ringing.

When Sly answered, he seemed relieved to hear my voice. "Miz Julie called here looking for you. Said you'd gone out to talk to that banker fella and she knew you were supposed to bring the truck by today. You okay?"

"I'll be fine," I assured him. "Had a little trouble, but it's taken care of. Sorry for missing our lunch date."

He laughed, and I could imagine the wide grin on his face. "Yeah, well, don't let that fella of yours know I'm beating his time. You be by later?"

"I don't know exactly. Boomer said he'd have someone drop the truck at your place and I can pick it up, but I don't know quite when. Might be tonight before I can get over there."

His chuckle died. "Sounds like more than a little trouble, girl. You *sure* you're okay?"

Jake held out his hand, gesturing at me to hand him the phone. I surrendered it reluctantly, afraid he'd reveal more than I wanted Sly to know.

"Sly, it's Jake." He listened a moment. "No, she's going to be fine. Bumped her head is all. Boomer and I both think she ought to be checked before she goes gallivanting around town."

Gallivanting? Did I actually hear Jake use that word? He was clearly starting to talk like a local. Next thing you know, he'll start saying "y'all."

"I'm taking her to the doctor now," he continued. "and I'll bring her by to get the truck as soon as the doctor says she's okay to drive."

He was silent again, listening as he pulled onto the county road. "I'll tell her," he said. "And I'll let you know when we're headed your way."

He hung up and tossed the phone back into the console. "He says for you to take it easy and not be in too big of a hurry about anything." He glanced over at me, then back at the road. "I didn't have to tell him that was completely useless advice, because you'll just do what you please anyway."

I started to protest, but he cut me off. "And don't try telling me any different. I know better."

Unfortunately, he did. I gave up trying to argue, and sat quietly the rest of the way to the hospital.

TYPICAL SUMMERTIME INJURIES CROWDED THE emergency room. Kids with cuts and scrapes, teens with extreme sunburns, retirees with heat stroke, and a middle-aged couple injured by a fender bender.

But I didn't have to wait. As soon as the nurse heard my name, I was whisked out of the waiting room and into a bed. "Boomer told us to take good care of you," she said.

Jake stayed by my side, but discreetly turned his head as she cut away the remains of my T-shirt and covered me with a clean sheet. No one questioned his right to be there.

"How did you know what to do?" I asked him at one point. "You sounded like you were in charge up there."

For a long moment I didn't think he was going to answer, but then he said solemnly, "I was a paramedic once, in another life. I guess it's time you knew about that life.

"I promise I'll tell you all about it. After I get you home."

I fully intended to hold him to that promise.

A nurse cleaned up my scrapes and iced my bruises. They sent me for X-rays and scans of my brain. They bandaged my arm and checked my blood for signs of the drugs Lacey had tried to shoot into me. The tests stretched into late afternoon. I sat in my bed, the curtains drawn for a modicum of privacy, and tried not to eavesdrop as patients came and went in the beds around me.

Jake stayed until I shooed him out. "You still have a store to run," I reminded him. "You can't just close for the day in the middle of the summer."

"I can do whatever I choose to do," he replied.

He finally let me chase him out, but only after Linda and Karen arrived in response to his calls. "Somebody needs to take care of her," he told them, as though I wasn't perfectly capable of taking care of myself.

Still, I had to admit I kind of like him fussing over me.

Boomer came in while I was waiting for the test results, and asked my two protectors to give him a few moments alone with me.

"Go get a Coke," he said, and they agreed.

Once we were alone, he pulled a chair close to the bed.

"If you keep this up," he said, "I am going to have to just give up and put you on the force."

I shook my head, and instantly regretted it. "No," I told him, "you really won't. It's not like I *want* to do this."

"Then why, Glory? Why do you end up in the middle of these things?"

I couldn't very well tell him it was Bluebeard's fault. Bad enough I'd shared that secret with my friends. I didn't want to share it with the police chief.

Instead I asked a question of my own.

"How's Buddy? None of the doctors will tell me anything."

Boomer seemed just as happy to change the subject. He told me Buddy was doing well, and was expected to make a full recovery. They'd removed the tube in his throat and he was awake and talking, though he was still weak.

"Lacey shot him full of something she got from the pharmacy," Boomer said. "Probably the same stuff she tried to inject you with." He cleared his throat, and lowered his voice. "We picked her up a couple hours ago, and when I left the station, she was still talking. Trying to blame it all on Francis.

"You didn't hear any of this from me," Boomer continued, "because I can't tell you anything, but Lacey said Francis went out to beg Bridget to help him keep his job and the house. Bridget knew him from the bank, so she let him in. But when he asked her to give him a second chance she said she couldn't. Francis pushed her, she fell and hit her head, he couldn't wake her. Francis called Lacey in a panic, and she decided she had to clean up his mess. Her words."

I remembered her saying something like that at the house when she attacked me. "And her idea of cleaning up a mess was to shoot her full of drugs?"

Boomer shrugged. "She was improvising, and drugs were the one thing she knew. She thought she could pass it off as an overdose—that everybody would be willing to believe it—and it almost worked. She figured it would give them time to sell off anything of value and make a run for it."

"If I hadn't spent some time with her, I'd have believed it, too." I left out the part about the postcards and Bluebeard. That part was personal, and he already had all he needed to put Lacey and Francis away for a long time.

He hesitated, as though deciding whether to give me any more information. "Did you know Lacey and Francis had a boat?"

"Nope."

"Had it moored over near Port St. Joe. That's where Lacey

was headed. Guess they were planning to head south." Boomer pushed himself up out of the chair. "Anyway, Buddy will be okay. We sent a unit out to pick up Francis, and I just got a call that they're on their way in with him in custody." He shook his head. "No job's worth that."

Chapter 37

JULIE AGREED TO WORK UNTIL I WAS BETTER, INSIST-ing I stay upstairs and rest. Jake agreed with her, and he checked on me several times a day to be sure I stayed out of the store.

At night he brought dinner and told me stories of his days as a firefighter, paramedic, and fire captain in California.

There was a lot to tell, including the fire that killed one of his crew, and forced his retirement on a partial disability. No wonder he'd been worried about making the grade in Key-hole Bay's volunteer unit.

But even with the constant company of Jake and Karen and Sly and Linda, and a short outing to Karen's for our regular dinner on Thursday, I was getting stir-crazy. A week of enforced idleness had nearly driven me nuts. When the doctor finally agreed on Monday afternoon to allow me go back to work, I was overjoyed.

Jake brought me home after my appointment and we let ourselves in the back door. Julie was at the counter with Mandy, deep in conversation.

"We need more," Julie was saying as she inspected a shirt with a large picture of Bluebeard on the front.

"I'll need three days, and that's if we put a rush on it," Mandy replied. "I think I can get my boss to waive the fee for it, just this once."

Julie noticed me and waved me over. "Is that okay with you?"

"Is what okay?"

"A reorder. We need more shirts."

I shook my head. "Not until these are sold," I told her. I thought about the gamble I'd already taken with my Buy-Out-Peter Fund. "I can't commit any more money to untested inventory."

Julie waved a piece of paper. "I started taking orders last Monday, when Mandy brought the prototype, and people have been picking them up all weekend. We're out of a couple sizes, and low on the rest. Oh, and the mugs are nearly gone, too."

Stunned, I looked across the shop at Bluebeard. If it was possible for a parrot to look smug, he did.

Jake slipped his arm around me. "It's time to start talking price with Peter," he said. "Thanks to Bluebeard."

From his perch across the shop, Bluebeard ruffled his feathers and struck a pose. Just like the one on the shirts and postcards.

"Pretty boy."

This time he didn't mean Jake.

Menus and Recipes

A cold supper usually consists of a variety of salads, along with bread and butter, a tray of pickles and olives, and sweet tea. While the salads require refrigeration, the flavors will be stronger and richer if the dishes are cool, not icy cold.

Glory's Childhood Cold Supper

Chicken salad can be spreadable for a sandwich or chunky for a main dish. Either way, the ingredients are similar: cooked chicken and vegetables in a creamy dressing. Although some versions use grapes, Glory's favorite recipe adds a bit of chopped apple for sweetness.

CHICKEN SALAD

3 cups cooked chicken, chilled and cubed
½ cup each chopped onion, celery, and apple
½ cup toasted pecans
¼ teaspoon caraway seed
salt and pepper to taste
1 tablespoon lemon juice
¾ cup mayonnaise

There are several options for the chicken itself: grill or bake chicken breasts and/or thighs, roast a whole chicken (or buy one already cooked at the supermarket), or buy precooked breast strips.

Toss the chicken, onion, celery, apple, and pecans lightly. Stir the caraway seeds, salt, pepper, and lemon juice into the mayonnaise; pour over the chicken mixture; and stir to coat. Refrigerate, covered, until ready to serve. Garnish with additional pecans, if desired.

For a luncheon, serve a scoop of salad atop a leaf of butter or iceberg lettuce. Or like Glory, you can serve family-style from a large bowl.

Deviled eggs are a favorite in the South. While a dozen eggs may sound like a lot, these are very popular. And if you do have leftovers, mash them into egg salad for sandwiches!

DEVILED EGGS

1 dozen eggs, hard-cooked
½ cup mayonnaise
1 tablespoon mustard
2 tablespoons sweet pickle relish
salt and pepper to taste
paprika, for garnish

To make perfectly hard-cooked eggs, refrigerate raw eggs for 3 to 5 days before cooking (they will be easier to peel) and bring them to room temperature. Place them in a single layer in a pot, cover completely with cold water, and bring to a rapid boil. When the water boils, remove the pan from heat, cover tightly, and let sit for 17 minutes (20 minutes for jumbo eggs). Drain and cover the eggs with cold water for at least 10 minutes. A trick for peeling eggs: after draining the cold water, leave the eggs in the pan, put the cover back on, and shake gently for 20 or 30 seconds.

When the eggs are cooled, cut them in half and scoop the yolks into a bowl. Mash the yolks with the mayonnaise, mustard, pickle relish, salt, and pepper. Fill the scooped-out whites with the yolk mixture, sprinkle with paprika, and chill.

Coleslaw is another Southern staple. It's a mainstay on BBQ platters and at picnics throughout the region.

COLESLAW

½ head each green and red cabbage, shredded
1 carrot, shredded
dressing (recipe follows), or use your favorite bottled dressing
parsley for garnish

Toss the shredded cabbage and carrot with the dressing. Chill for at least an hour to allow the flavors to mellow. Garnish with parsley.

Coleslaw Dressing

¾ cup mayonnaise
2 tablespoons vinegar
½ teaspoon sugar
½ teaspoon celery seed
salt and pepper to taste
¼ teaspoon caraway seed, optional

Mix well.

Everyone has their favorite potato salad recipe. In the South there is a wide variety of pickles, most of which can be used in place of the dill pickles.

POTATO SALAD

3 pounds potatoes
3-4 boiled eggs
½ cup each of celery, onion, and dill pickle, chopped
1 cup mayonnaise
¼ cup mustard
salt and pepper to taste
paprika for garnish

Cook the potatoes until tender, but still firm. Cool, peel, and cube. Reserve one boiled egg, and chop the remaining eggs. (See "Deviled Eggs," above, for instructions on cooking eggs.) Mix the potatoes, chopped eggs, celery, onion, and pickles. Mix the mayonnaise and mustard with salt and pepper. And a tablespoon of pickle juice, if desired. Pour the dressing over the potato mixture, toss gently, cover, and refrigerate.

When ready to serve, slice the reserved egg to garnish, and sprinkle with paprika for color.

Macaroni salad and potato salad are very similar, though macaroni salad usually does not include boiled eggs. As a variation, macaroni salad may be made with Miracle Whip, a popular mayonnaise substitute with a sweeter, spicier flavor.

MACARONI SALAD

3 cups cooked elbow macaroni
⅓ cup each of celery and onion, chopped
¼ cup chopped pimento, optional
½ cup mayonnaise or Miracle Whip
1 tablespoon vinegar
1 tablespoon sugar
salt to taste

Cook the macaroni according to the package directions. Rinse and run under cold water. Toss with the celery and onion. Add the pimento, if using. Whisk together the mayonnaise, vinegar, and sugar. Toss the macaroni mixture with the dressing. Refrigerate until ready to serve.

For three-bean salad, you can either cook your own beans or use canned beans. If you're trying to avoid heating up the kitchen, canned is the way to go.

THREE-BEAN SALAD

1½ cups kidney beans
1½ cups garbanzo beans
1½ cups green beans
1 red onion, thinly sliced

Recipes

½ cup vinegar

½ cup salad oil

salt and pepper to taste

If using canned beans, drain and rinse well under cold running water. Toss the beans and onion with the vinegar and oil. Add salt and pepper to taste. Refrigerate several hours, or overnight, to allow flavors to combine and mellow.

Fruit salad will depend on the season, and the region. Use whatever fruit is perfectly ripe when you visit your local grocery store. Better yet, seek out a local farmers' market for fresh, local produce. Experiment with different melons, such as yellow watermelon, Santa Claus, Crenshaw, or Persian melons. Red, black, or green grapes can also be added.

FRUIT SALAD

1 small watermelon

1 medium cantaloupe

1 medium honeydew melon

3 medium peaches

2–3 kiwifruit

1 medium pineapple

1 pint strawberries

½ pint blueberries

½ pint blackberries

dressing (recipe follows)
mint leaves, for garnish

Cube the melons, slice the peaches, and peel and slice the kiwis. Clean and cube the pineapple. Clean and hull all the berries—they can be used whole or cut into pieces, depending on size. Toss the melons and pineapple; gently fold in the berries. Arrange sliced peaches and kiwi on top, and drizzle with dressing. Chill. Remove from the refrigerator, garnish with mint leaves, and let stand about 20 minutes before serving.

Dressing

juice of 1 orange, about 2 ounces
juice of 1 lemon, about 1 ounce
juice of 1 lime, about 1 ounce, optional
1 tablespoon good-quality honey

Mix the orange and lemon juices (and lime, if using). Whisk in the honey.

We truly have no idea where these cookies originated, but they appear under many names in kitchens across the country. They're easy, tasty, quick to make, and require no baking—a real plus in a Florida summer!

LUNCHROOM COOKIES

3 cups oatmeal
½ cup peanut butter
½ cup milk
2 cups sugar
¼ cup cocoa
½ cup butter
1 teaspoon vanilla
¼ teaspoon salt

Mix the oatmeal and peanut butter in a large bowl. Set aside. In a saucepan, combine the milk, sugar, cocoa, and butter. Stir frequently, until the mixture makes a syrup. Bring to a rolling boil and boil 1 minute, stirring frequently.

Remove from heat; stir in the salt and vanilla. Immediately pour the hot syrup over the oatmeal–peanut butter mixture. Stir. As soon as the syrup is mixed in, drop the batter by teaspoonfuls onto waxed paper. Allow to cool for at least 1 hour before removing from the paper. Store in an airtight container.

Homemade ice cream is a wonderful end to any meal. Sweet, creamy, flavored with fresh fruit. Who could ask for anything more?

PEACH ICE CREAM

4 cups fresh peaches (about 8 small peaches), peeled and diced
1 cup sugar
12 ounces evaporated milk
1 package (3.75 ounces) instant vanilla pudding mix
14 ounces sweetened condensed milk
4 cups half-and-half

Mix the peaches and sugar; let sit for 1 hour. Puree the peach mixture in a blender or food processor until smooth. In a large bowl, stir the pudding mix into the evaporated milk. Add the pureed peaches, condensed milk, and half-and-half.

Place the mixture in the container of a 4-quart ice cream freezer and freeze according to the manufacturer's directions. When the freezing is completed, place the ice cream in an airtight container in the freezer until firm and ready to serve.

The standard Southern beverage, sweet tea, is served at every meal. Southerners like their sweet tea, and most traditional homes will have a pitcher or two in the refrigerator.

SWEET TEA

6 cups water
6 tea bags—traditionally, plain black tea
1 cup sugar
mint sprigs or lemon slices for garnish, optional

Bring the water to a boil, add the sugar, and stir to dissolve. Steep the tea bags in the sweetened water to the desired strength, and serve in tall glasses of ice. Garnish with mint sprigs or lemon slices, if desired.

A grilled dinner is a tradition across the country on Independence Day. But instead of the standard burgers and dogs, try these recipes for an exciting change of pace. Add a big jug of sweet tea or a cooler of beer, and you have all the ingredients for a spectacular Fourth of July.

Felipe's Grilled Gala

Shrimp in lettuce cups, or lettuce wraps, are a cool spicy/ sweet start to an evening of grilled goodness. The lettuce acts as a bowl or wrap, which makes these finger food.

SHRIMP IN LETTUCE CUPS

1 pound cooked cocktail shrimp

1 small cucumber, chopped

1 large avocado, diced

3 Roma tomatoes, diced

¼ cup cilantro, chopped

¼ cup white wine

¼ cup olive oil

salt and pepper to taste

1 head Boston, Bibb, or romaine lettuce (see instructions)

Toss together the shrimp, cucumber, avocado, tomato, and cilantro. Mix the white wine and olive oil, add salt and pepper to taste, and pour over the shrimp mixture.

For lettuce cups, use Boston or Bibb lettuce. Wash and dry leaves and arrange on a plate. Place a spoonful of shrimp in each lettuce "bowl" to serve.

For rolls, use romaine lettuce. Cut the bottom off the lettuce, wash and dry leaves, and cut in half crosswise. Place a spoonful of shrimp mixture on each half leaf, fold up one end about a half inch, and roll up like a cigar. Use a toothpick to secure each roll.

Serve with plenty of napkins!

This simple marinated and grilled chicken is the perfect antidote to a summer of hamburgers. Served with grilled vegetables, it makes a hearty, and healthy, summer meal.

GRILLED CHICKEN

¾ cup white wine
¾ cup melted butter
1 ounce lemon juice
5–6 cloves garlic, minced
2 tablespoons dried rosemary, or 2 sprigs fresh rosemary leaves
salt and pepper to taste, about ½ teaspoon each
2 chickens, 3–4 pounds each, quartered; or 6 pounds bone-in
chicken pieces

Mix all the ingredients except the chicken; reserve about 1 cup for basting. Pour the remaining mixture over the chicken in a plastic bag. Turn and shake gently until the chicken is completely coated. Force out as much air as possible, close the bag securely, and allow the chicken to marinate for several hours in the refrigerator.

Place the chicken bone-side down on a hot grill. Baste with marinade, and continue basting frequently while cooking. Cook for about 10–12 minutes, turn and baste, and cook another 10–12 minutes. Repeat turning and basting until the chicken is completely cooked (meat thermometer reads 180° when inserted in thickest part of the piece). Total cooking time is about 45 minutes.

Vegetable skewers, with their variety of colors and textures, are an attractive addition to any grilled menu. Use or omit any vegetable that you prefer, or do each skewer with a single vegetable and allow your guests to help themselves to their favorites.

SKEWERED VEGETABLES

2 each medium red bell, green bell, and yellow bell peppers

2 small yellow squash

2 small zucchini

1 red onion

24 cherry tomatoes

24 mushrooms

½ cup olive oil

½ cup lemon or lime juice

¼ cup water

¼ cup Dijon mustard

2 tablespoons honey

2 tablespoons minced garlic

2 tablespoons chopped fresh basil leaves

½ teaspoon salt

½ teaspoon freshly ground black pepper

Prepare the vegetables: remove the seeds and stems from the peppers, and cut into 2-inch squares; section the squash and zucchini into ¼-inch slices; peel the onion and cut into 2-inch squares; rinse the tomatoes; the mushrooms may be used whole, or halved if they are very large.

Mix the remaining ingredients, pour over the cut vegetables in a plastic bag, and marinate for 3–4 hours. Soak ten 12-inch bamboo skewers in water, or use metal skewers. (Be careful when handling metal skewers; they will get very hot!) Thread an assortment of vegetables on each skewer, place over a medium-hot grill, and cook 10–12 minutes, turning regularly and basting with marinade.

Eggplant does well on the grill. Be sure the eggplant is tender, but don't overcook it, as it can get mushy.

GRILLED EGGPLANT

2 eggplants
¼ cup olive oil
¼ cup balsamic vinegar
1 tablespoon minced garlic
¼ teaspoon each thyme, basil, dill, and oregano
1 teaspoon kosher salt, or to taste
½ teaspoon black pepper, or to taste

Slice the eggplants about ½-inch thick. Whisk together the remaining ingredients. Coat the eggplant slices with the oil and vinegar mixture (brushing works well), and grill on a hot grill, turning once, for about 15 minutes.

Tomatoes show up in lots of Southern dishes. They can be baked, broiled, fried, sliced, diced, made into sauce—or grilled. This basic recipe can be enhanced with herbs or spices such as oregano or pepper flakes, depending on your personal preferences, topped with fresh herbs such as basil or thyme, or garnished with grated Parmesan cheese.

GRILLED TOMATOES

4 large tomatoes
2 teaspoons salt
1 teaspoon black pepper
1 teaspoon garlic powder
⅓ cup minced garlic
¼ cup extra virgin olive oil

Cut the tomatoes in half crosswise. Mix the salt, pepper, and garlic powder; season the cut side with the dry mixture. In a small saucepan (you can do this on a side burner, or the back of the grill), sauté the minced garlic in olive oil and set aside.

Place the tomatoes cut-side down on a hot grill. Grill 3–5 minutes, turn over, top with the garlic and oil mixture, and grill for another 3 minutes. When the tomatoes are done, they can be topped with fresh herbs, bread crumbs, and/or grated cheese.

This grilled menu holds an array of vegetable dishes and aromatic chicken, a departure from the standard grilled meal. But we bow to tradition with the inclusion of the classic summertime dish: baked beans. And while a traditional cook would start with dried beans and spend a couple days cooking, this recipe takes a shortcut and starts with canned pork and beans, then improves them.

BAKED BEANS

3 15-ounce cans pork and beans
1 large onion, chopped
¼ cup brown sugar
¼ cup honey
¼ cup yellow mustard
¼ cup ketchup
1 ounce lemon juice
½ pound bacon, cut into small pieces

Mix all the ingredients except the bacon in a fireproof baking dish (a disposable aluminum pan works well). Sprinkle the bacon pieces on top. Cover with foil and heat on a grill for 1½–2 hours. All the ingredients except the bacon are already cooked, but the longer cooking time allows the flavors to blend and mellow.

After an excellent meal, this light dessert is a perfect finish. Sweet and juicy, it's like a little slice of peach heaven. Choose fruit that is still firm to the touch; too ripe and it will fall apart on the grill.

GRILLED PEACHES

6 medium peaches, ripe but still firm
¼ cup melted butter
¼ cup honey or brown sugar, optional

Halve the peaches and remove the pits. Peeling is not necessary but you may do so if you prefer. Brush the peaches with the melted butter. Brush on the honey or sprinkle with brown sugar, if you want a little sweeter dessert. Lightly oil the grill. Place the peach halves on the grill facedown. Cook for about 4 minutes. Turn. Brush on additional honey, or sprinkle with more brown sugar, if desired. Cook for another 4–5 minutes, until the peaches are soft.

Serve plain, or with vanilla or peach ice cream, yogurt, or whipped cream.